THE LOST DAUGHTER

Emily Slate FBI Mystery Thriller
Book 6

ALEX SIGMORE

Dark Woods Press

THE LOST DAUGHTER: EMILY SLATE MYSTERY THRILLER
BOOK 6

1st Edition

ebook ISBN 978-1-957536-22-4

Print ISBN 978-1-957536-23-1

Prologue

"WHAT WOULD YOU LIKE? YOU CAN HAVE ANYTHING YOU want."

Avery glanced up from her phone just long enough to give Mrs. Henderson *the glare*. The older woman smiled, though Avery knew she wasn't smiling on the inside. Whenever Mrs. Henderson often got upset or frustrated, she'd always produce the exact same smile. Avery didn't care about dinner, she didn't care about what they had, all she cared about was distracting herself from the fact her parents were out of town again, and it was her *birthday*. She turned twelve tomorrow and the only company she'd have were Mrs. Henderson and a couple of the bodyguards. Some birthday. Yasmin Barker's parents had rented out one of the local riding stables and everyone got to choose their own horse for *her* birthday. They'd had lessons on riding, not that Avery had needed them, along with a full party including inflatable castles and lots of fun stuff to do. And Yasmin's parents weren't nearly as rich as her own.

But when Avery had asked for a party, it had been the same answer she always got when her parents had to work: they'd do something small when they got back to celebrate.

Which meant they would forget entirely, and Avery would have to remind them.

That isn't to say they didn't get her *anything* for her birthday, she knew about the presents sitting in their bedroom closet that Mrs. Henderson would bring out for her tomorrow. But she'd already peeked in under the wrapping and knew none of them were what she really wanted.

"C'mon, you must be hungry," Mrs. Henderson said, her voice taking on that impatient tone that let Avery know she wouldn't last much longer. Fine. Let her sulk away back downstairs to where she could sit on the couch, drinking her parent's wine while Avery stayed up here in her room, where at least she didn't feel like a stranger in her own home.

"Maybe later," Avery finally said. "I had a big lunch."

Mrs. Henderson put her hands on her hips. "You call a bowl of soup and half of a Caesar salad a big lunch? You barely touched it."

Avery blew out a long breath, which lifted the strands of blonde hair off her head for a moment. Did she have to watch her every movement like a hawk? "I'm just not hungry, okay?"

"We talked about this. Come on now, we can order a pizza if you want. After all, it's your day tomorrow."

Was she crazy? Did she really think Avery wanted a *pizza*? She continued tapping away on her phone, knowing that if she ignored the woman long enough, she'd eventually go away. Finally, Mrs. Henderson let out a frustrated sigh and the sound of footfalls walking rapidly away filled the silence. Avery immediately got up and shut her door behind her. It would have been better if her parents had just left her here alone for the weekend; it wasn't like she couldn't handle it. As an only child, she'd been on her own a lot over the years, given the "importance" of her father's job. And since Mom never seemed to leave his side, and almost everything they did wasn't for kids—except for those rare times when he needed Avery to put in an appearance for the cameras—she was often left to fend for herself. She didn't mind; she'd become accustomed to it.

Just not on her birthday.

She'd already gotten a few messages from friends at school, wishing her an early birthday. But they weren't doing anything but being polite. Because of her family's name, it was hard for people to see her as anything other than her father's daughter. Even though most of the kids in her school had parents that were just as rich and or powerful as her father, there was something about the Huxley name that made people think twice. Maybe it was the rumors she'd heard that her father was a "cutthroat," that he wouldn't let anyone get in his way once he'd decided to do something. Or maybe it was something with *her*, maybe she just repelled people somehow. If that were true, she wished she knew what she was doing. It seemed like everyone else in school fit in. Why was it so hard for her to do the same?

Frustrated, Avery went into her en-suite bathroom, which, like the rest of the house, was spotless. The housekeepers kept it clean each morning, refilling anything that was out, and making sure all her needs were met before she even had a chance to realize something was amiss.

As was customary when she came into the bathroom, she avoided eye contact with herself in the mirror at first, as if not looking meant there was a possibility something drastic had changed since the last time she'd come in here. Eventually though, she relented and leaned over the counter, close to the mirror to begin inspecting all the imperfections in her face. She knew puberty was close, if not already here, and every morning she woke up terrified she'd find some large welp on her face, or a clogged pore that had turned itself into an unmistakable pimple overnight. She'd already procured all the tools she'd need to take care of it, sneaking off to the beauty store a couple of times during the middle of school. She had tweezers, extruders, needles and anything else she might need to keep her face looking flawless—at least until her parents began allowing her to wear makeup, then she'd just be able to cover it up.

Satisfied today was not the day she'd have to fight that battle; Avery stepped back and lifted her shirt to expose her midsection. She turned one way, then another, trying her best to get the lighting just right so that she looked as toned as all the other girls whose pictures dominated her social feeds. How did they make it look so effortless? All she saw when she looked at herself was what her mother had called "love rolls". Weren't those supposed to go away by the time she became a teenager? Even though eleven was technically "teen" tomorrow she'd be official. And the last thing she wanted was to begin her teens while still looking like a little girl. She needed to grow at least five more inches, which would help lengthen not only her legs but her abdomen as well.

Avery spent the better part of thirty minutes in front of the mirror, going back and forth, trying to pull parts of her skin back so that she could see her ribs, or to get rid of any of what she'd begun thinking of as "the jiggly bits". She may not be very popular now, but if she could just look the way she wanted in her head, she was sure people would begin to flock to her. That's what happened on Insta all the time. And if you weren't hot, you weren't anything.

But she had such a long way to go. There was so much to take care of. She wondered what Mrs. Henderson would say if she wanted to go out and get some lip injections or to the CoolSculpting place. Avery smiled, she did say *whatever* she wanted, didn't she?

Avery flopped back down on her bed, grabbing hold of Tomcat and squeezing him close. She hated this feeling deep inside her. It was like she wasn't even in the right skin, like she'd been born wrong, and now she had so much to fix before she really felt like herself. How did Yasmin and the others do it? Some of them had boobs already, which meant they'd attracted the attention of some of the cuter guys in her grade. But it was like they were able to look like movie stars without any effort. Last year, Yasmin showed up every morning, as perfect as she could be while Avery had to be content to come into school looking like a pressed lump. She couldn't even imagine what things would be like in a few weeks once summer break was over. Every girl in her grade would probably all be six feet tall and wearing full-size bras on the first day.

Avery rolled over, tears prickling her eyes. If she didn't do something drastic, she'd be left behind on day one. She was headed into sixth grade, after all. This was the big time, middle school. She'd have to head to different classrooms for each period, she'd have a locker and she'd have a lot more responsibility. She couldn't start the school year behind everyone else.

Shooting a quick look at the door like Mrs. Henderson had been listening in on her deepest thoughts, Avery picked up her phone again and sent Yasmin a text.

Hey

Yasmin responded a few seconds later. It was good to know Avery wasn't the only one glued to her phone on a Thursday night.

Hey

What's up?

Got a sec?

Sure.

Avery took a deep breath. This was a bit outside her comfort zone.

U started shopping for school yet?

My parents got me some things. All hideous.

Avery smiled.

Wanna get together? Pick out some outfits together?

Sure. When?

This weekend? My parents r out of town. U could come stay if u wanted.

Avery's heart hammered in her chest. She was taking a big risk here, and she knew it. Yasmin might think she was too desperate, or maybe she didn't even want to bother with Avery, since they had only ever really talked a few times.

Isn't it your birthday tomorrow?

Yea, they had to work tho.

Three little dots appeared then disappeared on Avery's phone. She sat, staring at the screen. Would Yasmin think it was weird since Avery wasn't having a party? Maybe she shouldn't have even bothered. She might have just committed social suicide.

Sure, sounds fun. Sat? 10?

Avery couldn't type fast enough.

Great! Do you know my address?

Lol, yeah. C ya Sat.

Avery pinched her eyebrows together. What was so funny about that? It didn't really matter. Someone popular was actually coming to her house! She'd have to let Mrs. Henderson know, who would have to let everyone else know. But the woman had told her whatever she wanted. If that meant a friend coming over and staying the night, then she didn't have any say in the matter. Now all Avery had to do was make sure her room was in order. The last thing she wanted was Yasmin coming over here and thinking she was a complete nerd.

After spending the better part of the evening re-arranging her room and putting away some of her old toys and trinkets that had been on her shelves, Avery climbed into bed without even informing Mrs. Henderson. She didn't want the woman doting over her, making sure she'd brushed her teeth or offering her an evening snack before going to bed. Avery's stomach rumbled, but she didn't care. She'd starve herself if she had to. Yasmin would know where to go to get the coolest new clothes, and Avery needed to be sure she could fit into them. Which meant eating only the essentials until Saturday.

Which also meant no birthday cake.

Exhausted, she fell asleep almost immediately, Tomcat in one arm. But some time shortly after, she was awoken by a loud noise. At first she thought she might have dreamed it, but then she heard it again, and recognized it immediately as breaking glass. Coming out of a deep sleep, it took her a second to realize what that meant. Had someone broken into the house? But if they had, wouldn't the alarm system have sounded? Maybe Mrs. Henderson just broke one of the flower vases on her way up the stairs after too much wine. That happened sometimes—she'd walk a little funny after she'd had a few glasses.

But then Avery heard another sound, a rumbling, like

heavy footsteps. It could be one of the other security guards coming to check on Mrs. Henderson, or Avery herself to make sure they were all right. But the footfalls came fast. Almost like the person was running. And something about that scared Avery. Enough that she jumped from her bed, Tomcat under one arm and went to her closet, closing the folding doors once she was inside.

Her parents had always warned her that if something didn't seem right, she was to hide until someone she trusted came to get her. Even if everything seemed normal, it was better to be safe than sorry. Avery did her best to slow her breathing as she heard doors being opened down the hall from hers. Something wasn't right—why were they looking in all the empty guest rooms? She wanted to call out for Mrs. Henderson, but knew saying anything wasn't smart, not until she knew it was safe.

She heard another door slam open, the one to the room right beside hers, which was nothing more than a guest room. But the door slammed open so hard it shook the wall between them, the wall Avery was leaning up against. Something was *very* wrong. She wished she'd grabbed her phone from her dresser before coming in here, but hadn't thought about it. Just as she was about to open the closet, her own door exploded open, the wood cracking and causing her nearly to scream out loud.

From her position in the closet, she caught a glimpse of a large man, dressed all in black as he searched her room. He went straight for her bed, where she was not more than a few minutes ago, and yanked off the covers. He then turned and Avery could see he had on a mask that covered everything but his eyes. She wanted to cry out. She wanted him to just go away. She held her breath, hoping he'd just pass the closet by and go to the next room. But instead he bent down, looking under the bed.

He was looking for her.

Tears began to stream down Avery's cheeks as she did everything in her power not to let out a sound. The man in black searched a few more corners of her room, before finally coming to the closet.

Just go away. Please…just go away. I'm not here.

He yanked open the doors, pulling them from their hinges and Avery screamed, dropping Tomcat from her arm.

A second later, everything went to black.

Chapter One

THERE'S NOTHING LIKE COMING HOME AFTER A LONG AND trying assignment only to find yourself staring down the business end of a Glock 18.

But perhaps what is more surprising is the person who is holding the weapon that's pointed at my midsection, only a trigger pull away from ending my life. The woman I've spent the better part of three months searching for stands right inside my doorway, sporting a large grin on those ruby-red lips of hers. The last time I saw her in person was back in the town of Stillwater, where she flashed me the exact same smile as we passed each other getting on and off the elevator. Little did I know then that she had just killed my primary suspect in a coverup. Or that three months earlier she had killed my husband and made it look like an accidental heart attack.

And now, here she is, less than five feet from me.

"I know what you're thinking," she says before I can even twitch. "And I wouldn't do it. Trust me, Agent Slate, I have no problem killing you right here."

"Then why am I not dead already?" I ask, trying to calculate if I have a chance to get that gun from her before she can pull the trigger. I know she's a trained assassin, someone who kills for a living, so my chances are probably low. If this was your ordinary, run-of-the-mill perp with a revolver, I could disarm him and have him cuffed in under thirty seconds with only a twenty percent chance of him hitting something vital. But this is a lethal killer, someone trained not to hesitate.

"Because that's what I've decided. Don't make me change my mind."

I move an inch out of place and I'm dead. "What are you doing here?" I ask.

"Is that really the question you want to ask me?" She chortles and motions for me to come all the way into the room as the front door is still open. My suitcase from my trip with Liam to Delaware lays on its side on the floor, right where I dropped it when I realized something was amiss.

I move slowly into the room, but don't leave the view of the doorframe. With any luck one of my neighbors might walk by and realize something is wrong. But the woman across from me keeps the gun trained and closes the door without looking away, sealing off the outside world. Now it's just me and her, and I have no chance to call for any help. My weapon hangs heavy on my belt. Maybe if I can get behind some cover I can find a way to disarm her.

As if she knows what I'm thinking she motions to my belt. "Remove the piece, slide it over to me. No sudden moves."

"If you're going to kill me, just get it over with already," I say.

"So eager to meet your maker, huh?" she asks. "Or even better, you can't wait to be reunited with your long-lost love. Maybe he can explain why he lied to you when you're both dead, huh?" Her voice is light, teasing, as if this is all some elaborate game.

"What is this?" I demand. "Are you just toying with me because you can? Is this what you did with Matt? And all your other victims?"

Her face turns serious. "My other victims never saw me

coming. If I'd wanted you dead, you would be," she says. "Piece. Now. Or I take something permanently. Like a finger."

I pull my blazer back to reveal my weapon still in its holster. I can't get off a shot before she puts one in me, and I can't take the risk her shot wouldn't be deadly. Unless I want to die at this very moment, I don't have much choice but to follow her instructions.

Unclipping the strap, I slowly remove my gun from its holster and place it on the ground, barrel facing me. I then slide it across my hardwood floors over to her. I have to believe she's being honest; if she wanted me dead, I wouldn't have seen it coming. It just would have happened.

She bends down, picking up the gun without taking her eyes or her barrel off me. My gun goes into one of her pockets. She's wearing what looks like a biker's outfit, all black leather, tight against her slim frame. But I don't doubt she's got some muscle under there. Still…if she didn't have that gun…

"Take a seat." She indicates my couch.

"How did you get in here?" I ask, walking over and sitting on the couch, slowly.

"How do you think? I copied your keys months ago. You never thought to change your locks? Even after you found the surveillance equipment?"

I shrug. "I figured it wouldn't do any good."

"Good guess," she says and sits in one of the chairs opposite the couch. I don't use those chairs very often, because usually I'm the only person here. But on the rare occasion someone does come over, they usually take that seat. Strange now, for me to be in this situation with the woman I've been hunting. "I suppose sometimes we just have to accept our fates, isn't that right?"

She has a peculiar accent, but I can't place it. And it isn't prominent; it just comes and goes with some of her words. My guess is she's probably fluent in a couple different languages

and dialects. After a while, those can begin to run together.
"So now what?"

"You are direct, I've always liked that about you," she says.
She's holding the gun a little looser, but I'm still not confident
I'd have enough time to get it out of her hand without taking
a bullet. This certainly isn't what I expected after all the shit I
just went through in Delaware. I thought I had begun to put
everything about Matt behind me, including the person who
killed him. The person who is now sitting in front of me, who
seems to want to examine me.

"I've been told it's one of my best qualities."

She chuckles. "Honesty, yes." Her tone turns malicious.
"Integrity. Special Agent Emily Slate, the darling of the
Federal Bureau of Investigation. The woman who always
makes the right choices. Who always gets her man. That
about sum it up?"

"I wouldn't say that's even remotely accurate," I say.
"Looks like you need to do better research."

"Let's see." She cocks her head. "In the past eight months
you've busted a human trafficking ring, uncovered not one,
not two, but three serial killers, rescued five women from a
brutal kidnapper, and dismantled two corrupt police departments. Does that about cover it?"

"What's your point?" I ask.

"My point is that you get results. You are driven, not
distracted by friends or family or anything else that makes so
many other people weak. You get the job done, even when it
costs you everything."

I lean forward, her sharp words stinging. But I'm not
about to let her see. "What is this, an interview?"

"Not hardly. I'm just saying you're effective. And for those
of us who need certain outcomes, that can be a very attractive
quality."

I stand, and pace in front of my couch. The barrel of the
gun follows me, but I'm satisfied for as long as I don't make a

sudden move, I'm in no immediate danger. She wants something. I rub my temple to get my head to stop pounding for a brief second. "Wait a minute," I say. "You're telling me that you're here, in my apartment, pointing a gun at me, because you want me to *help you*?" I laugh. "You might as well pull that trigger right now, because there's no way that's going to happen."

"You haven't even heard my proposal yet," she says.

"And I don't need to. You killed my husband. You destroyed my life and you've been hunting me ever since. You are the worst thing that has ever happened to me. Why should I do anything for you?"

"Oh, stop being so dramatic," she says, motioning with the gun that I should sit back down. "You take things so personally. In my business, you do that, and you end up dead."

"I'm not in your business," I reply.

"Maybe you should be. Because I heard you just got benched. Apparently, you're something of a liability to the Bureau at the moment, isn't that right?"

"If I am, it's only because I'm being hunted by a psycho who would rather play games than get to the point," I nearly shout. I hate that she's gotten the drop on me, again. Wherever I go, this woman always seems to be one step ahead of me. And I'm sick and tired of her always being just out of reach.

She smiles again. "You'll have to forgive me. I'm just not used to seeing you so flustered. Normally you're a stone in a turbulent river, unmoving, unaffected. At least on the outside. But we both know there's a lot more going on inside, isn't there?"

"Are you going to dance around this all night or are you going to get to it already?" I ask. I'm also frustrated because I just put all of this behind me. I'd decided that I didn't need to get justice for Matt after all, which meant I no longer needed to pursue this woman. Figures that as soon as

I no longer care about finding her, she shows up on my doorstep.

She zips the leather biker jacket halfway down, revealing compact body armor underneath. I've never seen anything like that before. But it means even if I could get a shot off, I'd have to go for her head to stop her. She reaches into the inside of her jacket and pulls out a vape pen, which she inhales for a moment, before exhaling again. At least now I know where the smell in my apartment came from. "Trust me, this wasn't my first choice. But given recent…circumstances, I've been forced to consider my options."

"Seems like we're both experiencing some difficulties lately."

She eyes me, then continues. "It turns out there are some…consequences to a job like mine. Consequences that really aren't in my power to control. Which means I need to adapt if I want to survive. You know a little something about that, don't you?"

I don't reply. This woman already knows more about me than anyone should. She's been following me for at least two months, maybe more, I'm not sure. What I do know is I can't trust a word that comes out of her mouth. But I need to play this out, see where it leads me.

"What sort of circumstances are we talking about here?"

"You're in a unique position to help yourself, Agent Slate. I am in need of certain information. A file, in fact, containing classified information about a current case." I start to move and she trains the gun on me again. "Save your objections. This is a one-time deal. You get me the case file I need, and you never see or hear from me again. I am gone from your life, like I never existed."

"No deal," I say. "I'm not giving you classified information of any kind."

"Think about this for a moment. The entire reason you've been sidelined is because you've been deemed a liability. Someone with a target on her back. I'm offering to remove that target. To get you back in the game. Because we both know the longer you sit here in this apartment alone, the worse it's going to get." She glares at me under hooded eyes.

"You've got some nerve," I say.

"You know I'm right." She takes another puff on the pen and replaces it back in her jacket pocket. "I know you, Emily. The thought of not working terrifies you. Because that's when the darkness begins to creep in. You and I are of a similar type."

I take a deep breath, trying to center myself. She wants to get under my skin. She's using this opportunity to get my emotions high, and I'm not about to let her win again. "If you actually think I'm going to give you classified information then you really don't know me at all," I say.

She gives me a hard grin. "I can't say I'm surprised. Though I'd hoped you would make this easy on yourself." She takes a few steps closer. Still not quite within reach, but almost. "Fine. I'll just go pay a visit to Agent Foley. And then to Agent Coll. Though, of course, neither of them will see me coming."

I make a motion to get closer to her, my blood pumping. But she flicks the gun in my direction, stopping me. "You wouldn't. They don't have anything to do with this."

"Au contraire," she purrs. "They're your motivation. You help me, and they both get to keep living their lives, oblivious. You refuse, and you get to walk away. But they don't. And then you'll have three lives on your conscience instead of one."

I grit my teeth, my fingernails digging into my palms. There has to be some way to get that gun out of her hand and even the score. If I could go toe-to-toe with her, I'm sure I could take her down. But right now, she's still got me dead to rights, and she's threatening the lives of two of the most important people in my life. "How do I know if I help you, you won't harm them?"

She throws me a quick sneer. "You don't. But do keep in mind I could have come here with one of their heads on a pike just so you knew I was serious. I didn't think that was necessary. Am I wrong?"

I have no doubt she's serious. I've seen what this woman can do, how silently she can move. It seems I have little choice but to cooperate. "No."

"Good." She reaches into another pocket and withdraws a syringe and a folded piece of paper. I take a step back.

"There's no way I'm letting you poke me with that," I say.

"Nor would I be so careless," she replies. "I get that close to you, and you might find a way to disarm me. You might even find a way to kill me. No, *you'll* be injecting you with that, not me." She tosses the syringe on the couch, where it lands, harmlessly. She places the piece of paper on the coffee table.

"What's it going to do to me?"

She lets out a frustrated groan. "My God, Emily. Had I known you were so squeamish I would have just injected you in your sleep."

"I'm not in the habit of shooting something into my veins that might kill me," I reply.

"It's a mild sedative, nothing more," she replies, taking another toke from the pen. "Otherwise, I'm sure you'll attempt to either follow me out or call some of your friends on me, which will only delay things, and not in your favor." She taps the piece of paper. "The case file information. Tomorrow. Drop off instructions are at the bottom. You're late, or you don't show at all, deal is off. You show up with a bunch of your buddies from the Bureau, deal is off. Understand?"

She's left me little choice. I nod.

"Good girl. Now sit down and inject yourself. I don't need you getting a concussion. You'll wake up in a few hours."

I stare at the syringe a moment. What have I gotten

myself into here? I always thought if I ever met this woman face to face it would be when I had my weapon out and she had her hands up. Or that the two of us would get into a fire-fight, or a fistfight. But not this.

I reach down and pick up the syringe, examining it. The liquid inside is a light amber, but that means it could be virtu-ally anything. I could be injecting myself with watered-down iodine for all I know. But if I don't do this, I have no doubt she'll hunt my friends down, if for no reason other than to spite me. And all because I refused her. If I have to go, I guess there are worse ways than trying to save people you love.

I take a seat, trying to control my breathing. Needles have never bothered me, but typically they're administered by a professional, not a trained killer. I remove the cap and find a vein in my elbow. Pressing the needle into my skin, I wince and depress the plunger.

"There, happy?" I ask, tossing the syringe aside.

"Very. Lie back. And when you wake up, drink a lot of water. You're on the clock, Agent Slate, don't forget."

I can already feel the room begin to spin. My head hits the back cushions of the couch just as the dizziness takes over. She walks over, picking up the spent syringe and replaces it in her pocket. She also puts her gun away, taking mine out and placing it out of reach on my mantle. I try to reach out to swat at her, but something is wrong with my arms, and I can't seem to make them do what I want them to do. "Wha…" The word is slurred before I can even get it out.

"Don't worry," she says, giving me a wink. "Sleep tight, Snow White."

I fight like hell to keep my eyes open, but whatever was in that stuff is strong. And before I know it, the world has dropped away and I'm falling in the other direction, untethered.

Chapter Two

A POUNDING ON MY DOOR WAKES ME FROM MY SLEEP. BUT IT takes me a few minutes to pull myself out of the grogginess, and by the time I open my eyes, I realize the pounding isn't on my door, but inside my head. It's my own pulse, though it feels like it's slamming on the inside of my skull two times a second. My mouth is dry and sticky, and I can already taste how bad it must smell. Rolling off the couch, I hit the floor and manage to push myself back up, fumbling at my pockets for my phone. Only, it isn't there. I look around the room, my eyes landing on the mantle where the assassin left my gun. My phone peeks over the edge; she must have taken it after she knocked me out in case I woke up early.

I push myself up on the coffee table, ignoring the note for a minute as I sit back on the couch and gather myself. When I finally feel like the room isn't going to spin away, I stand and head for the kitchen, filling a large glass of water from the tap. Whatever that stuff was, it was strong and potent. But as I drink the water, I start to feel a little more like myself. Part of me can't even believe that just happened. She was *here*, in this room, and I couldn't stop her. Somehow she manages to plan for every contingency. She even knew I'd been benched by

Janice, despite the fact it had only happened a few hours ago. I feel for my phone in my pocket, wanting to check the time only to remember, once again, that it is on the mantle.

Leaving the water behind, I grab it and my gun, taking them both back to the couch. I need to call this in, but I'm sure the assassin is watching. She's *always* watching. And if I do, the only thing that will happen is a swarm of FBI agents will show up here, do a forensics search, and come up with nothing, just like last time. But that sickly-sweet smell still hangs in the air from her vape pen. The only evidence she was here. I walk over to my front door and check it: locked. Of course.

What am I supposed to do? If I don't show up with this file, she's going to kill Zara and Liam. She might not even stop there. But I can't go steal the file either. That's exactly the kind of behavior Zara and I are working to change at the FBI. No more corruption, no more back alley deals, even if it seems called for. I really only have once choice; I have to call this in, even if she's going to see it. I've gone behind Zara's back in the past, and I won't do that again. She deserves to know what's going on, and how much danger she's in.

I sigh as I call up the numbers on my phone and dial. Some vacation.

Thirty minutes later I'm sitting in the front seat of my car as agents go in and out of my apartment, some of them clad in all-white clean suits, gathering evidence.

"This is a waste of time," I say.

Zara Foley sits beside me, her face drawn so that I can't tell what she's thinking. "You gotta move outta this dump. This is getting ridiculous. How many times in the past month?"

I shake my head. "Who knows? She comes and goes as she

pleases. It's like she has unfettered access to my life and I'm getting sick and tired of it."

"We should just booby trap the whole place. Next person that enters gets blown to kingdom come."

I suppress a laugh. Despite the joke, I don't feel like laughing. As soon as I informed my boss that the assassin had returned, she ordered another search of my apartment. We already went over this last month when I found the surveillance equipment. It didn't lead to anything then and it won't lead to anything now. This is all nothing more than a waste of resources and energy. I've been called back into the office, but I wanted to wait on Zara first. Given everything that's happening, she's taken the news quite well.

"So do I need to sleep with one eye open tonight?" she asks after a few beats of silence.

"Not tonight, but probably tomorrow, especially if I don't deliver this case file." I took a picture of the note the assassin left me before leaving it for forensics, but I doubt they'll find anything useful on it. My boss seems determined to hunt this woman down; but she can't accept what I already have: it's impossible. The only way to find her is if she wants you to find her. I wouldn't be surprised if she was watching this whole thing play out right now.

"Did she say anything else?" Zara asks. I know she's just trying to keep my attention off the half dozen agents swarming my apartment, but I'm not much in the mood for talking.

"No. She was pretty clear."

"How are you feeling?" I look over to see Zara's features are drawn. It isn't often I can get her to stop cutting up, but she knows this is serious. Not only is her life in danger, but it seems this woman is nearly unstoppable.

"I should be asking you, you're the one she threatened," I say.

She turns her attention back to my apartment. "But she

hasn't been watching me like she has you. She has no idea I can camp out in HQ for weeks at a time if I have to. In fact, I'd enjoy it. I could set up in the server room, it's nice and cool down there. Just throw down a cot and a sleeping bag. Brush my teeth in the convenient restroom next door. It would be perfect. You could even visit. We'd have sleepovers."

I can't help the smile this time. Leave it to Zara to lighten the mood when her own life is in danger. "I'm really sorry. If we had just found her earlier—"

"Hey," she says, placing a reassuring hand on my arm. "No one could have predicted this. We thought you were in the clear. Maybe it's a good thing you've been out of town so much lately, or this would have come a lot sooner."

"I don't know," I say, trying to think back to my conversation with her. She'd mentioned I was on a "clock" and that she hadn't wanted to do this so soon. I'm not sure she's not a little bit desperate herself.

"Ah, shit, here we go," Zara says. I look up to see Agent DuBois approaching my car. Despite the fact it's night, he still has his dark sunglasses on. Light from the parking lot reflects off his shiny head as he walks up, indicating I roll down my window.

"Agents," he says, standing stoically by the driver's side. I shoot Zara *the look* and we both get out of the car.

"DuBois," I say. "I told Janice this wasn't necessary—"

"It's our job," he replies. "The Bureau is still under a lot of scrutiny after what happened with Agent Green in New York. I wanted to inform you the forensics team isn't optimistic that they will find anything of use."

I blow out a frustrated breath. "As I tried to tell you."

"SAC Simmons would like to see you back at the office as soon as possible."

I suspected as much. It seems my little leave of absence will probably be the shortest in Bureau history. "We'll head over there now."

DuBois turns on his heel and heads back to the entrance to my apartment, handing out orders to the other agents on site.

"At least there's one good thing about this," Zara says. "Timber wasn't here."

I hadn't even thought of that. "You're right. She probably would have killed him before I'd even gotten in the door." The thought of my sweet boy being in that apartment when she broke in, and of her going after him causes me to choke back a sob. What's wrong with me? Why am I so emotional all of a sudden? It isn't like any of that actually happened. I guess maybe the fact that it could have makes it feel a little closer. "Looks like Dani was right. He is better off at their place."

"Are you going to tell them?" Zara asks.

My relationship with my in-laws has improved somewhat over the past few weeks, but we're not back to where we were before my husband died. I'm not sure we ever could be. And while we might have buried the hatchet, I'm not ready to divulge my deepest secrets to them. No need to tell them what they already know: taking Timber was the smart move. He's got more space over there, friends to play with, and they're at home a lot more than I am. I don't have to worry about him there; I know he'll be taken care of.

"Technically, it's classified. I'm not telling anyone outside the Bureau anything until we have this woman in custody." I take one last look at my apartment. The place that's supposed to be my refuge from the world. But it's lost that purpose. I think Zara's right. I need to move, if for no other reason than to re-establish a sense of security. But not until we've caught this woman. Until then, I won't be able to rest. "C'mon," I say. "It's going to be a long night."

Chapter Three

SPECIAL AGENT IN CHARGE JANICE SIMMONS HOVERS OVER the coffee maker in her office, three cups set to the side. She takes her time filling each one with a different brew, then turns and hands me one and Zara another. She takes the third and deposits herself behind her large desk without a word. Zara and I follow suit and take the two chairs on the other side. The mocha smell of the coffee isn't my preferred taste, but this late at night I don't even care. Who knows, maybe I'll find a new favorite flavor. I touch the cup to my lips, taking a ginger first sip, given how hot it still is.

"I want you to know, Slate, I've already informed Deputy Director Cochran of your situation. He and I are on the same page on how we want to proceed."

I glance at her over the edge of my cup. Despite the fact I was in this office not more than three hours ago being told I was being temporarily relieved of duty, somewhere in that time Janice has found the time to shower and change, while I'm still in the same suit I wore back from Delaware. Zara's in her workout sweats, as when I called I interrupted her evening workout.

"How do we want to proceed?" I ask.

"Obviously we have to take a threat like this very serious-ly," she says. "And we don't want to endanger the lives of either Agents Foley or Coll." I glance to Janice's open door as if to expect Liam to stroll right in at the mention of his name. Most of the office is dark, considering it's almost eleven in the evening. "I have yet to inform Agent Coll." She glares at me as she says it. "In fact, I would have preferred to keep both him and Agent Foley out of this until it could be resolved. But since you've already informed her of the situation, there's no sense in hiding anything further."

Zara raises her cup to our boss. "Appreciate that. It's always nice to know when your life is on the line."

"Then you are taking this threat seriously," I say. "Are you going to assign Zara and Liam protective details like you did for me?"

Janice leaves her untouched mug on a coaster. "Obviously that was ineffective. Given her mobility, I have to believe if that woman wanted to kill you, she could have at any time. Putting additional agents on guard duty would be waste of resources." Mentally I roll my eyes. This is exactly what I tried to tell her back when she assigned Liam to me. But at the same time, she's my boss, I can't exactly tell her how to run her own department. "Cochran doesn't like how much interest this assassin is showing in you."

"That makes two of us," I say.

"Given your accusations about what happened to Gerald Wright and your husband, and the data we've been investi-gating ever since New York, not to mention Agent Foley's attempts to uncover what we can only describe as an illegal business, there are a lot of moving pieces on this board."

I wasn't here when Zara almost caught up with the man who used to be my husband's boss. Both of them worked together, though the details around what kind of work they did and exactly *who* they worked for remain a mystery. Zara managed to track him down at a company that was being used as a front, but he slipped away. Apparently, his superiors didn't like the fact that she managed to find him; his body was discovered just a few days ago.

The investigation into his murder is ongoing.

I lean forward. "I don't know how all of this fits together, but I know wherever this woman goes, death follows. As I see it, we don't have much choice. We either give her the file, or we risk losing two more agents in what will sure to be a media nightmare." I'm trying to appeal to her practical side, because the thought of giving a known criminal and killer access to FBI records is a ludicrous notion on the surface. She and the deputy director will have to ultimately decide how much they want to risk.

"That's a cheery thought," Zara mutters, staring into her own mug of coffee.

"We don't want to put anyone's lives on the line," Janice says. "But at the same time, we can't let this go. We're not in the habit of turning over our case files to criminals and murderers."

"What's the case?" Zara asks.

Janice glances at her then turns back to me. "Cochran was very clear. He doesn't want anyone other than the assigned case officers working on this particular assignment."

"Must be important," I say.

"All our cases are important, Slate," Janice says, that hard edge sneaking back into her voice. "So then we're agreed. We are not turning the file over to your would-be assassin."

I share a glance with Zara. Neither of us agreed to that. If it were up to me, I would give it to her and not have another thought about it. That's not true, of course, but that's my gut feeling. To save Zara and Liam, I'd do just about anything. And the assassin knows that. But I also know when Janice phrases it like that, it's not a suggestion, that's the new law. We can't exactly argue with her. "So then what do we do? If we don't give her the file, she'll—"

Janice holds up a hand, stopping me. "I already know the stakes, Slate. We will deliver a file to your assassin, just not the one she wants."

"If you're looking to trap her, she'll see it coming a mile away. She said no other agents were to be present when I dropped off the package. The instructions are very clear." I glance down to the piece of paper sitting to Janice's left. The one the assassin left for me. Forensics didn't find a single fingerprint on it.

"I believe it. No, we'll deliver a dummy file, one with a tracker sewn into the folder itself, so we can apprehend her after the delivery has been made."

I take my seat again. "Can we get something undetectable?"

"You wouldn't believe what R&D has come up with over the past few years. She'll never even know it's there. You'll make the drop as scheduled. Then once she picks it up, we'll track her and make an arrest as soon as possible. Ideally within half an hour of delivery."

I don't like it, though I know we're limited by our options. Janice must see it on my face. "I know this isn't ideal. But you said she was desperate. We are never going to get a better shot at apprehending her."

"I never said she was desperate," I reply.

"You said her options were limited."

I nod. "Either she's playing a game with me, or she really has no one else to go to. But if that's the case, doesn't that make her even more dangerous? The last thing we want to do is make her realize she doesn't have any options left."

"With any luck, she'll be in custody by that point," Janice says. "And we'll have her on multiple felonies, not including the murders of Gerald Wright or your husband. If we find the evidence to convict on those, it will be nothing short of a miracle."

I have to agree. This woman isn't sloppy, and she doesn't make mistakes. Which makes me believe all of this is a bad idea. The idea of a dummy file isn't a bad one; I just wonder how long it's going to take her to realize she's been fooled. Because as soon as she does, I'm sure we'll experienced nothing short of scorched earth. She'll come after me too, for deceiving her. And I have the feeling she would do it with a smile. "I wish we had more time."

"I'm afraid we're limited by our options. If you have another suggestion, I'm listening," Janice stares, staring at me over the top of her black-rimmed glasses.

I try to think. There must be another way around this. "What's in the file?" I ask. "Why is it so important to her? If we can figure that out, maybe we can find a way to use it to our advantage."

Janice hesitates before reaching down into her desk and removing a brown manilla folder from the bottom drawer. It doesn't look like a typical case file, it's one that is sealed and has to be signed out to be read. As far as I can see, there are only two signatures on the file so far, one of them Janice's. "What I tell you doesn't leave this room. If this were any other situation this information would be classified above your pay grades."

Zara furrows her brow, shooting me a look before turning her attention back to Janice. She's as intrigued as I am.

"Last night the daughter of a US House Representative was abducted from her bedroom. No witnesses, despite the fact she had a full complement of security watching the house and a caregiver. One of the guards is in critical condition at GWU. Bullet lodged in his chest."

I sit up, the cup of coffee forgotten on the desk in front of me. "What? How did I not know about this?"

"I hadn't heard either," Zara says.

"That's because we're handling it discreetly. The Representative has an election coming up in November, and doesn't want any additional attention on this. He wants us to find her without going to the media."

I scoff. "Even for his own daughter?" I ask.

She nods. "Needless to say, we don't take orders from a single House Representative member. If we decide that media attention is warranted, then we'll take the appropriate steps. In the meantime, I've assigned this one to Sutton. He's only been on the case a day."

"If this case has been classified, how did she know about it?" Zara asks. "And what could she possibly want with it?"

I'm equally confused. I thought she'd be asking for a case that revealed some state secrets or incriminated someone she didn't like. But a kidnapping case? What could be the benefit? "She must be looking for some kind of leverage over the Representative," I say. "It's the only thing that makes sense."

"Which is why we can't give her any hard evidence that she could use against him," Janice says.

"What are the odds she was the one to abduct the girl in the first place?" I ask. "Setting this whole thing in motion."

Janice tilts her head toward me. "That's not a bad theory. But like I said, we don't have any evidence for it yet. To your knowledge, has she ever kidnapped anyone before?"

It isn't like she and I are besties. I barely know anything about the woman. But I wouldn't put it past her. "It's possible. No witnesses, clean, that's her M.O."

Janice nods. "Then apprehending her might be the best way to get the Representative's daughter back."

I sit back, a pit of anger forming deep within me somewhere. I'm not comfortable with the fact we have to protect him and potentially put two of our own in danger. "Does Sutton have any leads? Maybe if we can find the daughter before the deadline—"

Janice shakes her head, cutting me off before I can

finish. "There was little to no evidence left on the scene. Sutton has already given me a preliminary report and it's not looking good. The odds of finding this girl and returning her in—" She checks her watch. "—twenty-one hours is slim. We're better off putting our efforts into making a file that looks like what your assassin needs, while showing us her location." She stands. "You two go home, get some rest and I'll brief you first thing in the morning as to our progress."

Both Zara and I stand as well. "I guess this means I'm back on active duty?"

A small smile plays across Janice's lips. "I tried to tell Cochran not to take you off, that you'd find your way back in somehow. But even I was surprised at how quickly you've returned." She holds out her hand to mine. "Welcome back, Agent Slate. You almost made it four whole hours this time."

I smile and take her hand. "Thank you." She gives Zara a confident smile and shakes her hand as well before we head out. Once we're back in the hallway I turn to my friend. I can already feel the dark cloud settling around her.

"Hey," I say. "We're going to find her and stop her. *Before* she can do anything."

She shakes her head. "That's not what I'm worried about. It doesn't make sense."

"What doesn't?"

"Why would she kidnap the daughter, then get *you* to pull the case file? If she wanted leverage over him, why not just blackmail him directly?"

She's right. "I don't know. But it's been my experience this woman doesn't do anything without a reason. Something is going on here. I just wish we could find out what it is before the deadline."

Zara arches an eyebrow, then looks back at Janice's office. "What are the odds you think we could get that file away from her long enough to start an investigation of our own?"

"You're just itching to get me suspended, aren't you?" I give her a playful shove.

She shrugs. "It was worth a shot. But it looks like tomorrow is going to be a long day for everyone." She grabs my arm, wrapping her own around it. "C'mon, let's go get some sleep."

Chapter Four

GIVEN MY APARTMENT WAS DEEMED A "CRIME SCENE" FOR THE
second time in two months, Zara invited me to stay at her
place for the night after we swung back by and picked up my
suitcase from inside the front door. Since I didn't have a
chance to unpack there was nothing inside but dirty clothes
and my toiletries, but I really didn't care, given the events of
the evening.

After a night of restless sleep on Zara's couch, I got up
early and took a shower, digging out the cleanest set of clothes
from my trip to Mardel that I had. All of my suits need to be
dry cleaned, so I went with a simple t-shirt and dark jeans
which look professional enough for a Saturday.

"You look almost presentable," Zara says as I come exit
the bathroom, having pulled my hair back into a loose ponytail. I have a feeling today is going to be an especially
long day.

"I need coffee. Or maybe a stiff drink," I say, trudging to
the kitchen.

"Coffee is to your left, the liquor to your right. Feel free to
mix and match, I'll drive us in." She's on the couch pounding
on her laptop like there's no tomorrow.

"What are you working on?" I ask, retrieving a mug from one of her cabinets. I set it under the coffee maker and take a French vanilla cup from the carousel, popping it in the receptacle.

"I'm trying to find anything I can about the Representative's daughter," she says.

I circle around out of the kitchen while the coffee maker hums. "Do you know who it is?"

"Simple process of elimination," she says. "There are only four House Representatives up for re-election in November who have daughters. And only two of them live in Washington D.C."

"Well that's pretty easy," I say. "Who is it between?"

She presses her lips together and glares at me. "Do you really think I'm that sloppy?"

I chuckle. "Okay, smartass. Who is it then?"

"Representative Huxley," she replies. "Representative Arillo's daughter is in college, and just posted a series of selfies this morning on Insta."

"Could be the kidnapper trying to divert suspicion," I suggest. "Maybe someone took Ms. Arillo and prepared by stealing a lot of selfies to post so no one would question she'd been taken."

"I think this job is getting to you," Zara replies as the coffee maker beeps. I get back up and retrieve my mug, slowly taking a sip. It's better than whatever Janice gave us last night. "Ms. Arillo tagged half a dozen other people in her pictures. I checked their accounts, they all show similar activities, from different perspectives." I sit back down on the couch. "Trust me, it's Huxley."

"What if the kidnapper managed to steal photos from—"

"Stop," Zara says, taking the mug from me and taking a big gulp, despite the warmth. "I know you're just trying to piss me off. That's good, what flavor is that?"

I shrug. "I just grabbed the first one I saw."

"Huh," she replies. "I didn't even know I had that flavor."

"So Representative Huxley, huh? Isn't he the one who likes to pander to the 'silent majority'?" I manage air quotes; despite the fact the mug is in one hand.

"That's the one. And from what I can tell, he and his wife were at a fundraiser on Thursday night. Which explains why their daughter, Avery, was home alone."

"If you call a cadre of armed guards and a caretaker being home alone," I say.

"You know what I mean," Zara says, pulling up another website. "They've managed to keep Avery off social media as far as I can tell, so I don't have a lot to go on for her. And she doesn't have any brothers or sisters."

"So what's the angle?" I ask. "Revenge? Retribution for a vote the assassin didn't agree with? Or, more than likely, someone hired the assassin to grab the daughter, and is looking to swing Representative Huxley's vote."

"That's my guess," Zara says. "I mean, how often are people like her following their own agendas? She's a hired gun, right? So someone probably hired her for this job and now she's what…trying to control the whole thing by getting hold of our case?"

I shake my head. "I have no idea. It doesn't make a lot of sense to me." I don't like thinking about her, because every time I do, I can't help but see Matt's dead body lying in our kitchen. Sure, he lied to me every day he knew me, but that doesn't mean I didn't still love him. I had hoped I could put it all behind me, that I was finally ready to begin moving on with my life, that I could be content not knowing all the details, but it turns out life has other plans for me. It seems I am destined to do some dance with this assassin whether I like it or not.

"Hey, you okay?" Zara asks.

"I just can't believe she got the drop on me again," I say. "I knew it the minute I walked into the apartment. I should have…I dunno, checked it out or something first. I shouldn't' have just strolled in there."

"C'mon, how many times have you walked into your apartment and an assassin *hasn't* been standing right inside the door ready to shoot you?" She gives me a wide smile. "You had no way to predict that. So don't beat yourself up over it. You're already doing enough of that; you don't need to add anything to the pile."

I take a deep breath. "I guess you're right."

"And hey, this lady had her chance to walk away. She warned you to quit, and you did. If she's watching you as closely as she says she is, she should have known that. So she betrayed you again, by not letting you go off and be happy."

I take another sip of the coffee. "How are you so coherent this early in the morning?"

"It's the drugs. Speed with scrambled eggs. A sprinkling of coke on my French toast. Part of a balanced breakfast."

"You're terrible," I tell her.

She taps her chin a few times. "Maybe that's why every guy I have over here ends up bolting for the door as fast as he can."

"Wait, what about Ian? Your boy-toy from Switzerland?"

She types for a few moments before replying. "Yeah, just didn't work out."

"Zara, I'm really sorry. Was that before or after what happened with Brian Garrett?" I can't believe I missed that. Had I not been in Delaware, I would have been right there beside her, chasing down my husband's old boss. He'd been our only solid lead on the people my husband worked for.

"After," she says. "I think it freaked him out. You know how it goes."

I do. A lot of people have a hard time dealing with the demands of our job, but guys in particular. I think some of them feel emasculated when we're the ones out on the streets, chasing down suspects or getting into firefights. Matt was never like that, though. He was always very supportive. Though now, I have to wonder if that support was just so I wouldn't ever question what he was doing when I wasn't home.

"But enough about me, we need to talk about your motion on the ocean."

"We weren't even near the ocean," I tell her, getting back up to deposit the coffee cup in the sink.

Zara closes her laptop. "Okay, motion away from the ocean, then."

I suppress a smile, thinking back to my...encounter with Liam in the backseat of my car as we were waiting on backup. Probably not the most professional thing we could have done, but I'd just learned Matt had been lying to me for our entire relationship, and I was tired of holding a candle for him. To say I extinguished that candle, then stomped on it with a steel-toed boot would be accurate. "What's to tell? It happened, it was fun, and that's it. We decided to stay friends."

"You little liar," Zara says, standing up. "There's no way that boy mutually decided to stay friends with you. Especially after you gave him a taste of the honeypot."

"Z, don't be gross," I tell her.

"What's gross about it? Like the song says, *you and me baby ain't nothin but mammals*. It's natural! Who initiated? Had to be you, right?"

I can feel the heat in my cheeks already. "Okay, that's it, I'm done talking about this," I say.

"Nope, you can't wuss out," she replies. "Especially not after I got dumped. C'mon."

I huff, washing out the mug in the sink. "Fine. It was...I'd just gotten off the phone with you...where you'd told me about Garrett."

"Ohhh," Zara says. "That makes sense." Her face falls. "I wish I could have told you in person. That wasn't the kind of news I wanted to deliver over the phone."

"It was rough," I tell her. Finding out the one successful relationship in my life had been nothing but a lie was a little more than rough. But I don't want her to feel any more guilty than she already does. "But he was there for me when I needed him to be."

She pinches her features. "Wait, weren't you at the coroner's office when I called you?"

"Yes, but—"

"You dirty dog!" she yells. "In the coroner's office? Em? Ew! How could you stand the smell?"

"We didn't do anything in the office," I say, hoping she'll lower her voice. I don't have any idea of how thin the walls are here. Though, if they're anything like my place, a freight train could be driving through the next apartment over and I'd never know. "It was in…the backseat of my car."

A grin a mile wide spreads across her face. "Nice."

"Is that all you have to say?" I laugh.

"I don't think anything else needs to be said. Did he let the big 'L' slip while you two were all wrapped up? Guys can't help it."

"No, he managed to practice some restraint in that regard," I say. "Actually, he was surprisingly quiet."

"I'm sure you can fix that next time," she says, pulling her shoes on.

I grab my badge and my sidearm, along with my ID and keys. "No, there's not going to be a next time. That was it. One and done."

"Uh-huh," she replies, gathering up the rest of her things.

"Z. I'm serious. I told him that it wasn't going to happen again."

"Sure," she says in that way that tells me she doesn't believe a word of it. Hell, maybe I don't believe it either, but I don't think it's a good idea to start a relationship like that right now. Especially not when Liam's life could be in danger.

"Hey," I say, taking her by the arm. "I'm serious. Not a word of this to him."

"C'mon, would I really do that to you?" she asks.

"I dunno, who made me get on a roller coaster, or go sing karaoke to a crowd of half-drunk strangers?"

She taps me on the shoulder with one finger. "That's because you lost some bets. Now if we were to place a friendly wager—"

"*No.*"

She breaks out into hysterical laughter as she opens the door. "Em, you are too easy."

Chapter Five

"Agent Slate, are you in position?"

Janice's voice crackles in my earpiece. I made sure to let my hair back down once I settled the tiny device as I don't want anyone knowing I've got the rest of the FBI in my ear. Still, even if I were to pull my hair back it would be difficult to see. Thankfully it's not one of those wire models the Service uses. I rub my clammy palms on my jeans; I'm not entirely comfortable with this. The assassin said no other FBI, and while there are no agents in the immediate area, they're stationed all around on different cross streets to follow the signal I'm about to plant.

"I am," I tell her as I sit in my car, staring at the MTA station ahead of me. The parking lot is filling up quickly as commuters park in preparation to take the train in for an enjoyable Saturday night. I'm at the Brookland-CUA station in University Heights. The instructions on the sheet were very clear for me to drop the case file in one very specific trash can on the station line. I check my phone. It's almost seven p.m. We've had half a dozen agents working on this operation all day, with Janice at the helm. Zara is back at HQ, keeping an eye on things from our surveillance there, while I do as I'm "supposed" to and drop the file in the designated location. I'm then to leave and hopefully suffer no more contact from the assassin. But my nerves are tingling as they have been all day. I know I can't trust a word out of that woman's mouth.

"You are clear to proceed," Janice says.

"Acknowledged." I get out of my car and begin walking toward the station. A couple trots past me, dressed in what I can only describe as "clubbing" clothes. I can't help my heart pounding in my chest. If all goes right, I could be sitting across an interrogation table from the assassin in only a few hours. Though I don't expect her to talk, not unless she knows it's going to get under my skin.

One step at a time, Emily. Let's just catch her first.

As I head for the station, I can't help but feel her eyes on the back of my head, watching and waiting to see what happens. Does she suspect it's a trap? Or does she think I was dumb enough to get a classified file from the Bureau and bring it to her? So far this woman has been one step ahead of us at every turn. Why should this be any different? At least if she's watching she won't see any other agents, that much I'm sure about.

I head down the stairs into the underground portion of the station and that familiar tang that's present in every station in the city hits my nostrils. It's like a combination of wet garbage and mold and no matter what they do, it's never completely gone. "All clear," I say as I get to the bottom of the escalator. More passengers fill the station, and there's a short line to get through the turnstiles. I wait, my heart pounding as I do everything I can not to look around me suspiciously. This woman can't be everywhere at once; either she's here, in this crowd, or she's out there somewhere, watching from afar. Either way, I've got a job to do. I can't let her see that I'm rattled.

Swiping my card, I push through the turnstile into the other part of the station. The file is in a small bag on my shoulder. I take the escalators back up to where the trains stop on the platform, filing in behind all the others. The sun is low in the sky, but it's still light enough that none of the outdoor lights are on yet. At least fifty people are already waiting in the immediate area, and I see even more further on down the platform. But none of them look anything like the assassin. "No sign yet." My assumption is she's concealed herself in this crowd somewhere so she can retrieve the file and disappear. But we have people at stations in both directions, waiting to jump on the trains if necessary.

"Proceed as planned," Janice says.

I head south along the station, stopping at the third trash can. There I rummage in my bag, pulling out a couple old tissues and a brown plastic grocery bag that's been wrapped to cover the file itself, but looks like nothing more than ordinary trash. I discard them all into the can, then continue walking down the platform. The last thing I want to do is draw attention to myself throwing something away. There's also the remote chance someone might decide to dig through the trash and accidentally take the file, so I take a seat at the next bench, where I can keep an eye on the trash can for a minute to make sure no one goes fishing for something they shouldn't.

"Package has been dropped," I say. "Awaiting confirmation."

"Stand by," Janice says.

I take a deep breath and try to calm myself. People stroll by in both directions, some stopping close to me, but none are her. They're all turned away from me, either looking at their phones or staring down the tracks, as if that will make the train come any faster.

It's taking all my willpower not to think about what the next few days could be like if we apprehend her. I would finally be able to relax for the first time in four months. I could take a bath without worrying if someone had a video camera on me or eat at a restaurant without looking for a sniper's laser.

As I sit there, contemplating, I realize just how much the past few months have been weighing on me. The relief from this burden can't come fast enough. Someone coughs and I nearly jump, but I manage to maintain my composure, keeping a sharp eye. Still no sign of her.

"Signal acquired, you're clear to leave," Janice says in my ear.

I nod, more to myself than anyone else just as the southbound train approaches the station. I get up with some of the other people and as people begin to crowd the platform waiting for their chance to get on, I take the escalators back down into the underground portion of the station. A few people run in my direction, putting me on alert, only for them to take the up escalator in an attempt not to miss the train. I can already hear the telltale sounds of the doors chiming their final chime before they close, indicating these people will be too late. I feel my shoulders start to relax. It's done. Now all we have to do is wait and see if she takes the bait, or if she realizes the ruse and decides to come after Zara and Liam.

I only hope it's the former.

"Slate?" Janice's voice crackles in my ear again.

"Go ahead." They can't be getting movement on the package already, can they?

"Head back up to the platform, there seems to be a problem. I need eyes on it."

I turn back before I reach the exit turnstiles. "What sort of problem?" A scream filters down from the platform and I bolt up the escalator, squeezing past other passengers craning their necks to get a good look at what's going on.

When I reach the top, the train is right where it was when I left only moments ago, stopped in place. The doors are closed, but it isn't moving and there's a crowd of people gathered around the front of the train.

"Let me through," I say, holding up my badge. "FBI, move please." People part and I get to the edge of the platform only to see a young man lying on the tracks. He only looks unconscious, but he's touching all three lines, which tells me he's already dead, the electricity flowing through his body is enough to kill anyone.

"Janice, we've got a body on the tracks up here, the train isn't going anywhere." Immediately I'm on full alert. This looks like *her* handiwork. I turn to the nearest onlooker. "What happened?"

She's a young woman, no older than twenty with a smattering of freckles across her cheeks. "I—I don't know. I didn't see it; I just heard the commotion."

I turn to the rest of the crowd. "Did anyone see what happened?"

"Slate, please repeat, there's a body on the tracks?" Janice asks just as half a dozen people start yelling things at me. I hold up both hands.

"One at a time, please," I tell them. "I need everyone to back up."

"I think he was pushed!" one man with a baseball cap calls out.

"No, I saw him trip," someone else says.

"Alright, everyone, just back away from the platform." I walk over to the front of the train and tap on the conductor's window, showing him my badge. He slides the window back. "Have you notified anyone yet?"

He nods. "Just called it in."

I continue motioning the people back. Some are groaning, more upset at the inconvenience rather than the fact that a man has died. I tap my earpiece again. "We've got a possible homicide up here," I tell Janice. "I can't get a clear consensus from the crowd. Conductor just called it in."

"We're receiving the reports now," she says. "Emergency services are on the way."

It's tragic, but I can't let myself get distracted. That's exactly what *she* wants. "What about the package, has it moved?"

"Foley reports no movement on it so far," she replies. "If this was a ruse, it was a bad one."

Still, I can't get the feeling that the assassin orchestrated this somehow. But for what purpose? Why kill some random innocent stranger? It's just another charge we can bring against her once we apprehend her. "Keep everyone on high alert. This woman doesn't do anything without a reason."

"You sure it was her?" Janice asks.

I can't say with a hundred percent certainty that I am, but it seems like too convenient to be a coincidence. "Maybe. How should I proceed."

"Emergency services are close; the MTA will want to shut down the tracks until they can clear it. Start funneling people out of there."

As I make the announcement I'm met with even more groans and complaints. *Have a little humanity here, people.* The sad fact is someone lost their life for no good reason. I can't wait to have this woman in custody, just so I know more people aren't going to be killed.

Some of the crowd begins heading back down the escalators to pass under the tracks on their own, though a significant portion remains for the northbound train. I help manage the crowd, even after additional security and police show up. I'm happy to let them take over; I'm not great with crowd control. But given there was no other authority on the platform at the time the job fell to me. I wonder if she was counting on that? And if so, for what purpose? All she seems to have done here is to delay a train by a few hours and inconvenience a lot of people. As far as we know, the file is still in the trash can. If she was going to use this as a distraction, wouldn't she have taken the file during all the commotion?

I poke my head up, though it's difficult to see above the

heads of everyone else. I can't make out anyone in the crowd that looks like her, but I can practically *feel* her presence around me. It's like she's right here, always behind me.

The crowd grows thicker and it's almost as if I've been caught in a human wave, being pulled and pushed along in a thicket of human resentment, powerless to move in any direction but forward. People all around me are grumbling at the situation, some of them shooting me dirty looks. Since I'm on my way out anyway, I keep pace with the people, not letting them get to me. It's not my fault their night was ruined. Or is it? Is all of this because of something I did? Does the assassin know about the tracker?

As I'm contemplating it, I feel a familiar pinch in my neck, like a bee sting. When I turn to swat it, the edges of my vision go blurry, and I feel myself collapse into someone's arms.

For the second time in two days, darkness takes over.

Chapter Six

THE PUNGENT SMELL OF VANILLA AND LILACS WAKES ME, drifting into my subconscious like a ghost becoming corporeal, and eventually rousing me into a state of alertness. The first thing I notice is my throat is dry as a bone, and I have a massive headache.

The second is that I've been tied to a chair with nylon ropes.

Adrenaline floods my system and I immediately begin yanking on the ropes, panic setting in. I had been in the crowd of people, and I'd felt a presence behind me, someone who was too close. And then there had been the pinch. Just like when I'd injected myself. My eyes, though dry and scratchy, tell me I'm in what looks like a bunker. It's nothing but concrete blocks on all walls, though there's a door at the far end. A single light bulb is suspended from a wooden ceiling. Across from me a ratty green sleeping bag has been stuffed next to the wall. And there are discarded coffee cups and other bits of trash strewn around the room.

I try to rock the chair back and forth, only to realize it's been bolted to the cement floor. It's not hard to figure out what happened, though my brain still feels a little foggy from the drugs. But even though I know this is *her* work, I'm more worried about what will happen to Zara and Liam now, since things obviously didn't go to plan. Somehow she knew all along, just like I suspected she might.

I continue to struggle, but it's no use. She has restrained me in a way that the more I pull on the ropes, the tighter they become. I stop struggling, and close my eyes, hoping to stop my head from pounding.

Stars explode across my vision as my head is rocked to the left by a blow from behind. It takes me a full second to register what just happened as white spots dance across my vision. I cry out in agony, my headache now multiplied by a factor of ten.

"That's for not listening to me," a familiar voice says from behind me. I didn't realize she was in the room, though I should have suspected it. I can't see anything behind me, so I'm not surprised I missed her. Still, I thought I would have felt her presence, like I did back in the crowd.

"What—" is all I can get out before the dizziness takes over and I list to one side, suspended by only the ropes. I'm at this woman's mercy, and I hate I can't even control my own reactions.

"I knew you weren't going to *steal* the file for me, that much I was willing to accept. But I had hoped you'd use your powers of persuasion and the threat of death on your friends' lives to motivate you to bring me the actual file. Was that really so much to ask?" She walks around so I can see her, and she's clad in the exact same outfit she was last night, though her blonde hair looks more frazzled today, like she's been out in the heat a lot.

"Can't...classified...the Representative—" I manage to get out while trying to sit back up under my own power.

"So they told you what was in it, I wasn't even sure you'd get that much," the assassin says. "Did you think I couldn't detect that tracking device in whatever you left in the trash can? What was the plan, wait for me to take it and then have one of your FBI teams take me down?"

I take a few deep breaths, as deep as I dare, anyway, which begins to clear my head. I'm at least able to sit up under my own power. "You—you can't have really expected this to work."

"Expected, maybe not. But I had hoped. For your sake. And now you've wasted another day, putting me behind schedule."

"Sorry for the inconvenience," I say, though from the tone of my voice it's obvious I'm anything but. I'm starting to feel more like myself and were it not for the sucker punch to the back of my head, I'd probably be feeling a lot better by now. "So what's the plan, ransom me instead?"

"What?" The assassin looks at me like I've lost my mind.

"You were planning on using the file to blackmail the Representative, weren't you? Because you were the one who took his daughter."

The assassin pinches the bridge of her nose, then retrieves her vape pen and takes a few long puffs on it. "Emily, you disappoint me. Your prejudice toward me has affected your critical thinking ability."

"Can you blame me?" I ask as the dizziness finally abates. "You destroyed everything I had."

"I saved you, whether you want to believe it or not," she spits back at me, leaning down so she's right in my face. I take a moment to study her features; I'll need them if I can get back in front of a sketch artist. High cheekbones, smooth skin, pointed eyes. When this woman looks at you, you can feel a sort of magnetism, and it makes you want to look back. I don't know if she does that on purpose or it's something she's learned over the years as she's increased her skillset, but it's damn hard to look away. "I didn't take the Representative's daughter. I'm trying to find out who did."

"Why?" I ask. "So you can capture her yourself to sway his vote?"

She chuckles, standing back up. "I don't care about the American political system. No more than I care about the Russian, or the Chinese, or any other country. I'm not bound by a border, nor am I loyal to any country. No, this has to do with the people who hired me to kill your husband."

A stab of pain shoots through me at her words confirming my worst fears. But at least now I am sure, and no amount of doubt will ever change that. She's admitted to it, just as I had always thought. But now I also know that she's always been a hired gun. That someone else wanted Matt dead. "What about them?"

"They're the kind of people who expect anonymity. You can appreciate that."

"I can't, actually, considering it's all illegal," I reply. Were my legs not bound to the legs of the chair, I could attempt to sweep hers out from under her, perhaps even knock her out on the concrete. But that would do me little good as I see nothing in her possession that will cut through these ropes. Nor do I have a way of moving myself closer to her unconscious body. Still, I can't help but fantasize about it.

Panic grips me as I realize I don't know how long I've been out. Has she already had time to go after Liam and Zara? "What day is it? How long have I been here?"

"You've been out a grand total of five hours," she replies. "It's now Sunday morning. And the clock is still ticking."

"You don't seriously think I can get you that file now, do you?" I ask.

"Clearly you can't. You don't follow instructions very well, do you?" She glares at me, and I get the sense something very bad has happened.

"Where are Liam and Zara?"

She ignores the question. "Here's what's going to happen

now. Since you are obviously incapable of obtaining this file for me, you have now volunteered to find Avery Huxley yourself. Once you do, you will inform me and your part in this will be over. But you now have less than two days to do it." She takes another puff from the pen, not removing her eyes from mine.

"I'm not doing a thing until you tell me where they are and what you've done with them," I say.

The woman sighs. "Agent Foley is fine, still at work, searching for you. Agent Coll, however..." she trails off and pulls out her phone. When she turns it to me, I see a picture of Liam restrained in a chair very much like the one I'm in. It looks like it could be the next room over.

"Where is he? Is he still alive?" I demand, pulling once again at the ropes holding me down.

"For now," she replies. "However, if he stays that way will depend all on you."

Dammit. I should have warned him; at least let him know that it was a possibility. With only a still image to go by, there's no way of determining his condition, but either way, he's been restrained and possibly assaulted. He's not in a good way. It was a picture from what looked like a security camera. He could be dead already and I wouldn't know. It's not like I can trust her word.

I yank at the restraints again and she only laughs. The sound enrages me, and in the heat of the moment I forget all my training, all my morals. All I want to do is throttle this woman. Who does she think she is? She can't just play with people's lives like this, pretending to be God.

"Calm down or I'll have to knock you out again and then you'll really have your feet to the fire," she says, taking another puff. I've begun to hate that vape pen. I just want to smash it all over the ground.

"I don't work for you," I finally growl.

She shakes her head. "No, but you do work for the FBI,

and as I understand it, finding this girl is a high priority, though it's to be kept very hush hush."

"If you know so much, then why do you need me?" I ask.

"My sources only go so far," she replies. "And since you obviously won't deliver the file to me to let me do my own investigation, you're going to need to do it for me."

"And what's so important about finding this girl? Why does it matter so much to you?" I ask.

"That's my business," she replies.

I shake my head. "No. I need to know what all this is about. I'm not playing anymore games. You wouldn't have come to me unless you were desperate. So tell me what this is all about or I'll refuse to help."

She arches her eyebrow. "And risk Liam's life?"

I square my shoulders. "I don't know what you're going to do with that information. I don't know if you're going to murder that child if I find her or use her to try and influence her father. I don't know anything, which tells me whatever you're planning is worse than not finding her. Liam knew what he was getting into when he signed up. We all did. And if it costs our lives to save other innocents, then we're all prepared for that."

She appraises me for a moment. "That's...unexpected." She crosses her arms and taps her toe against the concrete for a few moments. "But then again, sometimes you manage to surprise me."

"Glad I can be of some amusement," I reply.

"Only some," she replies. "The reason I need to find this girl is because I believe she will lead me back to my one-time employers."

"Why can't you just contact the person who hired you?" I ask. "And what do you want with them anyway?"

"It's simple," she says. "I want to kill them. I want to kill all of them."

Chapter Seven

IT'S LIKE I'M IN A DREAM. SOME ALTERED STATE WHERE things seem real but aren't. I stare at the woman who took my husband's life, who drained his very last breath from him, and I feel nothing but rage. Despite everything he did to me, I can't help but want to drag her kicking and screaming into the FBI and charge her with first-degree murder. I want to put her away forever, without any possibility of parole, and watch her as her days tick by and she can do nothing but wait for the end.

But it's not that simple either. She apparently wants to go after the people who ordered my husband's death. As she's pointed out, she's a contract killer. That's something I trust her on, at least. I don't believe she cares one way or another if someone lives or dies, she only cares about a paycheck. And someone came to her offering her a big payday to make my husband's death look like an accident. I need to know why.

"No," I tell her.

She sneers at me. "No?"

"No, you're not going to kill them all. *I'm* going to charge and arrest them. *That's* what's going to happen."

She cranes her head back and lets out a long laugh, like it's the funniest thing she's ever heard. "Emily, don't be so naïve. These are not the kind of people you bring charges against. These people are above any law, beyond the reach of any government."

"No one is above the law," I say, dead serious. "But first things first, I want to know why they wanted my husband dead. I'm not going to let you kill them before they can tell me."

"Isn't it obvious?" the woman asks, grinning at me. "He worked for *them*."

Her words don't quite register. "What?"

"He was part of the organization. That was why they called me in. They wanted him dead."

I try to sit up. This is information I've been searching out for months now. "Why? Who are they?"

"That's the big secret," she replies. "Even I don't know. I told you, they like their anonymity. Which means no names, no official organization. No big conference room in the middle of some skyscraper where they all meet and discuss... whatever it is they discuss. These people are entrenched, and they are cloaked to resemble normal, everyday people. But I just need to find one. I find one, and I can find the rest."

"Why do you want to find them so bad? Did they stiff you on your payment?" I ask.

"No. Because they've put out a contract on my head now as well," she replies.

Now it's my turn to laugh. It starts small, but I can't help myself and it bubbles out of me. Even though it's not legal, my internal sense of justice meter has flipped over to the green column for the first time in a while. "Seems fair to me."

"Yes, it's all very funny," she replies. "But take a second and think about *why* they want me dead."

"You obviously must have screwed up somewhere," I reply. "Not carried out some assignment." She's looking at me pointedly, and I realize that there's something written in that gaze.

All of a sudden it hits me. "Wait. Is this because of me?" She doesn't deny or confirm. "Is this because you warned me to lay off investigating Matt?"

She takes another three puffs on the vape pen, and for the first time since I've seen her in person, she seems unnerved. Her features have become pinched and she's holding herself a lot tighter than she was before. Not someone who is completely in control, despite what she would like me to think.

"You were supposed to kill me, weren't you? But instead you warned me to leave it alone. Why?"

She gives me a pinched smile. "Let's just leave it at that, why don't we? *Now* you understand the stakes here. Not only are they after me, but they're still coming after you. No doubt they've hired someone else to take you out, especially after they find out what I've told you. This is as much for self-preservation as it is for anything else."

This whole time I thought she was always watching me through the end of a sniper scope, but her denial confirms it: she could have killed me at any time and yet she didn't. She'd even been ordered to and decided against it. And yet it seems like she killed Matt without hesitation. Why spare me? What makes me so special?

"No," I say, standing my ground. "Tell me. You owe me."

"I don't owe you anything," she replies. "This is how it is. Are you really willing to let the people who not only employed him, but decided he needed to die, get away?"

Now that I know who ordered him to be killed, I feel a renewed sense of focus. But at the same time, I feel like I have more questions than when I started. "Don't think this changes anything," I say. "You're still the one who took his life. Someone else may have ordered it, but it was your hands."

"Trust me, I'm under no illusions of that," she replies. "Will you find the girl?"

"How can you be so sure this missing girl will lead you to these people?" I ask. My mind is spinning, but I focus on the task at hand, trying to shove everything else into a back corner of my brain. I'll deal with that later, when I'm not tied up and I have my weapon on my hip.

"So many questions!" the assassin yells, clearly exasperated. "Can't you just do the job?"

I shake my head slowly. "I. Don't. Work. For. You."

"Fine. I know, because I've seen this before," she replies.

"Seen what?"

"The daughter of a powerful man or woman abducted. No witnesses. Sometimes it's a Billionaire CEO, or a head of state. Or it can even be a state governor. Anyone who has power and influence and who can be manipulated by the suffering of a loved one."

"Explain," I say.

She sighs. "It's always the same. The girl is always Caucasian, blonde, twelve-years-old."

"What happens to them?" I ask.

"They're usually returned. Though in worse shape than they were taken. Maybe not physically, but psychologically, at least."

"And you know this...how?"

"I hear things," she replies, avoiding my gaze.

"But you don't know how to get in contact with these people who keep hiring you for jobs? I find that hard to believe." Something about all of this doesn't make sense. But given all I've learned; I'm going to need some time to sort it all out.

"These people aren't the trusting type, for good reason. Look at me, I betrayed them, after all. Had I already known who they were, I could have infiltrated their ranks by now, and silenced them all for good. But apparently, I'm going to have to do this the hard way."

"The hard way—as in getting me to do your dirty work for you."

She leans down so she's in my face again. I get a full whiff of the lavender and vanilla. "I tried to make this easy on you. All you had to do was deliver a simple file. That's it. But you decided you'd try to trap me instead."

"I don't control what my superiors tell me to do," I say. "But yeah, I wanted you in handcuffs by now."

"Then neither of us got what we wanted," she replies.

"I think they call that a compromise." She walks behind me again and I can hear her rummaging on a table or some other elevated surface. "What are you doing back there?" The pinch bites at my neck again.

"Find the girl," she whispers in my ear as the darkness begins to take over. "You have two days before she's due to be delivered. That's always how it works. When you do, I'll find you."

I fight like hell to keep my eyes open. I still have a hundred questions for her. One of these days I'm going to be the one holding the syringe. I fall into unconsciousness thinking about how sweet that day will be.

"Ma'am, ma'am, can you hear me?" My eyes flutter and my pounding head reminds me I'm not dead. Still, wherever I am, it's dark. I look up to see a figure a couple of feet away. He's got a long, graying beard, and is covered in tattered clothes. In my half-awake state a surge a fear runs through me, and I scramble back, my arms and legs flailing.

"Whoa, whoa there, you okay?" he asks, holding his hands up. As my vision clears, I see he's nothing more than a man, probably homeless by the look of him. I glance around; I'm under a highway bridge, lying in something wet in a ditch.

I groan once and he approaches before I hold a shaky hand out. "Stop right there, FBI."

"Didn't mean nothin'," he says. "Just tryin' to do a good deed." He takes hold of an old shopping cart I'd missed earlier and pushes it on down the road, heading into the darkness.

I appreciate him waking me, but I don't know where I am or what time it is. I feel for my phone in my pocket, and find it's still there, as is my weapon. She's returned everything to me just like before. Surely she knows if she took my phone it would delay things even longer.

I rub my temple a minute trying to get the headache to subside before I dial the office.

"Dispatch."

"Slate calling in. Put me through to Simmons," I say.

The line clicks once, then twice before it's picked up again. "Slate? Where the hell are you?"

"I have no idea," I reply. "I just woke up. She grabbed me at the station, took me somewhere. I don't even know how long I've been out."

I can hear her snapping her fingers in the background. "Give me your location, are you in any danger?"

"No more than normal." Cars thunder on the roads over-head. I pull the phone away from my ear and open my maps app. "I'm on Stoneybrook, right under the beltway."

"I've got a team headed to you now. Are you hurt?"

In the dim light I can see deep marks on my wrists from where the rope had me bound. "Not seriously."

"Do not move. Slate, I'm serious. We need to gather any evidence we can from the site if we're going to find this bitch."

That's the most impassioned I've ever heard Janice get about something. It's good to know she's still in my corner. She probably also feels somewhat responsible for losing me at the station. "I'm not going anywhere. It's not like I'm about to hike."

Chapter Eight

I GRUMBLE AS I PULL ON A PAIR OF GRAY SWEATPANTS WITH BIG, blocky yellow "FBI" letters emblazoned along the leg. The sweatshirt isn't much better, as it has a matching logo along the sleeve. All my clothes and my shoes were taken as evidence to try and determine where I was while I was being "interrogated". It's a little after two in the morning and I'm exhausted. After the stresses of the day, along with being injected with who-knows-what twice in a row, my body is wrecked.

Still, I had to go through debrief before I can go back home. I've already given my statements to Janice and Deputy Director Cochran via video conference, but there's a procedure to follow no matter what time of day it is.

I grab a pair of sneakers and pull them on with my sweats, and grab what few items I have left. Forensics has just about everything I had on my person while I was captive, including my phone, which they're trying to use to triangulate the assassin's location.

It's all useless. I know it, Janice knows it. But we have to follow procedure.

I head out of the locker room and take the elevator back

up to my floor, finding most of it dark this time of night. I feel like a walking zombie, like I'm going to collapse any minute. The adrenaline from earlier has worn off and all my body wants to do is sleep.

Janice's light is still on, so I head back into her office, only to find her in there already, working on her laptop.

"Don't you ever sleep?"

"Wait until you're a Supervisory Agent in Charge. You'll wish you had about twelve more hours in every day."

"No thanks," I say, taking one of the seats across from her.

Janice stops typing and moves the laptop aside, folding her hands in front of her. "I know you're exhausted, but I need your read on this situation. If everything in your statement was accurate—and I have no reason to believe it wasn't—then we have a decision to make."

"Have you had any luck contacting Agent Coll?" I ask.

She shakes her head. "Neighbors didn't hear or see a thing. He was just…gone. DuBois found his phone still in his apartment. No sign of a break in, nothing else missing. His car is still there."

"Dammit," I say. "He could be anywhere."

"Not anywhere. More than likely within a twenty-mile radius of the city. You said that his room looked a lot like your own. That would lead us to assume he's somewhere she can transport him back and forth easily if she needs to. Just like you."

I sit back and rub my eyes. "How did she even get me out of the MTA station? The last thing I felt was that stupid needle in my neck."

"We're still going back over the footage to try and find out. It seems there are some gaps in the data. She could have hoisted you out with the crowd, explaining that you'd just had too much to drink."

"And the civilian on the tracks?" I ask.

"Eddie Ramirez," she replies. "Construction worker, two

kids, wife. Lives out in Riverdale. Apparently, he was headed out to meet some friends for the night. And your new best friend decided he'd make as good of an excuse as anyone to cause the station to fill up with people. We suspect that was the only way she could get you out of there unnoticed. Had there been fewer people, and had they all not been so angry at the situation, someone might have picked up that you weren't exactly conscious."

I let out a deep sigh. "It's like I said, she does everything for a reason."

"Do you believe her; her claims about this organization your husband allegedly worked for?"

I shrug. "Who knows. The only thing we know about them is apparently they eliminate anyone they think is a security risk. She seemed pretty adamant about tracking them down, I believe her life is in danger from them. The rest of it…I don't know."

Janice looks out her window at the city sparkling in the distance. "We've already devoted significant resources to finding the organization your husband worked for. After what Agent Foley found last week and now this, I don't think this is an opportunity we can ignore."

"Which means what?"

"That you need to find this little girl." She removes the actual case file from her drawer and tosses it across the desk, where it lands right on the edge.

"You can't be serious. You're going to give in to what she wants?"

"We've already seen that we can't risk another sting. She'll see it coming a mile away. I should have listened before; you were right about her." My shoulders drop and I realize I've been waiting to hear those words since I got back. The validation feels nice, but Liam is still out there somewhere, possibly dead already. And it's my fault because I didn't follow her instructions properly.

"But you can't seriously—"

"I'm not saying we bow to her wishes, but she does have a hostage," Janice says. "And for the moment, our goals align. Not to mention we do have a young girl's life that is possibly on the line here. I don't see we have much choice, not until we can secure Agent Coll's safety."

"So I'm just supposed to work the case like normal?" I ask, taking the file and staring at the signature lines on the front. It hasn't been opened since Janice showed us yesterday.

"There's nothing normal about this," she replies. "Didn't she say the girl only has two more days before she's delivered?"

I nod. Those were the last words I remember before waking up in that ditch. "Delivered where I don't know. I assume to her former employers. Has Sutton made *any* progress?"

"Go see him first thing in the morning," she tells me. "He hasn't updated the file since I gave it to him, but that doesn't mean he hasn't made some headway. You know Sutton, he's not the best with his paperwork."

I scoff. That's an understatement. He's known around the office as the man with a million stories because he'll get so involved in one, he'll forget to do his other work. But he's great with witnesses; really finds a way to relate to them.

"Got it, so find the girl, then what? Wait for the assassin to contact me?"

"Your priority will be Agent Coll's safe release," Janice says. "But my hope is once you locate the girl, we'll have a chance to move in before the assassin can do any of her dirty work. You have the entire Bureau at your disposal, per Deputy Director Cochran's orders."

"Wow," I say. "That's high praise from a man who had no problem relieving me of duty."

She leans forward. "You realize how irregular all of this is. The Bureau is in a tough position here, especially with an election year coming up. Everyone's always walking on eggshells right up until November. And if we have a new administration come in, you can bet things will change, *especially* here."

It takes considerable effort not to say exactly what's on my mind. "I hate politics."

"I know." Janice opens her desk drawer and places my phone in front of her, sliding it across the desk to me. "I had them run this through as quick as possible, seeing as you'll need it. Your girl is thorough, no fingerprints, no dust particles. Apparently, she turned it off and removed the SIM card while she held you captive, as there's a full hour missing from the location data. She knew exactly what she was doing."

I take the phone and turn it back on, the blue screen popping back to life. "She's a professional. That much I'm certain about. It seems like she has eyes everywhere."

"Don't worry, Slate. We will get her, eventually. No one can be perfect all the time. She'll screw up, and when she does, we'll be there to snare her. I only hope we can do it before Agent Coll's situation grows any worse."

I take the file and stand. I still need to gather the rest of my effects from processing. "I'll get started on this right away."

She shakes her head. "No, you're going to sleep first. I need you clear-headed. And we should have the tox screen from your blood back in a few hours, at least then we'll know what she gave you. And not that I expect it, but any other evidence from your time with her."

"But the clock—"

Janice stands to match me. "Slate. Get some sleep. I'll get you a hotel room if you want. But if you are the only one who can work this case, which seems like the hand we've been dealt, then I'd rather you sleep so your mind is clear rather than trying to zombie your way through it. Understand?"

I give a half-hearted nod. Part of me understands the

urgency of this, but another, possibly stronger part just wants to close her eyes for a few hours. "I'll just go back home."

"You don't have to do that," she says. "I'm sure we can find you alternate accommodations."

I shrug. "What's the difference? She's going to follow me either way. I might as well stay in my own apartment with my own things."

Janice nods. "Fair enough. Check back in first thing in the morning." I give her an appreciative nod, then head to the door. "And, Slate?" I turn back to my boss. "You said you called her out during her interrogation, dared her to kill you and Agent Coll."

I nod. "I think I was just angry. And still a little messed up from the drugs in my system."

There's a strange look on Janice's face, one I can't seem to place. "Angry or not, it tells us one thing. She might need you more than she's letting on. For a cold-blooded killer, she doesn't seem to have a problem sparing you."

She's right. Based on what the woman told me, that was the second time she had spared my life. I wish I knew what that meant.

"Goodnight, Slate."

I take my cue. "Goodnight."

Chapter Nine

THE NEXT MORNING, I ARRIVE BACK TO WORK IN A CLEAN SUIT for the first time in three days. After a long, hot shower and six straight hours of sleep, I finally feel more like myself. I've also managed to tame my hair, which had been a mess after my ordeal. It's just one more thing that was out of my control for those couple of days. I'm not sure if this is how it is for everyone else, but when the things I don't normally think about are messed up, like my attire or my appearance, it becomes a distraction I'm not used to dealing with and I can't think as clearly. The whole reason I don't wear a lot of different clothes is, so I don't have to dedicate a lot of brain-power to what I wear each day. I'd rather focus that energy on my job. It's the same with food, though half the time I forget to eat anyway, like this morning. I just grabbed a cup of coffee on my way out of my place before I drove into the city.

But the entire time I couldn't help but look around, seeing if I could spot her out there, watching. I'm sure she got a big kick out of me trying to find her. Even though she says she needs me, I still feel like I'm being watched through a sniper's scope.

"Hey," Zara says, getting up from her desk as I come

through the double doors into the main office. The place is the opposite of last night, a buzz of electric energy seems to crackle through the air. People are on edge, moving quickly, not offering the normal friendly platitudes and there are more agents in the office for a Sunday than I've ever seen before.

Zara wraps me in a quick hug. "Are you okay? I'm sorry I couldn't be here last night, Janice was adamant she talk to you alone once your debrief was over."

"I'm fine," I say. "No permanent damage." Though in the shower this morning I could still see the red marks all over my body from where the ropes cut into my skin. "You didn't go home, did you?"

She shakes her head. "Are you crazy? After what happened to Liam? No, I set up in the server room, like I told you I would. And I slept great. The hum of the machines and the cool temperatures are perfect in there."

I let out a breath. "Good. Because if something happened to you too——"

"Stop," she says, then averts her eyes. I can tell from the way Zara's face is drawn her own guilt is eating away at her. "I don't know what happened. We had full surveillance on the station, including in the underground portions. She shouldn't have been able to snag you. But the feeds went in and out there right at the end, like something was interrupting the signal. Whatever she used, it was high-tech." It's not her fault.

"Listen to me, you're not going to feel guilty about this," I say.

She cracks a smile. "I think that's my line. You're the one who is always sending herself down the guilt spiral."

I nod. "That's right, and I can tell you from experience that you're only going to end up drowning at the bottom. You couldn't have done anything to stop that from happening. She would have found a way to get to me eventually, no matter what anyone did."

Her face relaxes and I can see she's relieved I don't blame

her. But it's almost immediately replaced by anger. "I just can't believe she killed an innocent man for it."

"We will bring her to justice," I say. "One day. She's not getting away with this, any of it. And we're going to find these people Matt worked for. Even if it kills me."

"That reminds me, I need to bring you up to speed," Zara says.

I look over to Janice's office, but the lights are off and as far as I can tell, it's empty. "Where's—"

"She had an emergency meeting this morning. She told me to get with you so we could get started. But first, I spoke with Caruthers. They didn't find anything on any of your clothes. No hairs, DNA, nothing. And the dirt on your shoes didn't show anything significant. Basically, she knew not to leave any evidence behind."

"So we're no closer to finding Liam," I say.

She shakes her head. "I wish I had better news."

I've got the case file from last night tucked under my arm. I'd considered trying to go over it last night, but it just wasn't happening. I was too tired. I'm anxious to begin so we can find our victim, but at the same time, I don't like playing the assassin's game. "Please tell me you don't have any other pressing cases right now."

She shakes her head. "I'm all yours, baby."

I breathe a sigh of relief. For a second I thought I might have to work this case all on my own. Normally that wouldn't be a problem, but given the high-profile nature of this one, not to mention everything that's riding on it, it's nice to have some backup. "Janice told me last night I have the resources of the Bureau at my disposal."

"Free coffee and pizza indefinitely?" Zara asks, hopeful.

"I think she meant something else, but I'm not going to say no," I chuckle. I can already feel the stress of everything beginning to roll off my shoulders. Which is good, because it's hard to work when I'm freaked out like that. "But what I meant was we can pull anyone we need for the case. I think right now it's better we start with just the two of us, but we may want to exercise that option in the future."

"Look at you, slinging your power around," Zara says, taking a step back and putting her hands on her hips. "Anyone you want to fire?"

"C'mon," I say. "Let's get started."

Ten minutes later after we've procured some breakfast burritos from the hot vending machine, Zara and I have set up at our desks, going over the details of the case file. I need to familiarize myself with what we have so far before we move forward.

"Doesn't look like Sutton got very far," Zara says.

"He's going to be our first stop once we get a handle on this thing," I tell her. "Then we're going to see Representative Huxley. I want to get a look at that house."

"Should I prep a team?"

I scan what little is in the matching electronic file on my computer. "Yes. There's a possibility Sutton already did it and it's not in the system yet, but there's no sense in not being prepared." Everything else in the file is basic information: victim's age, history, and a report of the incident, including anyone who was present at the scene when it happened.

"Any cameras on the property or around it?" I ask.

Zara types on her computer a moment, only taking a break to chomp a bite of the burrito. "Cameras at the house were disabled, as were those on the outside property. The only other ones are cameras from neighbors, but given the size and distance between these houses, I'm not sure those are going to be any use."

"Start on requisitions to pull them, from any neighbor

within a thousand yards. This house is too far out there for someone to take her and walk. They had a vehicle."

"On it," she says.

I go back over the details on the victim: Avery Huxley. It's just as the assassin said. She's Caucasian, blonde, and turned twelve-years-old the day she was abducted. So much for a happy birthday. But as I read the information on her, I can't help but think why people Matt worked with would want her. What was he into and what did they do to pre-teen girls? The assassin was adamant this wasn't the first time something like this had happened. Did Matt know about this? Had he helped or participated in some way? The thought makes me sick to my stomach. No wonder he never told me anything about who he really worked for. Because if all of this is true, he's more of a monster than I thought possible.

"I've got records with two of the three big security companies, on two neighbors," Zara says, breaking me from my thoughts. "They're sending over the data now. But there are two other neighbors that are within that radius that aren't with any of the big companies. I know rich people aren't stupid, so my guess is they probably use private security companies."

"Was the security team protecting Avery contracted or do they work directly for the Representative?" I ask. Depending on their affiliation, we might be looking at an inside job here. Someone obviously knew their way around the house and how to disable all the security measures.

"Contracted," Zara says. "Mansfield Tech. They're expensive, and not for the middle class or anyone who doesn't pull in two million per year. Strictly rich people and politicians. But that doesn't mean he didn't go through and vet these people personally."

I'm surprised. A hawk like Huxley strikes me as the kind of man who has no problem working with private militias. But then again, maybe that's all just for the campaign trail. He might think a little differently when it comes to his own family's personal security.

"And what about this caretaker, Irene Henderson?"

"Looks like she's worked for the family for about seven years, ever since Avery was young."

I consult the file again. That looks like all we have as far as witnesses go, despite the fact their initial statements already saying they didn't see who it was. But they might have seen *something*. We're going to need to interview all of them. "We've got some legwork on this one." I also can't let myself forget this is no ordinary case, which means we don't have time to sit back and contemplate.

"There is one update from GWU," Zara says. "The security guard who was shot is out of surgery and stable. We should be able to talk to him too."

"Good," I say, and take a few large bites of the burrito all at once. We need to get moving, which means I don't have time to eat.

"Hey," Zara says, turning to me just as my cheeks are as full as a chipmunk's. As soon as she sees me does everything she can not to laugh.

"What?" I say, my words half muffled. "I'm hungry."

"I can see that. What I was going to say is do you think this has anything to do with that trafficking ring you busted back in January."

I stop chewing, all thoughts of hunger gone from my mind. I hadn't considered that possibility. We busted that ring and sent a lot of people to prison. But it was only one cell of many across the eastern seaboard. We tried to coordinate with other departments to make a simultaneous strike, but by that time I was on leave and didn't have any involvement in the Bureau's operations. From what I understand it was partially successful, but some things always slip through the cracks. Then again, it could be a completely new operation out there, connected to this organization the assassin mentioned. But right now we don't have enough information to make that kind of assumption.

I finish chewing and swallow. "Let's put that on the back burner for now, but we'll keep it in mind," I say. As if I didn't need any more pressure from this case. If it is somehow connected to that ring, I'll need to tread very carefully.

"Grab everything, I'll drive," I say.

"Yep." She gathers what little we have, along with the remainder of her burrito as we head out. I catch looks from some of the other agents. Everyone knows how much is riding on this. While I try to give them reassuring nods, I'm not feeling very reassured myself. If we don't come through with this, there's a good chance Liam is dead.

I only hope I'm up to the job.

Chapter Ten

THANKFULLY, ZARA DOESN'T OFFER PASSENGER-SIDE commentary on my driving as we make our way to Agent Sutton's house. Unlike Liam, who always seemed to have a word to say about how I operate a vehicle. I can't seem to get him off my mind, though I know I have to if I want to find Avery and hopefully secure his release. I can't be thinking about how much I miss him and that night in the back of this very car. I shoot a glance to the backseat and feel nothing but a stab of pain, so I instead turn back to the road and try not to think about it.

Agent Sutton has always been someone I've looked up to in the Bureau. He's one of those career agents who somehow manages to balance both his work and life and not go crazy in the meantime. I was surprised he wasn't in the office with everyone else this morning, but then again, those of us with families do our best to carve out time for them. Not every agent is as...hardcore...as Zara and me. Not everyone spends all their waking moments at the Bureau, some agents actually go home and spend time with other people.

I don't know why, but that just doesn't sound like something I could do, especially with the kinds of cases we work.

Being a Special Agent with the FBI to me means putting everything else in your life on hold and working the cases until you find a resolution. Because often, especially in our department, lives are on the line. I can't just sit around watching TV or reading a book when I know someone is out there suffering. But at the same time, I know this is exactly what leads to burnout, and why so many agents retire or quit early. Thankfully I'm still less than five years into this career, and I feel like I still have a full tank. I can go like this for a long time to come.

Agent Sutton's house is a nice brick two-story, situated right in the middle of a neighborhood with a cul-de-sac. It's what I expected, honestly, given what I know about the man. It seems he lives the perfect domestic life, or at least keeps up appearances.

As we step out of the car, I notice for the first time in months the air isn't as muggy as is typical for August. A sure sign that fall is right around the corner. Personally, I can't wait until summer is over. I don't do well in warm weather; I'd much prefer layers and a cool breeze blowing in the afternoons. Maybe once all of this is over, I can find a nice new place with a balcony where I can wrap up in a warm blanket with a similarly-warm drink and relax between cases.

"Nice house," Zara says as we make our way up the sidewalk.

"Think he's taking a cut under the table?" I tease.

"No question. They sure don't pay me enough to have a house like this." She looks up at the second floor above us. The brick has been painted an off-white color, and all of the window casings are done up in black, to match the black roof. It's a statement, considering most of the other houses in the neighborhood are unpainted brick or siding.

"Hey now, you never know. Sutton's wife might be a surgeon." I ring the doorbell and take a step back. A few minutes later a blonde woman with an apron wrapped around her waist answers the door. She's in a baggy sweatshirt and leggings, but rather than looking casual, it somehow makes her look more sophisticated. Her hair is pulled back just right, so that only a few strands fall down, framing her face.

"Not a surgeon," Zara whispers. I shush her.

"Oh, hello, you must be Bill's colleagues, please come in." She steps back, making way for us.

"I'm Emily Slate, this is Zara Foley," I say.

"Juliette," she says, shaking each of our hands. "This way, we're all out back." I shoot Zara a look and she just rolls her eyes as we follow Mrs. Sutton through their house. This is what I don't understand. Had this been my case and someone else had been assigned to it, I would have been prepared with everything I had when they arrived. But it looks like Bill Sutton is preparing for a family cookout. He's out on his back deck, up under the large grill that's been built into the surrounding deck structure.

"Bill, your friends are here," Mrs. Sutton says.

Sutton pokes his head out from under the grill. "Oh, morning. I didn't realize you'd be here so soon." He gets up and wipes his hands down with a nearby rag. He's filthy, covered in charcoal. "Sorry about the mess, the grill has been on the fritz. Slate, how are you? Foley?"

"Hey Bill," I say, taking his hand quickly. Zara does the same. "We're on the clock here. Zara and I have already been over the file. But we wanted to check with you to see if you'd made any headway you hadn't reported in yet."

"Right, of course," he says, turning to his wife. "Jules, can you see if you can get this thing lit? We'll be in the office." Bill Sutton is in his early fifties, and his gray hair has begun to bald, but he's not a bad-looking guy. He's managed to keep his gut to a minimum, though like most of us the job has aged him prematurely. He's probably got twice the number of crow's feet a person of his age should have. Still, he moves quick and with purpose to a set of double doors off the far end of the porch.

The doors open into a home office, which, unlike the rest of the house, is something of a mess. Shelves line both walls, and there's a door at the far end leading into the rest of the house. Sutton has a home computer set up, but it's covered in paperwork. "Sorry," he says as he brings us in the room. "I gave up trying to keep this place organized years ago. I usually end up bringing most of my work home with me and so it ends up here."

Now I feel bad; I think I've misjudged Sutton. Whereas I usually have something of a separation between my work and my home life, it looks like he's merged the two together. I guess maybe we're not that different after all, we just have different approaches to the job.

Sutton pulls a series of file folders out from under a pile of papers, opening them. "I went ahead and copied everything in the secure file. Didn't feel like checking it out every time I had a question. Not to mention most of what we do is electronic these days. I don't know why they still bother with those archaic things."

"That makes two of us," Zara says.

"I was only on the case for about thirty-six hours before the word came down from Janice to put a hold on the investigation," he says. "Then they informed me last night you'd be taking over, so I didn't go any further. Something about special circumstances?" He hands me one of the manilla folders.

"We're in something of a bind here," I say. "And Agent Coll's life is on the line."

"Jesus, I had no idea," Sutton says. "I'm sorry. He's a good agent. Anyway," he turns back to the file folder. "I'd scheduled a few interviews, but no one got back to me. Two of the neighbors had security systems using the big three, and the other two had private security: Mansfield Tech and LiveGuard Systems."

Zara shoots me a satisfied smile. At least that cuts down on some of our work.

"I called to get the footage from them, but they said it was only available through the homeowners; that they don't keep a central station. How dumb is that? If someone hacks into their security system, they can erase all evidence they were even there, without a backup copy at a centralized location. Not to mention it relies on cell service to call out. What if someone breaks in while there's a bad storm?"

"It does seem foolish," I admit, anxious to get any other information he has.

He keeps searching through more papers, looking for what, I don't know. "Damn right. I once had this cousin—this was back before cell phones were the norm—and he had a security system that didn't even have a battery backup. So all the thieves had to do was cut his power, and the system just died, like that. Took him for everything. And because he hadn't disclosed that on his insurance forms, they denied any coverage. He had to use furniture from his neighbors for years before he could get everything replaced."

Bill is headed into story mode. I need to get this back on track. "So was that all you found on the case so far?"

"Almost," he says. "You'll want to check with that care-taker. I found out she used to work for Senator Parnell back in the early nineties, doing the same job. So she's used to the work—it isn't like she doesn't have experience."

"Got it, thanks," I say. "Everything in here?" I hold up the folder.

He continues to shuffle through the papers. "Yeah, just about. Wait, here it is." He pulls out one last sheet and hands it to me. It looks like a printout of an email.

"What's this?"

"Read it."

The door flies open, startling me and I jump back as a girl probably no older than nine runs in the room. "Daddy!

Mommy said she got it working!" She stops short when she sees Zara and me. My heart is going a million miles a second and I force myself to breathe.

"That's great, honey, but Daddy's doing something important right now. Can you go play for a few minutes? I'll be right there."

"Okaaay," she says, then gives us a little smile before running back out again, leaving the door wide open.

"Sorry about that. My daughter, Katie. She's a little fireball. Anyway," he points to the paper in my hands. "That's from Cochran."

"Deputy Director Cochran?" I ask.

He nods. "He sent this not more than fifteen minutes after I was handed the case by Janice. It's an 'advisement' to keep any information about the case close to my chest, that the details of what's going on shouldn't go any farther than I need them to. In other words, keep a lid on things and don't let people know what you're working on."

I know Janice said this was a sensitive matter, but this seems a little on the paranoid side, even for Cochran. "Did you reply?"

"No, but I did make a physical copy of the email in the event the digital one magically 'disappeared'." He uses air quotes. "There's something strange about this case. Never before have I been told to keep things hush hush. Especially not when it involves such a high-profile victim. Frankly, I'm glad to be done with it. It seems to me like the kind of case where you put one toe out of line and you're working a desk in Montana the rest of your days."

"Thanks," I say. "We'll keep an eye out."

"One more thing," he says, stopping me from leaving with a brief touch on the arm. "Watch out for Cochran. He's always been ambitious. I heard what he tried to do to you, but I'm glad to see you beat it and are back on active duty. Just… watch out. He's a man with an agenda."

"What kind of agenda?" Zara asks.

"I don't know for sure. But I can tell you he will go wherever the wind blows to gain points. He wants the top job."

I give Sutton a solemn nod. "Thanks for your help, this saves us some time."

"I know it's not much," he says. "If they hadn't tied one hand behind my back I could have done more." He holds out his hand again and I shake it. Zara follows suit. "I'd offer you both a burger before you go, but they're going to take twenty minutes at least."

"Thanks anyway," I say. "Enjoy what's left of your weekend."

"Good hunting."

Chapter Eleven

"According to Sutton's file, he never got a chance to order any forensics on the Huxley home," Zara says as I take the exit off the beltway that will take us out to Potomac, on the Virginia side of the line. "I can call them now and have them meet us over there. Caruthers has them prepped and ready to go."

"Not yet," I say. "We need to speak with Representative Huxley first. If he's as skittish as everyone is making him out to be, a team of FBI forensics personnel showing up in a big white van will only freak him out and probably cause him to clam up. He's already going to be somewhat resistant because he wasn't even there when she was taken. I'm sure his pride will be a factor. If it looks like he's going to be cooperative, then we can call in the backup teams."

Zara shakes her head. "It's been two days already. There's no way they haven't destroyed what little evidence was left."

I agree. Waiting this long to dust for prints or look for other evidence is not only detrimental to the case but it's downright irresponsible. Sutton probably tried to get some of this started but either ran into resistance from Huxley or maybe even Cochran. Either way, I'm not about to let some politician in an FBI uniform run this investigation from his wingback.

"We gotta get reassigned to another office," Zara says. "I don't know how much longer I can deal with all these snakes."

"Let's just work the case," I say, though I absolutely agree with her. I've done everything I can to stay away from any politicians, but when you live in D.C. it just comes with the territory. This was always going to happen eventually. I just wish it hadn't happened with Liam's life on the line.

As we drive, my thoughts drift back to him. What is he thinking? I know he was disappointed how we left things, but he's not the kind of guy to push his will on mine. He's respectful of my wishes, and I appreciate that. He's also one hell of a detective, and from what I've heard, is already making a name for himself in the Bureau. To lose him now would be a travesty. But really, deep down, I do care for him. If there was ever anyone I could see myself with after Matt, it would be him, but I'm just not ready yet. And now I've put his life in danger, which is worse than what happened to my husband. Matt's death wasn't my fault. But Liam's will be if the assassin goes through with it.

Even more reason to wrap this case up as soon as possible.

We pull up to the gates of the Huxley home and the differences between this and Sutton's house couldn't be starker. It's a stone manor, set way back from the street, with matching stone columns framing a massive iron gate that screams opulence. I have to lean out my window to touch the small button on the microphone mounted in the ground.

"Go ahead," a hard-edged voice says on the other end.

"FBI," I say.

"Please present your credentials."

"Oh, for—" I grumble as I search for my wallet, finding it and pulling it out, showing the badge to the camera built in beside the speaker.

A second later there's a high-pitched beep and the gate

begins to roll to one side. I pull myself back into the car and stuff my wallet back inside my blazer pocket.

"I can tell this is going to go swimmingly," Zara says, not bothering to hide her sarcasm.

"I guess they got their cameras back up and working," I say. "I don't care if they were off when Avery was taken, I still want to see what footage they do have."

"Works for me," she says as I drive up the long driveway. It winds and I notice in a couple of spots the earth is disturbed right beside the pavement. I stop the car and hop out, wanting to go in for a closer look. "What is it?" Zara asks.

"Maybe nothing," I reply getting on my hands and knees. It looks like a tire went over the edge of the pavement into the soft earth and tore it up, which means it would have had to have been going relatively fast. I wonder if this could be from the getaway car, or just one of Representative Huxley's staff being careless.

"You there! Stop!" I look up to see two men dressed all in black running in our direction. Both of them are sporting AK-47's around their shoulders. I stand up and pull out my badge, holding both hands up before they're fifteen feet away. My badge is easily visible in my left hand.

"FBI, we're investigating the disappearance of Representative Huxley's daughter!" I yell. Zara is out of the car, but she's still behind the door. I can't tell if she's drawn her sidearm.

The two men stop jogging, and instead walk up to us. Their weapons aren't pointed at us, but I do notice the safeties are off. What were they going to do, shoot us?

The nearest one takes a close look at my badge. "Agent Slate?"

"That's right," I say. "May I put my hands down now or are you planning to put a bullet in me?"

He flips the safety of his weapon back on and slings it around to his back on the strap. His partner does the same.

"Sorry about that, we're a little jumpy around here after what happened."

"Who are you?" I ask, putting my badge away. "And didn't they tell you they let us in at the gate?"

"Wallace Armstrong, LiveGuard Security," he says. "This is my associate, Duke Hoover. The Huxley's decided to hire our company after their last security team failed to stop this tragedy."

So it turns out my hunch about Huxley wasn't wrong after all. "I see. Do you realize that pointing a weapon at a federal officer could be considered a serious crime?"

"Sorry, ma'am, but you hadn't identified yourself," Hoover says from behind Armstrong. "We were just doing our duty."

"It's the middle of the morning and I'm in a chevy," I say. "I highly doubt I'm here to abduct anyone. You two need to lay off the trigger fingers. And I better not see those safeties shut off again unless you're being fired upon, get me?"

Hoover nods but Armstrong just looks over to Zara then back to me. "Are you here to see the Representative?"

"That's one of the reasons, yes," I tell him.

"We'll escort your vehicle up to the house," he says. "We can't be too careful given the circumstances."

My willpower is just about maxed out, but somehow I manage not to roll my eyes. I get back into the car with Zara as Hoover and Armstrong trot ahead of us, "escorting" us up the rest of the driveway.

"Trigger happy military wannabes," I mutter.

"Careful," Zara says. "They'll shoot you if they hear you disparaging what they've clearly made their life's mission."

"I'm sure they've been using the local wildlife for target practice," I say. I've met men like Armstrong in the past and they're always the same. They tend to live by one creed: freedom through firearms. Unfortunately, a lot of guys like this get hired by private security companies and are given more legitimacy than they should have. I could technically confiscate those weapons from them, but I know they probably have a hundred more. And the last thing I want to do right now is antagonize Representative Huxley when we need his cooperation.

We pull up to the house and Hoover and Armstrong stand on either side of the car, like they're part of some vehicle escort in Afghanistan. The house looms large, and we've pulled the car under what I can only describe as a two-story carport, like the kind they have at hotels to keep people from being rained on when they're loading and unloading their cars. Except this one is all stone, matching the house. In front of us is a series of stairs leading up to massive iron doors.

Without another word to our personal militia, Zara and I head up the stairs and ring the doorbell. I'm almost surprised they didn't want to escort us inside.

A moment later one of the doors opens to reveal an older woman, probably in her early sixties, her gray hair pulled back in a tight bun and a serious expression on her face. "Ah," she says with a light English accent. "You must be the FBI."

"Agent Slate," I say. "This is Agent Foley."

"Please, come in," she says, holding the door for us. "I first want to confirm this matter is being tended to discreetly."

"May I ask, are you Irene Henderson, by chance?" Based on the description we have in the file, she matches perfectly. I can't imagine this is anyone else, unless the Huxley's have a pair of twins working for them.

"I am," she replies, shutting the door.

"We'd like to have a word with you, if we could," I say.

"What about the Representative?" she asks.

"He wasn't here Thursday night. You were," Zara replies.

"But I've already given a statement over the phone," she says. She appears hunched, like something is wrong. I don't know if it's because she feels guilty in some way, or if she's really hiding something. But I plan on finding out.

"Still, if you wouldn't mind," I say, trying to keep my voice as sympathetic as possible. I don't always succeed in that area, especially when I'm under pressure. "It will only take a few minutes of your time."

Mrs. Henderson sends a furtive glance down the hallway. "Very well. In here, please." She directs us to a sitting room, not far from the front door. "How can I help?"

She's got the demeanor of someone who is used to being in control. Very terse, rigid. Like a strict schoolteacher. I imagine she imposes a lot of discipline on young Avery. But there's something else in her eyes, a fear, I think. Either of the repercussions of letting this happen on her watch, or possibly something else. "Just tell us what happened that night, from your own perspective," I say, taking a seat in one of the plush leather chairs.

Zara follows my lead and we're both sitting, looking up at her. She purses her lips, then moves over to the chaise lounge on the far side of the room, tucking her hands under to smooth her long dress skirt as she sits. "It was past ten, because I had already turned off most of the lights. I normally make one last round of the house before I retire. When I reached the security system, I noticed none of the lights were on. Usually, the system shows a green light when unarmed and a red one when armed. I went to go inform the head of security for the property—Mr. Moran, and that's when I heard the gunshot."

"Where did it come from?" I ask.

"Somewhere out on the grounds," she says. "I ran to Avery's room to check on her, but she was gone. Outside I could hear some of the other security personnel yelling."

"Okay," I say. "Where were the security personnel normally stationed?"

"One at the door you came in, another at the back door near the pool. And then two on patrol around the property, they work in shifts before returning to the gate house you passed on the way in. The only people in the house were Avery and myself."

I know the answer to this next question, but I ask it anyway to try and alleviate some of her nervousness. "And Representative Huxley and his wife were out of town?"

"Yes, at a fundraiser in West Virginia." She wrings her hands together, whether that's a conscious move or not I don't know.

"All right," I say, keeping my voice light. This woman is on edge and I'm not sure it's just about the little girl. "What happened when you heard the shouting and realized Avery was missing?"

"That's when I called...our security company," she says, correcting herself.

"You didn't think to call the police?" Zara asks.

"I did...but our company is closer and can respond quicker. I didn't realize Robert had been shot, otherwise I would have. Obviously when we realized what happened we called emergency services."

A quick glance to Zara tells me she's thinking the same thing I am, this woman's adherence to her boss's rules might have cost them precious time. A private security firm is no replacement for the police. "I see from the men outside you've hired a new company."

She nods. "The Representative thought it was prudent, given what happened."

"So then you're the only one who was here that night who is still employed by Mr. Huxley," Zara says.

Henderson cuts her gaze to Zara. "Yes, *Representative* Huxley has always valued my service."

I look down at my phone like I'm checking some notes, while in reality it's just a blank screen. "Have you received any threats, any suspicious mail, or noticed anyone watching you or Avery when you're out of the house?"

"Goodness no. I would have reported it immediately. I take Avery's safety very seriously, and I'm always on the watch for predators out there. I don't have to tell you the world is a dangerous place, Agents. Little girls don't understand that yet."

"I understand, I just have to ask all the pertinent questions," I say. Given my own experience with the assassin I'm very aware that someone could have been watching Avery or the house and no one would have had any idea. But what bothers me more is Mrs. Henderson didn't even notice something was wrong until she saw the security system was disabled. That means the kidnapper got in the house and got back out with Avery before anyone noticed a thing. I need to find out how and where they came in.

"Did you ever have any problems with Mansfield Security before this?" I ask. "Any of their employees not performing to their standards?"

She shakes her head slowly. "Not that I recall. They're a national company with a fine reputation, and if it were up to me, I would have kept them on board."

I stand. "Thank you for taking the time. We'd like to see the Representative now."

She stands as well, patting down her long skirt. "Yes, please wait here for a moment. I will come fetch you."

She leaves us and Zara turns to me. "What are you doing?" she asks in a hushed voice. "We need to take a look at the entry and exit points."

"We will, but I suspect this is a matter of…timing," I reply. First I want to get a read on Representative Huxley and hopefully get him on our side. Then we'll take a look at the place.

"Agents," Mrs. Henderson says, coming back around the corner. "The Representative will see you now."

Chapter Twelve

Mrs. Henderson leads us back through the large house and I catch glimpses of every room. Each one is spotless, with minimalist décor, though the walls are covered in pictures of the Representative with other famous politicians. Above the fireplace in the great room is an oil painting of him, his wife, and a much younger Avery, probably no more than two.

We reach a pair of French doors that lead into a home office that isn't much unlike Sutton's, except this one is tidy, with rows and rows of law books on the shelves, as well as a smattering of additional pictures along with some awards. I don't bother to let any of it distract me, I'm focused on the man sitting behind the desk, a cell phone at his ear. Representative Adam Huxley is smaller in person than I would have guessed, especially from the way that painting looked. He's clean-shaven, with silver hair that's combed to one side. His gray eyes are bright and alert, and glance over at us as we enter, even though he's clearly in the middle of a conversation. A pair of reading glasses sits on a laptop in the middle of his leather-top desk, which holds little else other than a small paperweight and a pen station with an American flag bolted to the middle. Additionally, both the American and West

Virginian flags flank either side of him, framing the windows that look out on the back of the property.

"Yes, Jack, I understand that. But I'm dealing with a crisis here. You can make the vote without me, can't you? My daughter is missing, for Christ's sake!" He's practically yelling. It doesn't take much for me to assume he's talking to Jack Hirst, the House Committee Chairman. He holds up a finger for Mrs. Henderson to hold us outside the room for a minute, even though we can hear everything through the open doors.

A pained look comes over his face. "Yes, yes of course. No. Fine. See you then." He hangs up the phone and slips it into one of the desk drawers. He then motions for us to enter, standing and buttoning the middle buttons of his blazer. A tiny American flag pin hangs on his left lapel.

"You must be with the FBI," he says, extending his hand.

I introduce us while Mrs. Henderson excuses herself, closing the French doors behind her. Huxley offers us the seats as he takes his seat again. "What's the word, have you found her yet?"

"I'm afraid not, Representative. We're still gathering evidence, which unfortunately has been few and far between. That's part of the reason we're here. We'd like your permission to take a look at Avery's room, see if we can find any evidence the kidnappers left behind."

"Both the police and my security team have already done that," he says as if that closes the matter. "That's nothing but a waste of time. You need to be out there looking for my daughter."

I already don't like this guy; he's just rubbing me the wrong way for some reason. "To be honest, sir, it's as if we're working with our hands tied behind our backs. If you'd allow us to contact the media, we could get her face out there, which would improve the chances—"

He shakes his head vehemently. "Absolutely not. I won't have Avery's disappearance used against me in the polls.

Besides, those mass media campaigns never work. You just end up sorting through a pile of calls from people who want nothing more than attention."

"Do you have any idea of who might have wanted to abduct your daughter?" I ask.

He pauses for a second before answering. "None."

"Any political enemies you've made over the years? Someone looking to hurt you?"

"No one would dare. They know what kind of power I wield on the floor." He's acting as if he's the one performing the investigation here, as if none of this information could be important or vital.

"Representative Huxley, I can understand this is a stressful period. But if you don't give us something to work with, we're going to have a very difficult time finding your daughter. As you say, you have a lot of power on the floor. If someone were looking to coerce that power to their own ends, what better way than to hold your daughter ransom?"

He bristles. "Because they know I don't negotiate with radicals."

"Even for your own daughter?" Zara asks.

"Agent, you may not realize this, but the minute you give into those animals they will never stop coming after you. Which is why I need *you* to do your job and find her. Because I'm not about to violate my oath to the United States Constitution. Whoever took her made a bad calculation on that."

I'm not what you'd call someone who is very comfortable with kids. I used to be, but recent events have made me more skittish than I'd like. Even then, I don't think I could be this coldhearted toward any child, especially my own. "Have you ever had anything like this happen before? Any close calls, anyone who tried to hurt you or your family?"

"Beyond the normal chatter on social media? No."

"Very well, then," I say, pretending to look down at my

phone again. "When did you and your wife return from your fundraiser?"

"As soon as we got the call," he replies. "We hopped on a flight from Charleston that night. Arrived shortly after two in the morning."

"We spoke with Mrs. Henderson," I say, attempting a lead. "She informed us she didn't call the police immediately when the incident occurred."

"That's correct. Our security company can respond quicker than the police can. She did exactly as instructed. The security company had a better chance of intercepting the kidnapper before they got too far away rather than the police, which would have taken precious minutes to arrive."

"But they don't have the authority to arrest anyone, or fire their sidearms if necessary," Zara says.

"I've found that in any instance where that is required, it can all be sorted out later. My priority is how fast someone can respond to my house. And that's not Alexandria Police. I'm sorry if you have friends on the force."

I shake my head. "Not at all. I just find it curious that it wasn't your first thought."

"When you work in my field, you learn that in order for people to do what you need them to do, you have to pay them. And since I can't put our local precinct on my payroll, I go with the next best thing. Besides, they arrived not long after to tend to the security guard that was shot."

Maybe he's right, but what strikes me as odd is he's either pre-planned for something like this, or it was decided near or in the heat of the moment, which makes me wonder about his priorities. Most people I know would call the police out of sheer habit, but it seems like Representative Huxley is cut from a different cloth.

"Any ransom demands? Has anyone contacted you about Avery?"

He shakes his head. "If they had, you would already

know about it, Agent. I don't know why you're wasting your time with me. You should be out there looking for her." The man stands in a huff and turns to a small bar inset into one of his cabinets and pours himself two fingers of Kentucky Bourbon.

"How often is Avery left with Mrs. Henderson here?" I ask.

He glares at me over the edge of his glass. "Why?"

"I'm trying to figure out if anyone would have recognized a pattern," I say.

"Listen, Agents. I represent the great state of West Virginia. In fact, I live there, in a very nice home. But because most of my work is here, I keep this residence for my wife and daughter. It's too disruptive for them to travel back and forth so much, at least for Avery, it is. However, I *have* to travel; do you understand that? It's my *job*. Between that and the different fundraising events all over the city, you can see why we hired Mrs. Henderson in the first place." He takes a long drink from the glass, nearly draining it.

"I never said you didn't, but if someone was watching your house, or they knew your schedule—"

"Tell you what, why don't you talk to those imbeciles at Mansfield? They're the ones who let this happen, get on their case about why they didn't do their jobs properly." He drains the rest of the glass then pours himself another.

"We plan on doing that," I tell him, keeping my voice even. "In fact, we're headed to the hospital after we finish here."

"Then by all means, go," he says, waving us off. "I don't know what you want from me."

"As we said before, we'd like permission to search Avery's room," Zara says again. "And to bring in a forensics team. Maybe there's something LiveGuard missed."

Not to mention the fact they're not even qualified to be here, I think. If they've already been in her room then Zara is right, the whole place is probably useless as far as evidence goes. But we need to check and make sure.

"I don't need a hundred FBI agents swarming all over my house," Huxley says. "My wife is upset enough as it is. We need this taken care of quietly."

That's the second time someone has told me that about this case and it's beginning to piss me off. We don't take care of cases quietly when we have missing children out in the world. We need to make as big of a stink as possible.

"We'd also like to look at your security footage from that night," I say.

"The police already reviewed when they came in. There was nothing there," he says.

"That doesn't mean we don't need to review it as well," I tell him. Does he really have no concept of how any of this works? It's like he's decided that he doesn't need to abide by or participate in the rules surrounding something like this. Like he can just make unilateral decisions regardless of if he has the authority or not. I wonder if all Representatives and Senators are just as cocky.

"Fine," he says. "Mrs. Henderson will show you how to access the footage. And she can show you Avery's room, though I really don't know what good that will do. You should be out there, using the full resources that *I know* the FBI has to find her, not traipsing around my house."

Zara and I stand. "I think we've taken up enough of your time today. Thank you for meeting with us."

He's about to respond as his cell phone rings again. He gives us a curt nod and I lead us out through the French doors just as he picks up.

"That went better than I expected," Zara says.

I can't say I'm as optimistic.

Chapter Thirteen

WE FIND MRS. HENDERSON IS POURING HERSELF A CUP OF TEA in the kitchen. The whole house feels dark and moody, like a castle. Maybe it's just because it's so empty.

"Oh, I didn't realize you'd be finished so soon," she says, setting the cup to the side. "Was your meeting with the Representative productive?"

"He told us you could show us where we could review the footage from that night?" I ask.

She nods. "Of course, this way." We take a staircase that's hidden behind a wall adjacent to the kitchen down to a lower level.

The basement is finished, and I can see what looks to be a bar-slash-entertainment area off to our right as we come to the bottom of the stairs, but Mrs. Henderson leads us to the left instead, into a small room. Inside is what looks to be a miniature version of the server room we have at the Bureau. Large computer cores line the side of the wall, while blinking lights indicate that all systems are still running. "This is the main control room, where everything in the house is routed," she says. "It controls all the breakers, the sprinkler system, the alarms, even the primary temperature controls come through here." She indicates a monitor mounted to the wall showing four different feeds at once. "It used to be unmonitored, but we have a new man from LiveGuard who is supposed to be in here watching everything, but I'm not sure—"

As if an answer to her question, a bearded man who can't be more than twenty-five appears at the door, zipping his pants up. He freezes when he sees us. "Mrs. Henderson," he says, startled. It's the same voice we heard when we entered the property.

"Mr. Cassidy, these are the FBI agents, here to investigate Avery's disappearance. I told you to inform me if you needed to be off duty," she says with a schoolteacher's discipline.

"Yes, ma'am. Sorry, ma'am. It was less than a minute."

"Don't let it happen again," she says, then turns to us. "Agents."

"We'd like to see the feeds from Thursday night," I tell him as he edges his way past us to the monitor.

"I've gone back and looked myself," he says. "There was a power interruption to the system, which caused all the cameras to go down." He types something in below the monitor and all four feeds change, their timecodes indicating Thursday around ten p.m.

"Someone would have needed to access this room to do that, wouldn't they?" I ask Mrs. Henderson.

"Not necessarily," Zara says. "This is a Tonyo, CR17. It's not exactly the top of the line in the security world. All the cameras are connected via the same feed and if some are accessible from outside then someone could interrupt them all without cutting the system. But they would have to be familiar with this system itself."

"Is that true?" Mrs. Henderson asks, more to Cassidy than to us.

"Well, I'm not exactly sure, ma'am," he says. "I've never worked with this type of—"

Mrs. Henderson pulls out a notepad from her skirt. I

imagine she's writing down something about buying a new security system for the house.

"Keep running it forward," Zara says. Cassidy nods and speeds up the feeds. At ten minutes till eleven, they all go dark. When they come back on, the timecode shows nine a.m. the following morning.

"See?" he says. "Nothing."

Zara turns to me. "It's a long shot, but we need to get a team to investigate all the access points. I doubt our unsub left any evidence behind, but maybe we'll get lucky."

I direct my attention to Mrs. Henderson. "Is that something you can authorize? Or do we need to go through your boss?"

She hesitates a moment. "No, I think given these revelations it's a prudent course of action." I can see from the sour look on her face it pains her to go against what she believes are her boss's wishes, but we might be leaving a potentially vital clue here if we don't have a full team inspect this place.

"Call Caruthers," I tell Zara. "In the meantime, may we take a look at Avery's room?"

"This way," she says, and we follow her back up the stairs, Zara on the phone with headquarters. By the time we reach the third floor, she's confirmed that they're on the way. Hopefully they'll be able to get what they need without disturbing the good Representative downstairs. Though I'm somewhat unnerved that he seems less interested in us finding his daughter, and more concerned with his image, or what he thinks will be best for him in the polls. That's why I never wanted to be a politician, I believe after a certain amount of time, it just begins to rot your soul. This only adds further proof to that theory.

"Here it is," she says, indicating a door decorated with pink and green flowers.

"I need to know every person that's been in here since she went missing," I say, inspecting the door frame. The wood is cracked around the handle on the door, and the frame itself looks to be damaged as well. There's no question the kidnapper came in through here.

"The police performed an initial investigation, then the gentlemen from LiveGuard came through for a look, on the Representative's suggestion," she says, though her tone tells me she might now believe that was a mistake.

I sigh. "Anyone else?"

"No."

Zara and I pull on a pair of gloves, which I use to open the damaged door. Avery definitely didn't do that herself. It's a bright room, with the midday sun streaming through a pair of doors that look like they lead to a private balcony. I smile. Not many kids have their own balcony to look off.

The room is in relative order, though the sliding door to the closet has been pulled off its rail, causing it to sit at a crooked angle against the doorframe. The bed is a mess, looking like someone jumped out of it quickly. I spot a laptop on a desk, though it sits alone. There's not even so much as a pen on the desk. For a little girl's room, it's surprisingly sparse and clean.

"I can't imagine what possessed whoever came in here to take all her things off her desk and shelves. She's usually so adamant about keeping what she wants up there," Mrs. Henderson says. There's a longing in her voice, though I suspect it's more for the days when Avery would do whatever she said rather than question everything.

"The kidnapper didn't do this," I say, looking at the desk a little closer.

"What?" she asks.

"No kidnapper is going to take the time to do anything other than get their victim and leave," I say. "Avery must have taken everything down since the last time you were in here."

"Why would she do that?" Mrs. Henderson asks. "Avery

loves her things. She still sleeps with a stuffed tiger. Something my mother would have whipped me for at that age."

"When did you last see Avery?" I ask, making a cursory inspection of the room, making sure not to touch anything unless I have to. Zara is over by the doors to the balcony, inspecting another door which I assume leads to the bathroom.

"Earlier that evening," she says. "I was trying to get her to tell me what she wanted for dinner, though it turned into an exercise in futility," she says. "She locked herself in her room and wouldn't come out."

"Did something happen that upset her?" I ask.

"Nothing more than normal. I think she was just missing her parents since it was her birthday and all."

Understandable. What kid would want to be left alone on their birthday? Another strike against her father. "I'm curious. Where is Mrs. Huxley?"

"She is…indisposed at the time. I'm sorry. If you'd like to speak with her, I can arrange an appointment."

"Indisposed doing what?" Zara asks. "What could be more important than this?"

Mrs. Henderson leans forward, dropping the timbre of her voice. "If you must know, she has taken a sleeping pill and is on bedrest. She's been nigh inconsolable for the past two days. Sleeping is the only way she is making it through."

I arch an eyebrow. "Doctor prescribed; I hope."

"Of course. I wouldn't allow her to take anything that might harm her."

We go back to searching her room. I take a close look at the closet. From the way some of the things in the bottom have been tussled around, it looks as though Avery might have tried to hide here when she realized something was wrong. The door off its hinges is further proof of that. "I assume this door wasn't always like this."

She shakes her head. "No. We don't allow things to fall into disrepair here."

"Did Avery have a cell phone?" I ask.

She nods. "We haven't found it."

"Which means they either took it with them, or they destroyed it," Zara says. "I wouldn't count on finding it. If they were smart enough to cut the camera feeds, they're not about to leave a cell phone lying around."

She's right. I don't see much here we can work with. "Anything in the bathroom?" Zara shakes her head. I walk over to the balcony doors. Pulling them both open, I'm greeted with an expansive view of the backyard and the pool. Woods surround the property, which is bordered by a high hedge. "Is there a fence hidden in that hedge?"

Mrs. Henderson joins us on the balcony. "Very good. The builder decided it would be more aesthetically pleasing to look at greenery rather than an iron gate. But yes, an eight-foot wall hides behind there."

That would have been difficult to scale, but not impossible. The abductor could have used this balcony to escape, either by a ladder or other apparatus. It makes getting out of the house quick and easy. "Were these doors open when you came to look for Avery after you heard the shot?" I ask.

Mrs. Henderson hesitates. "I…I don't remember."

I glance out to the yard beyond. "Where was the man shot?" I ask.

Mrs. Henderson points down to the left of the pool, in a patio area surrounded by chairs. String lights hang above the area, creating an intimate atmosphere out of a large space. "There, right at the edge of the patio."

"You thinking the abductor went off the balcony?" Zara asks.

"Maybe. Were there any ladders or anything else found nearby?"

Mrs. Henderson lets out a frustrated sigh. "I don't know.

There was so much going on at the time and I didn't even come back up here until after the police had taken a look. They worked with Mansfield regarding the rest, I stayed out of it."

I'm going to wait for the forensics team to do a full investigation, but as far as I can tell, there's little to go on here. Except…I head back into the room and walk back to the door, inspecting the damage again. "Didn't you say Avery locked herself in that night?"

Mrs. Henderson draws herself together. "Yes."

The handle isn't the kind that needs a key either. Which means the kidnapper more than likely kicked it in without even trying it, meaning they were in a hurry. "Was it open when the police came to take a look?"

She holds out her hands. "I really don't know, I'm sorry."

I glance back at the balcony again. So the kidnapper came in through the door, but left with Avery over the balcony. Not an easy thing to achieve, especially given there's nothing but a concrete patio below us. It would have been difficult to drop down holding a child, but not impossible, especially if our unsub has good balance. That may be something to consider. We could be looking for someone who has some physical training, possibly someone who has been in the military or even a local fire department.

Now that we know how they took Avery, I need to figure out how they got into the house. "Were all the doors of the house locked that night?"

"I lock the doors every night," she replies. I shoot a glance to Zara. A non-answer.

"Do you know how the kidnapper got into the house?"

She shakes her head. "I'm sorry, I don't." I'm getting really sick of people stonewalling me, especially when we have a missing child. I push past Mrs. Henderson and head back down the way we came to the main level of the house.

"Wait a moment," she says. "You can't leave without an

escort." She hurries behind me. I'm sure Zara is doing exactly what she should be doing, which is watching Mrs. Henderson's body language while my back is turned. Something is very wrong about all of this, and I don't like it. I head back to the front doors, which are made of solid wood and about eight feet high. They're also heavy, which I noticed when Mrs. Henderson let us in the house. Even if one of these doors was unlocked, it would have been difficult and cumbersome to get in through here. Not to mention the foyer offers no cover at all.

"How do I get to the back of this maze?" I ask, turning to finally face Mrs. Henderson, who has followed me down the long staircase that lines the wall.

"I don't understand what you're looking for," she says. "I thought you just wanted to see Avery's room."

"I want to know how someone got in this house without you noticing," I say. Henderson narrows her eyes for just a second. She's not going to tell me a thing; for some reason she's back on the defensive.

"I'll find it myself," I say, and I weave around her, heading back through the labyrinth as Zara catches up with me.

"That way leads back down to his office," she says as we come to what seems to be a second foyer where two hallways intersect. There's a vase with flowers atop a marble table in the center of this space. I look up and a skylight two floors above shines light down into the space.

"It has to be this way," I say and head forward.

"Agents, if you please," Henderson says behind us. "I think that's quite enough."

Finally we reach the back of the house where there's a galley kitchen off a main dining room, which leads to a door that seems to go to the west side of the property. This isn't the house's main kitchen, it must be a smaller, prep kitchen for events and gatherings. Thus, it's not very fancy or as upscale as the rest of the house.

I still have my gloves on from Avery's room, so I carefully open the door and inspect it, looking for any signs of forced entry. There's a deadbolt on this side of the door, but it can only be accessed from inside.

"Really, there's nothing more to see here," Henderson says again.

"Is this the only exit that goes to this side of the house?" I ask.

"Yes, why?"

I point out the open door. "This area is covered with high, heavy shrubs. If someone wanted to wait in there without being seen, it wouldn't be difficult. You said there's a patrol around the house, but I bet they walk right by these without a second glance."

Henderson gives us a pinched look.

"Hey, Em," Zara says, bending down. I do the same and notice there's a scratch on one of the floor tiles. I swing the door closed again, but even though the scratch follows part of the door's path, the door has enough clearance not to scratch the floor when it opens and closes.

I pull my phone out, turning on the flashlight, and get down on all fours, sweeping the ground. A reflection of light catches my eye right under the dishwasher which is close to the door itself. I reach in and my fingers barely manage to pull the small piece of glass out. It's a shard about a quarter of an inch long. I hold it up, staring at Henderson. "Forget to sweep this one up?"

"One of the kitchen staff, they broke a glass a few—"

"Mrs. Henderson, do I have to tell you it's a felony to lie to an FBI officer?" I hand the piece of glass to Zara. "This glass has no curvature, nor does it have any features of dishware. This came from the broken window out of this door, didn't it?"

She bites her lip and looks up a moment, as if she's making a pact with God before finally nodding.

"What really happened?" I ask.

"I was…I had consumed a few glasses of pinot," she says. "That girl can be so infuriating sometimes." She takes a deep breath. "When I heard the glass break the first thing I did was run downstairs and hide in the server room. I thought maybe I could see what was happening on the cameras—"

"Without putting yourself in danger," Zara says.

She nods. "But they were already dark. I knew someone was in the house, but I thought they just wanted to rob it. I never thought for a minute they'd actually take Avery. I never even heard the gunshot from down there."

The truth finally comes out. It seems Mrs. Henderson isn't as altruistic as she seems. "You fixed this door quickly."

She nods again. "I didn't want the Representative to know what I'd done," she says. "It was fixed the next day."

"Our unsub came through here after he'd turned off the security system from outside," I say. "Then had a clear path upstairs to get Avery. But instead of chancing coming back down through the house, he decided to go off the balcony."

Henderson doesn't say anything. She's obviously ashamed that she let this happen on her watch. But at least now we know it wasn't an inside job. At least not from her. The security company is a different matter altogether.

"I need a list of every person from Mansfield that worked here for two weeks leading up to the abduction." I give Zara the signal that we're ready to go as I hand Mrs. Henderson my card. "As soon as you can get it to me."

She nods, wiping both her eyes once. "I'll compile the list now. I can send it in a few minutes."

"Thank you," I tell her. We allow her to escort us back to the main entrance. Once we're outside we see an unmarked white van pull up. The two guards from LiveGuard remain on alert, though I notice they're not running down the driveway, pointing their guns at this vehicle on the property.

Caruthers gets out of the passenger side. "Zara fill you in?" I ask.

He nods. "Full workup. I've got three other agents. We'll make quick work of it."

"Make sure you do, you know what's on the line here," I say and hand him the piece of glass from the back entrance. "Entry point looks to be the back galley kitchen." He gives me a quick nod and Zara and I head back to our car, ignoring the militiamen.

"You think Mansfield had something to do with this, don't you?" she asks.

"I don't see how they couldn't have. It's too clean."

"Maybe our unsub is just that good," she replies.

I roll my eyes. "No one is *that* good."

Zara opens the side door and slips into the passenger seat. "Is it time to go beat up some people in the hospital?"

I chuckle. "I'll let you do the beating. I just want to ask the questions."

Chapter Fourteen

IT ONLY TAKES US ABOUT FIFTEEN MINUTES TO GET FROM THE Huxley Manor to Inova Hospital, where they took the Mansfield officer after he was shot. According to the file from the police, the bullet entered in the upper chest, which required some extensive surgery. He was lucky to pull through, though I don't know how long they'll be keeping him.

Zara and I threw a few theories back and forth on the way here, but we don't have anything concrete, not yet. And I couldn't help but glance at the clock the whole way here. Part of me feels like we're wasting time, that we should be doing more. But I know this is how it works, and if there's ever any chance of finding this girl, we have to follow where the evidence leads us. Unfortunately, things are looking slim at the moment. I only hope the security guard can offer us some additional insight into our revelations at the Huxley house. Because he was in surgery during the initial inquiries, no one else has spoken with him yet as far as I know. Maybe he'll give us the missing piece of this puzzle we'll need to find Avery.

After identifying ourselves with the front desk, we take the elevator up to the third floor, where he's being kept for observation. He's in room four-nineteen, which is dark, despite the time of day. As we knock on the half-open door, I can't stop a flashback of the last time I was in a hospital like this, where I would later learn the assassin had killed my only suspect. It only serves to remind me that she's still out there, waiting for me.

"Come in," a hoarse voice says after the knock. We push the door open slowly to reveal a man lying in a hospital bed. He's deeply tanned, and his exposed forearms look like they're about the size of tree trunks. He has dark hair and a trimmed beard and moustache, reminding me of a nightclub bouncer. Who knows, maybe he moonlights as one when he's not on duty with Mansfield.

"Mr. Hayden?"

He looks up, though I can tell his eyes are bloodshot, even in the low light of the room. "Who are you?"

"Agent Emily Slate, FBI. This is Agent Zara Foley. We'd like to ask you some questions about Thursday night."

He gives us an errant wave of his hand. "Sure. Why not. It's all anyone seems to want to talk about. Why not add the FBI to the list?"

"Who else has been speaking with you?" Zara asks. She knows as well as I do that no one should have questioned him yet.

"LiveGuard Security, my boss, the doctor, a handful of nurses. Why not get the ATF in here too, I'm sure they'd like to hear my story for the hundredth time." He shifts in his bed, which causes him to wince. I see a large patch of gauze sticking out from under his hospital gown near his neck.

"LiveGuard spoke with you?" I ask.

"Yeah, had a guy waiting here as soon as I got out of surgery. Though I don't know if I was making much sense; I was still pretty out of it."

"Do you remember his name?" I ask.

He shakes his head. "Sorry. I barely remember the guy at all."

That's strange. I can understand LiveGuard has a vested interest in this, given they're the new security consultants for Huxley. But their job is protection, not investigation. I'll need to follow up with LiveGuard in order to determine their true motives.

"What's your recovery time?"

"About twelve weeks," he replies. "As soon as they let me get out of this bed."

"We'll try not to take up too much of your time." I know how annoying it can be to have people pestering you when all you want to do is rest, especially in a hospital. When I was in after inhaling all that smoke, I had the benefit of needing to write down answers to every question to give my lungs time to heal. No doubt Hayden wants us out of here as soon as possible. "Can you tell us what happened?"

"I was on patrol around the house, like every other night," he says. "I'd just finished checking some holes around the outer fence. Just a fox or something, trying to get under the fence. It's not a big deal, but we have to check them out, you understand. So I was off my time by about two minutes when I come around the back of the property, and there's a guy, dressed all in black, with a hood over his face standing right outside the back doors."

"Where, exactly?" I ask.

"I don't know, near the right side, over near the patio. Underneath the girl's balcony. He looked like a cat burglar from what I could tell."

"Can you describe him," I say. "Height, weight, build?"

"Maybe six-two, two hundred pounds. Pretty big guy." He winces again as he tries to shift in his bed unsuccessfully.

"Did he say anything, could you hear his voice?"

Hayden shakes his head. "Never said a word. Pulled a gun on me before I could even react. One shot, right to the chest."

"Did you see the girl?" I ask.

He sighs. "I'm not sure, maybe. She could have been behind him, but it was so dark it was hard to tell. Everything happened so fast, and after he shot me all I could think of was if this was how I was going to die. I didn't sign up to get shot at, just to watch some rich guy's house, you know?"

"You didn't think that someone as high-profile as Representative Huxley might carry more risk than your average person?" Zara asks.

"Not for them to get past the gate guards and on the property, no," he replies. "I still don't know how he did it. None of the alarms ever sounded."

"We think he interrupted the feeds before he broke into the house," I tell him. "Do you remember anything after you were shot?"

He turns away from us. "Nah, it's pretty much a blur after that."

"And you can't confirm if he had the little girl with him when you spotted him," I reiterate. I really don't like how little we have to go on here. This man is our only witness, if you can call him that. If we're ever to have a chance of finding Avery, he's it.

"Sorry, no," he says. "I wish I could remember, but it was dark back there, the pool lights were off, and I couldn't see much unless it moved. If she was there, she was staying still."

I tamp down my frustration and reset. No witness to the actual crime. No footage to speak of. And we still don't know how our kidnapper got Avery off the property. I can feel the pressure of this case crushing down on me. All I can think about is if we don't find the answers we need, Liam is dead. And there's nothing I can do about it. I should be out there retracing my steps, trying to find out where she's holding him and let Sutton or Zara take the lead here. But I know if I do, *she'll* find out. And even though she might not be willing to kill me, I have no problem believing that courtesy doesn't extend to anyone else.

"Let's talk about Mansfield," I say, starting over. "How long have you worked there?"

"Why does that matter?" he asks.

"Just answer the question," Zara says.

"About a year," he replies.

"And what other jobs have you worked for them?"

He tries to take a deep breath, but stops short, tightening up for a second. It's going to be a while before Mr. Hayden is going to be comfortable again. "Standard stuff. I've done some commercial guard duty, transport security, stuff like that. No big deal."

"Any personal security before this?" I ask.

He shakes his head.

"Are you trained to use a firearm," I ask.

"Why does that matter?"

Zara steps forward, her arms crossed. "You seem to have a hard problem answering simple questions."

Hayden sighs. "Not professionally. But I have a license to carry."

"Doesn't that require training?" I ask.

"A buddy of mine does training and certification. I got it from him."

I stick that in my back pocket and move on, though I'm disturbed to learn an "instructor" might be out there, handing out licenses without adequately certifying their students. "Concealed?" He nods. "But you didn't shoot back, or even think to draw your firearm on the intruder?"

"There wasn't time," he says, protesting. "Like I said, I came around the building and he was already there."

"He had time to draw his weapon, or was it tucked away?" I ask.

"No, he pulled it," Hayden admits. "What are you getting at?"

I admit this is probably not very productive, other than providing me with a modicum of self-satisfaction. These private security firms aren't trained to deal in live-fire situations, even when they think they are. Any other cop would have been able to assess the situation in an instant and had a weapon on the intruder immediately. But it furthers my theory that our unsub might be former military if his reflexes were that quick. "Nothing," I finally say. "What about your co-workers, had you worked with them long?"

He shrugs, though it's not very pronounced. "A few of them. We get shuffled around all the time. But the Representative had a regular contingent, which I think is standard for someone like him. That way he knows each of us personally."

"Any new faces in your group?" I ask.

He tries to sit up. "What are you saying? You think someone from Mansfield did this?"

"I'm not saying anything. I'm just asking a question." I stare at him, looking for any clues that he might be hiding something. While I don't think he was involved in this, I can't overlook the possibility it was a coordinated job that got out of hand. Maybe one of them was only supposed to fire off a round in the air and they either got nervous or scared. Or something else could have gone wrong. Either way, everything we have so far points to this being orchestrated by someone who knew the location and the vulnerabilities. They knew which door would be best to go in through, and how to get back out of the house fast, without alerting anyone. If Mr. Hayden had been on time during his patrol, the kidnapper would have gotten away without a soul seeing him. We're going to have to look at everyone in Mansfield.

"We've had a couple new hires come in, yeah. But what company doesn't? There's always going to be turnover."

"Who are the new hires?" Zara asks.

"I don't know their full names. Just last names from their

uniforms," he replies. "Gates and Moreno. They've only been with the company a few weeks."

"Either of them match the description you gave us?" I ask.

"Lady, most the guys I work with match that description," he replies. "The company has certain expectations when you go through hiring."

I consult the notes app on my phone to see if there's anything we've missed. Looks like our next stop is going to be Mansfield corporate offices. They're going to fight us tooth and nail, I know it, but it's the best lead we have so far. Unless Caruthers comes up with something better.

"Alright, Mr. Hayden. Thanks for your time," I say, giving him a reassuring nod. "We'll let you get some rest."

"Hey, there's one other thing, though I don't know if it's important or not," he says.

Zara and I stop near the door. "Go ahead."

"When I was close to the guy, right after he shot me, he walked over, I think to make sure I wasn't getting up. And I swear I could have smelled coolant on him."

"Coolant?"

"Yeah, like engine coolant. Like he was a mechanic or something. I just thought it was odd. I also could have hallucinated it. I was going in and out there for a while."

"Okay, thanks, Mr. Hayden. Best of luck on your recovery." As we leave, I hear him lowering the bed back down. For a shot like that right through the chest, he really is the luckiest man alive.

"Hey," Zara says, once we're back in the elevator. "What was all that stuff about his firearm training?"

"Oh," I say, waving it away. "I'm just so tired of all these wannabees thinking they can do what we do with little or no training. Maybe it's a pride thing, I don't know. But look at how both Mansfield and LiveGuard have both screwed this up already."

"Rich people hire private security," she says. "It's going to happen."

"Yeah, I know," I say. "I just wish they were better at it."

"Then you and I might be out of a job," she says with a grin. I give her an easy shove as the doors open and we head off to get some answers from Mansfield.

Chapter Fifteen

"DAMMIT, COME ON!" I YELL OUT THE WINDOW. THE CAR next to us puts on its blinker, indicating they want to cut in front of us. "Nope, no way," I say. We're already at a standstill, every car that gets ahead of us is just that much more of a delay. "Why does Mansfield's corporate office have to be on the complete other side of the city?"

"Em," Zara says, putting her hand on my arm that's got a death grip on the steering wheel. "There's nothing we can do. We'll get there as soon as we can."

I grit my teeth. "Can't we call someone to clear this mess away? An Agent's life is on the line here," I say.

"You know it doesn't work like that."

I glance at the clock on my dash. It's already one-thirty. It's been half a day already and we've barely made any progress. I lay on the horn, as the traffic ahead of us inches up and the person next to us tries to merge in.

"Want me to pull my gun on them?" Zara asks. "Would that make you feel better?"

"Maybe," I grumble. I feel like I'm barely holding things together here. The longer we go without finding Avery, the worse this all becomes. "Do you think Janice could get another agent over to Mansfield before we do?"

"Hang on," Zara says, checking her phone. "It's going to clear. There's a wreck about five hundred feet in front of us. A few more minutes and we'll be on our way." I can't see that far ahead because we're coming around a bend, which means I have to trust her information is accurate. Though she's never let me down before.

I lean my head back against the headrest and close my eyes, tears stinging them. I feel like I'm going crazy here. How could I have let this happen; how could I have let her get so much leverage over me?

"Hey, it's okay," Zara says. "We're going to find her. And we're going to get Liam back. Let Janice worry about tracking down the assassin. Let's just focus on the job at hand."

"I've been trying," I say, glancing at the clock again. Another two minutes gone. "But I just can't quit thinking about it."

"Is that why you were so hard on Hayden back there?" she asks. "And why your tact with Representative Huxley wasn't exactly kosher."

"Please," I say. "That man wouldn't know manners if they kicked him in the balls."

"You're not wrong about that, but he could still get you in a lot of trouble. Both of us. People like him have a lot of strings they can pull."

I turn to her. "So what, we're just supposed to bow down to him?" I wipe my eyes, clearing the excess tears away.

"No, but you don't have to be so abrasive either. You're usually really good at it. It's just now—"

"—now everything's screwed up, and it's my fault."

"Em, don't do that," Zara says. "You know what happens when you start to guilt yourself."

"I know," I say. I'm not looking for pity and I'm not trying to make excuses. It's just the facts of the case. If it weren't for me, Liam wouldn't be in this position. But for some reason this woman seems to have some strange obsession with me. She said I was her assignment, but I think there's something else there, though I can't say what. Maybe she feels guilty about what she did to Matt? Though, she'd never admit it. From what little I know of her she's not the kind of person to open up and show her vulnerability.

Still. She could have just killed me at any time and moved on. So why all the games? Why all this with Liam? I don't understand.

"There," Zara says, pointing ahead. "It's moving." She's right. The line of cars slowly begins to creep forward, and I stop, letting the car next to us in. The driver waves once they're in front. "Aww, look at that. They appreciated your kindness."

"I guess."

"They could have thrown you the finger instead." She grins.

"Not if they want to keep all their fingers intact." Which reminds me, I never told Zara about what I did to Sherriff Black while Liam and I were down in Mardel. While it wasn't exactly proper procedure, I at least got the man off my back. But now's probably not the time.

As the traffic clears, we finally get moving again and the pressure on the back of my neck releases a little. Zara is right, we can only do this as fast as we can do it. And while I'd love nothing more than to march into Mansfield with a battalion of agents at my back, I know that will only be counterproductive. We need to message these people, better than I did with Representative Huxley. I can't let my impatience or my emotions surrounding this get in the way; that won't help Avery and it won't help Liam.

I just hate feeling like both their lives hang on my next few decisions.

We pull up to Mansfield, which sort of feels like a fortress in itself. The building is about seven or eight stories tall, but the base is clad entirely in concrete, like they think someone's going to run a truck full of fertilizer into the ground floors. Or maybe it's just all for show. Maybe this is what they want clients to see when they first drive up. A large, secure facility. It's a good marketing technique.

"Wow, overcompensate much?" Zara asks as we get out of the car.

"They just want to you to know how big it is," I reply.

She turns to me, a big smile plastered across her face. "There was a time when I couldn't beat a euphemism out of you. How the tables have turned."

"What can I say? I'm spending too much time with you, I suppose."

"I think you mean not enough," she says. "C'mon, let's go break some steel balls."

I can't help but giggle. Every ounce of me is on high alert, which is making me react in extreme ways to everything. I need to calm down and find my center, as my trainer used to say. He'd reiterate to me that I would never be able to effectively strike my opponent if I wasn't focused. In the last eight months I've been the opposite of focused, I've been distracted at every level. Maybe it's time I take up lessons again; they might be good for me.

When we walk into the lobby we're greeted by two large men in black suits, both with their hands clasped in front of them. Beyond them, people stroll back and forth in the large, expansive lobby, which is lit from a triangular glass ceiling high above us.

"Do you have an appointment?" One of the men asks.

I pull out my badge, showing it to him. "No. And I don't have time to wait on one either. We're here to speak with the person in charge of residential or high-net-worth security."

"One moment," one of the men says and turns to a small

desk near the door. He picks up a phone and speaks into it for a moment before hanging up and returning to us.

"So do we get into the club, or do I need to slip you both a fifty first?" Zara asks.

"What's this regarding?" the same man asks.

"That's a classified matter," I reply. "Regardless, your company was engaged in protective services for a client. I need to speak with the person in charge of that division."

"That would be our Director of Residential Affairs, Mrs. DuPont. But she's off today. It is Sunday, after all."

"As I said, this is of some urgency." I can already feel myself losing what little cool I've established. "We'll need to speak with whoever is here today that can assist us with this matter."

The man exchanges a glance with his compatriot before returning to the desk and speaking into the phone again. A moment later he returns. "If you will have a seat, Mr. Sandoval will be with you shortly." He indicates a bank of chairs off to the side of the room, beside tall windows flanked with curtains. Beyond the windows is the outer base of the building.

"How long?" I ask.

"Not more than a few minutes." He indicates we head in that direction. "I presume you're armed."

"As are you," I say, noticing the small indentation under his suit coat. "Is it a problem?"

"Normally we don't let anyone carry into the building. Just letting you know we're aware," he says.

"In case what, two trained FBI agents decide to start blasting people?" Zara asks. The man doesn't respond and so we go and sit down, waiting for this Mr. Sandoval. "Man, I think *you're* rubbing off on *me*," she says. "I see what you mean about these people. It's like they expect us not to be able to handle ourselves, when we've had years of training. How long have they had, a twelve-week course at some online university?"

"Frustrating, isn't it?" I take a seat looking out the window, but all I can really see is concrete. "Great view."

"Maybe it's better from a couple stories up," Zara says. As we wait I notice my leg begin to bounce. I'm not usually so full of energy, but the longer we have to waste time here waiting on someone, the worse I'm going to get. I keep thinking maybe we should just call Janice to bring more people in, but what good would it do? What else can they work on that we're not already doing? The unfortunate thing about all of this is we're actually moving quite fast. If this were any other case, I'd be much happier by now.

The same man who met us at the door comes over about fifteen minutes after we sit down. "Mr. Sandoval will be right down," he says. Please wait here."

"What does he think we've been doing?" Zara asks. Finally, a man appears in the lobby having come from the opposite side. He's trim and fit despite his age, and his slim gray suit fits him perfectly. He's wearing rimless spectacles and his head is entirely free of hair. Somewhere inside of me I start thinking of a nerdy Mr. Clean and I crack a smile that I can't hide.

"Agents," he says, his step quick and sure he reaches us. "I'm Elian Sandoval. What can I do for you?"

"I'm Agent Slate, this is Agent Foley," I say. "We're investigating the event at Representative Huxley's home this past Thursday evening."

"Ah," he says, after taking each of our hands with a strong grip. "Yes, of course. You know that we are no longer employed by the Representative."

"We do," I say. "But we still have some questions. We just finished interviewing Mr. Hayden over at Suburban."

He nods. "I can assure you his bills will be paid in full by the company. We aren't in the habit of leaving our employees high and dry, especially when it comes to injuries on the job."

"Not your typical Worker's Comp policy, I take it."

"No, something a little more specialized. But rest assured, each of our employees are well taken care of."

"That's good," Zara says. "Because we have some questions about a few of them."

"Oh?" he says, his near-non-existent eyebrows raising.

"Specifically, two employees named Gates and Moreno. Do you know them?"

"We're a large company, Agent Slate, I can't possibly keep track of every single employee, even just in this division. We cover most of the Washington and Baltimore area from this office, which means we have thousands of employees out there, keeping people safe. However, I'd be happy to look them up for you."

"We'd appreciate that."

He leads us back through the lobby and to the hallway he came from, leading us to an elevator that takes us up to the fifth floor. Once we arrive, he escorts us down a series of offices, all with large glass windows allowing us to see inside. Most of them are empty, save a few.

"Weekends are pretty slow around here," he says, showing us into his office where he takes a seat behind the desk. I notice he lets out a breath of relief when he does.

"I'm sorry, we didn't mean to make you—"

He waves me off. "No, no, it's fine. I just finished a round of basketball in our gym. Working here comes with a lot of extra perks."

I can't help my curiosity. "How is your employee retention?"

"I'd say we're better than the national average," he replies. "It can be a stressful job. We try to provide our employees with a plethora of amenities. I'm sure the FBI has something similar."

"You'd be surprised," Zara mutters.

He gives us both a grin. "I've worked for Mansfield ever since it was a fledgling company out of Texas. And now, here we are the second largest private security firm in America. I like to think I've had a hand in that, even if it is just with something as simple as gym access. Now, you were looking for information on Gates and Moreno, correct?" I nod. He types the first name into his computer, which I notice is an older model PC.

"Mr. Sandoval, do you happen to know who installed the security system at the Huxley house?"

"I'll have to check," he says, "But I believe we did. Huxley hired us back before he even moved there, so it would make sense that we would have pulled out whatever system was in place and replaced it with our own, especially if we were going to be working the property too." He searches his screen for a moment. "Here we are. Colby Gates. Twenty-nine-years-old, been employed with us for three weeks. Came over from Lansdowne. Former military, a staff sergeant in the Army. He came highly recommended by his C.O."

I shoot a look at Zara. Former military. It could explain the precision shot. Maybe he was good enough to know it wouldn't kill Hayden. Then again, maybe that had been his intention. "Any special notes in his service record?" I ask.

"Not that I see. He did one tour in Afghanistan, then came back home. Before that a high school career with a focus on math and science. Not much else to note."

"Where does Gates live?" I ask.

"Am I allowed to give you that information without a warrant?" Sandoval asks. "I feel like I've already been very forthcoming."

"You have," I say. "But you understand we don't have a lot of time here. And a little girl's life is on the line." Technically, yes, we should have a warrant before requesting any of this information as it's private. But given the circumstances, I'm willing to bend the rules a little bit. If Sandoval really starts to put up a fight, I'm sure Janice can fast-track us one. But I'm not even sure we're headed in the right direction yet.

"7076 Poplar Hills Rd. Crescent Heights," he says. "Do you need his phone number?"

"It probably wouldn't hurt," I say, writing it down as he rattles it off. "Okay, how about Moreno?"

"Just a moment." Sandoval types again. "Here we are. Anthony Moreno. His work history is a little more...unorthodox. Personal security for high-net-worth individuals and not much else. College graduate, major in psychology. Great GPA. He's twenty-seven, though his references are...well, see for yourself." He turns the monitor toward me and my mouth just about falls open.

"Is this right?" I ask. "Is Mansfield in the habit of hiring mobsters?"

"Of course not," Sandoval says. "There must have been some sort of mistake in the hiring process."

"What?" Zara says. "I missed it. What's going on?"

"Anthony 'Tony' Moreno's very first reference is Santino Toscani," I say. "Of the Toscani Crime family."

Chapter Sixteen

"ARE YOU SURE?" ZARA ASKS AS WE SPEED DOWN THE BELTWAY, headed for Brentwood. "What about this Grant guy? Former military?"

I shake my head. "It's Toscani, I'd bet my pension on it." We've tangled with Toscani before. A couple months ago I had suspected Santino of using his new position as head of the family for kidnapping a judge's daughter. It actually turned out to be someone who was working with the FBI and from all appearances, Toscanis business was legitimate. But there is no way this is a coincidence. Someone who just happens to know Santino Toscani—enough to use him as a reference on his application—has to be involved in this somehow. "Remember how Hayden said he thought he smelled coolant? The Toscani's run an air conditioner manufacturing plant here in D.C. And what do air conditioners use a lot of?"

"Coolant," Zara says, sounding defeated. "But we still don't have a direct connection between them. And even if this Tony Moreno did take Avery, how is going over there going to get her back?"

"I want to put some pressure on Santino," I say. "Show him how bad this can get for him. More than likely he'll deny knowing anything about it, but he might be willing to roll on Moreno. I just don't understand what Toscani would want with Huxley's kid. Unless he's outgrown his ambitions and has decided he needs to start blackmailing state representatives."

Zara scoffs. "Do you buy Sandoval's explanation of how he got hired in the first place?"

"Not a chance," I say. "They knew exactly who they were hiring, and they didn't care. Unfortunately, it's not an isolated problem. Security work, and police work for that matter, are hard jobs, and sometimes they tend to attract the wrong kind of person. Moreno got hired because he had experience in the arena, and a background check would have been worthless. It either would have come up blank or been glowing with a bunch of made-up statistics. I'd be willing to bet Moreno got himself hired so he could infiltrate Huxley's place, and then when the timing was right, kidnap his daughter."

"But what's the motive?" Zara asks as I swerve around a slow-moving car.

"That's the million-dollar question," I say. "Let's just make sure we have backup this time. I don't want to go in there without some cover nearby."

"Working on it now," Zara says, her phone up to her ear. My heart is pumping; if my hunch is right then this means we'll be able to track down Avery, hopefully before the day is over. Though it's already mid-afternoon. Toscani is a slime-ball, but he'll do anything he can to avoid even the appearance of guilt. Which is why I have no doubt he'll roll on his man.

"Janice just confirmed two more teams are on the way," Zara says, hanging up. "Do you think she might be in the building?"

She's thinking the same thing I am, that Toscani is keeping Avery close, just in case. We have to operate under that assumption, otherwise we'll put her life at risk. "That's a good point. Tell the other teams to stay back until we're ready to call them in. If Toscani sees five FBI vehicles pull up all at once, he'll panic. He might even do something stupid. You and I need to go in there, keep him calm until we know more."

"I don't like this, Em. We're going in there blind," she says.

"I know, and you're right. If we had time maybe we could do some reconnaissance, but given the situation I don't think we have the time."

"Dammit," Zara mutters under her breath. "Dammit, dammit, dammit."

"Hey," I say. "It's going to be okay. You've done this before."

"Last time was a lot less combative," she says. "We were just there to ask questions. I get the feeling this time might not be as amicable."

I shake my head. "No, same deal. We're just asking questions. Let's just hope he has the answers we want."

"And if he doesn't?"

"He has to," I finally say. "We're running out of time."

We pull up to the warehouse marked C-4 on the side. An ominous sign if I've ever seen one. The factory is still running, and the lights are on, though there aren't many trucks in the yard. A few trailers sit butted up against the building, no doubt being loaded for transport later tonight or tomorrow. A shiver runs through me when I think that poor Avery could be on one of those trailers and we'd never even know it. Hell, if Toscani wanted, he could have transported her halfway across the country by now. I just hope that's not the case.

Strangely, though, the assassin never mentioned anything about the Toscani Crime family. I wonder if she even knew they were involved. Though, I guess I don't know that they're involved yet, other than two pieces of circumstantial evidence. But I think I can rattle Toscani enough that something falls through the cracks.

At least, I hope I can.

We park and get out of the car, headed for the main building offices. Last time we were here, a pair of men flanked either side of the doors. This afternoon, there's only one. I wonder if Toscani is having the same trouble hiring as other businesses are.

"Where are the other units?" I whisper as we make our way to the door.

Zara is flexing her hands open and closed. "Two minutes out. Waiting on your signal."

As we approach the door, I recognize the man standing outside. He's one of the guards that was here last time. Looks like he hasn't had a promotion yet. "Toscani can't give you a better gig than guard duty?" I ask.

"I'm happy to do whatever Mr. Toscani wishes," he says, shrugging. "What do a couple of Feds want?"

"Just a quick chat," I say. "His name came up in conversation. Just looking to confirm or deny a lead."

The guard pulls a phone from his pocket and speed dials a number, and then explains why we're there in not so many words. A few moments later he slips the phone back in his pocket, motioning to the door with a nod of his head. "Warn ya. He's not happy."

"Is he ever?" I ask.

He opens the door for us, and we weave through the front offices until we get to the factory floor. This is the exact same route we took before. The sounds of the machines are deafening, so I don't even bother trying to understand what the man who comes trotting up to us says. He points up at the manager's office that overlooks the factory and I nod. He then turns and we follow him through the equipment area, and the entire time I'm looking up, wondering if something is going to fall on my head. Finally, we climb the stairs that lead to his office. I give the man a nod of thanks as I open the door into Toscani's office which he closes behind us, shutting out the noise.

Inside, he's sitting on one of the two couches, reading a newspaper. He lowers the newspaper just enough so that his dark eyes land on us as we come in. He then raises it again in an attempt to look nonchalant. "Agent Slate, my favorite person," he says. "I assume you have a good reason for disrupting me on a lovely Sunday afternoon."

"Having a quiet weekend, Santino?" I ask.

"Quiet enough. Until now, that is," he says, not lowering the paper again.

"Sorry to interrupt."

Finally, he folds the paper and takes his feet down from the ottoman. Full height, Toscani probably isn't taller than five-five. But he has an imposing presence, nonetheless. He's dressed to the nines, his suit probably costs more than six months of my salary, though the coat is hanging off the back of his chair. His vest has silk inlays, and compliments his stark white shirt beneath. Surprisingly, he doesn't have a holster or weapon on him, at least not that I can see. Then again, he's sure to have one hidden in his desk. Stepping behind the desk, he slaps the paper on the desk as he sits down. "Somehow I doubt that."

"How's business?" I ask as Zara takes a closer look at some of Toscani's decorations on the wall.

He eyes her a minute then turns his attention back to me. "Fine. Why? Want to come bring some more false charges against me?"

"How about some real ones this time?"

He glares at me. "What are you talking about?"

"Do you happen to know Anthony Moreno? Goes by Tony."

Toscani hesitates a moment before responding. "Yeah, I know Tony, why?"

"Do you know what he's been up to lately?"

He shrugs, leaning back in his chair. "Not really. I haven't seen him in probably six months or so."

"Are you sure about that?" I ask. "He used you as a reference on a job application to Mansfield Security."

Toscani's eyes flash, but he keeps an artificial smile on his face. "That's right. I forgot about that. How's he doing over there? I hear they have a good dental program."

"You haven't seen Tony since Thursday have you?" I say, ignoring his obvious attempt to get under my skin. He knows exactly what he's talking about and just playing dumb. But that's only going to get him so far.

"Nope, can't say that I have."

"He's not here?"

Again, Toscani shakes his head, this time slower than normal. Zara is still in my periphery. I know she's got my back if something happens. And unfortunately, it looks like I'm going to have to put the screws to Toscani.

I take a seat on the edge of his desk; letting my blazer hang open to reveal my weapon. It's not an overt threat, but it's not a subtle one either. "See, we think Tony has gone and gotten himself into some trouble with a very important person in the political arena. We just want to find him to sort all of this out before it gets messy."

Toscani scoffs. "Messy how? Like you're going to do anything other than arrest him."

"C'mon Santino," I say. "You don't want to get mixed up in this, do you? Tony is in a heap of trouble. No sense in you going down with him."

He leans back a little further in his chair. "How could that happen seeing as I don't know what you're talking about? And even if I did, none of this has anything to do with me."

I furrow my brow like I'm thinking really hard. "Well.

Seeing as you were the one who helped him get the job, all I really need to do is prove that you knew what he was planning to do this whole time. And given the D.A.'s penchant for organized crime, I'd be trying to get as far away from Tony Moreno as I possibly could right now. That is," I say, in mock concern. "If you really didn't have anything to do with this."

"You can't just make that up," Toscani says. "I don't even know what you're accusing him of."

"Sure, we can go that way," I say, slipping off the desk. "Or I can argue the two of you came up with this plan on your own and you helped him infiltrate a company that would allow him access to high-profile political figures. Based on your family history, how do you think that's going to go?"

He glares at me like he wants to kill me. We both know I have nothing here, but at the moment I'm willing to do almost anything to keep Avery and Liam safe. If that means trumping up charges on Toscani to get him to talk, I'll do it in a heartbeat, and I think he can see that conviction in my eyes because he sighs and leans forward, opening a drawer on his desk.

"Easy," I say, my hand on the butt of my weapon.

"It's a schedule," he says. "Nothing more." Before he pulls it out, he pauses. "You're playing fast and loose with the rules, Agent Slate, and one day it's going to bite you in the ass. And on that day, I'll be there, standing over you, laughing."

His threat sends a chill down my spine, but I don't bother to respond. Instead, I only continue to stare at him as he pulls out a schedule from his desk. "Tony drives for me on occasion," he says. "Does it on the nights when he's not working for Mansfield. Here's his schedule." He tosses the ledger across his desk. "I'd like to reiterate here; I got no clue what you think he's done. I don't want to know, either."

I grab it before it can slide off to the floor and I can feel Zara's presence closer behind me. The ledger has a full list of drivers, starting with all the fully employed individuals and then moving on to the contracted ones. Tony Moreno's name is halfway down the contractor list, and given his other job, he doesn't have very many runs. His signature is on the ledger beside all the routes he's driven.

"Has Tony been here since Thursday?" I ask.

"Are you blind? Do you see his name on there between then and now?" Toscani asks.

His last scheduled run was last Wednesday, though he has another one tomorrow, beginning at eight in the morning. "He's scheduled to come in tomorrow?"

He looks at me like I've been struck dumb. "He should be in by seven."

"Ledger only shows a pickup time. Where's he driving to?" I ask.

He extends his hand for the ledger, and I give it back to him. He licks a thumb and flips a few pages. "He's listed for the Oriole run. Which means he'll be headed to BWI and drop off the trailer there."

I check my watch. That's a little over nineteen hours from now. "Where would he be right now?"

"Fuck if I know," he says, putting the ledger back. "Are we good here?"

I place both hands on his desk, leaning forward. "No, we're not good here. I don't think you understand, I need to find him *right now.*"

"Well, I can't help you with that, now can I?" He stands, matching me. "I feel like I've been more than cooperative here, Agent. And unless you'd like to talk to my lawyers about threatening to make up some bullshit charge just to get what you want, I suggest you leave."

It seems I've pushed Santino Toscani as far as I possibly can. I feel my phone buzz in my pocket, but I ignore it, staring into the other man's eyes. "Thanks for your time," I say in a low voice.

"Get the hell out of my business," he says, the threat palpable on his lips. I don't let him see that it rattles me a little.

I'm in his territory, and even though we have backup close, there's no guarantee they could get here in time if something went sideways. Based on what I've seen, I don't think Toscani does know what's going on with Tony. He seems oblivious to Avery's plight, which makes my heart drop. This won't be as quick of a resolution as I had hoped.

I turn to Zara and motion that we should leave.

"Agent Slate," Toscani calls to me as we reach the door. I shoot a glance over my shoulder. "Don't ever come in here without a warrant again."

Chapter Seventeen

"IS IT JUST ME, OR WAS THAT A LOT SCARIER THAN THE LAST time we were in there?" Zara asks once we're back in the car and away from the warehouse. The other units stayed close until we were sure Toscani wasn't going to try and send anyone after us just for fun.

"It seems like little Santino is growing into his big boy pants," I say. I was impressed with him this time; he held his own. Something I wasn't expecting. Part of the reason I had no qualms about going in there to ask about Tony Moreno was because in our past meetings, Toscani was less ferocious. But it seems like he's been tempered over the past few months. I'm not sure what to make of that, other than if we ever have to tussle with him again, there's a good chance blood will be drawn.

"So now what?" Zara asks. "If Toscani doesn't know about the operation—"

"—we go after the source," I say. "We'll check Moreno's home first, then any other places he's known to frequent. If nothing else, we know his schedule. If he's making a run for Toscani first thing in the morning, then he'll be close."

"You really think he'll still drive the route? If he's got Avery?"

"I think he'll have delivered her by the time he's scheduled to go out on his next route, which doesn't give us a lot of time." I check my phone again out of nervous habit. "The assassin said we had a day. That might not have meant a full twenty-four hours."

"I've got his address as 6026 Highland Ave," Zara says. "Apartment B."

"*Apartment?*" If he's keeping Avery there, it would be almost impossible for someone not to notice. Unless she's been unconscious the whole time. Even then, there's a much higher risk of someone seeing him transport her in and out of the apartment.

"Are you still sure this is our guy?" Zara asks again. I'm sure she's having the same doubts about the situation. "I think we should check on the ex-military guy."

"Call DuBois. Tell him to check on Grant," I say. "Because you're right, maybe I am barking up the wrong tree, but I don't think so. Still, it wouldn't hurt to be sure. We might as well use all these extra resources Janice allocated, right?"

"Got it," Zara says, calling it in. With DuBois' help we'll be able to hit both locations at the same time. Still, the apartment aspect is bothersome. I assumed Moreno would have a freestanding building somewhere. A private place where he could hold Avery without the risk of being caught.

But as I'm puzzling it over in my mind, my phone buzzes again. I immediately recall it rang while I was in with Toscani, and I forgot to check on who called. "Slate," I say, turning a bit so that Zara and I can hold conversations at the same time.

"Slate, it's Caruthers," the man on the other side says. "Just finished with the inspection of the Huxley house."

"I assume you wouldn't be calling unless you found something," I say, my pulse picking up.

"It's not much, but we have a partial shoe print," he says. "It's in the soft ground near the edge of the patio where the water collects. Looks like he might have taken a misstep when he shot at the security guard. So far, it's the only evidence we've found."

"Man's shoe?" I ask.

"Weight from the depth of the indentation would seem to indicate that much. Size twelve. We're running the sole pattern right now; looks like a sneaker."

"I guess it would have been too much to ask for a *NIKE* indentation in the ground," I say.

"Just a little. I'll keep you updated if we find anything else," Caruthers says. "Best of luck in the investigation."

I thank him and hang up just as Zara gets off the phone as well. "DuBois is taking his team to investigate Grant right now," she says.

"I don't want to alert Moreno at his place if he really is there. We'll have to do some recon first, just to make sure."

"I still don't get this whole thing," Zara says. "We still don't have a motive. What does a low-level creep like Moreno want with a Representative's daughter? He can't be part of this organization the assassin mentioned, could he?"

I shake my head. "I wish I knew. I don't know if Moreno is working for this organization, or if he's decided to do this on his own, but either way, I think he's got her."

"And what about the assassin?" Zara says. "If we take Moreno down before he delivers her, then won't the assassin lose her chance to find this organization?"

I grip the steering wheel tighter. "Frankly, I don't care what she does. If it weren't for Liam…" I look over and catch Zara's eye.

"I know," she says. "It's going to be okay, Em."

"The thing I can't figure out is why she went after him instead of you," I say, allowing the car's GPS to guide me to our destination. "She knows both of you are important to me.

And yet she chose to take him. Even after threatening you both."

"Maybe it was a matter of convenience," Zara suggests. "I didn't leave the Bureau after the operation went bad. She couldn't get to me in there. But Liam…"

"Maybe," I say.

"Or maybe she thinks you'll work harder to get him back. Since, you know, your little *encounter* in Mardel."

"That's not funny," I say. "I would work just as hard, if not harder for you. You've been there for me when no one else was, and I care about you just as much. If not more."

"Aww." She leans over so our shoulders are touching. "Does this mean you *love* me?" she teases. "Enough to pull me into the backseat of a chevy?"

I shake my head. "I knew I should have kept that to myself."

Zara chuckles. "C'mon, it's kinda hot. You have to admit. The fact that you won't go into more detail just makes me want to know more."

"Sorry to disappoint," I say. "But you're right about one thing. It was pretty hot."

Zara leans back into her own seat, smirking. "I wonder if she has video. Maybe I should try to contact her to make my own deal."

"You will not!" I shout, causing her to bust out laughing again. "Oh, God, do you really think she does? I hadn't even thought of that."

"She seems to have everything else," Zara says. "Why not? In case she needed to blackmail you."

"I just don't understand her obsession with me," I say. "She's had more than ample opportunity to kill me, and yet I'm still here. What's the deal?"

"Who knows why disturbed people do what they do? You can ask her once we have her in custody." Zara puts one foot up on the dash, relaxing back into the seat. I wish I felt as calm as she does about it, but it gnaws at me.

"Here, we're only a few minutes away," I say, checking the GPS.

"How do you want to play it?"

"What kind of car does he drive?" I ask.

"Uhh…" Zara searches on her phone for a minute, before calling in to the system to confirm. "A black Camaro, Z28."

I pull into the apartment complex, which is a two-story place made up of three different buildings. Each building looks like it only has four units, which really just makes this a set of quadplexes. Apartment B is in the first building, on the first floor. Easy entrance and exit access if he was transporting Avery.

"I don't see the car anywhere," Zara says.

"Me either. Let's check with the office."

The apartment complex office is little more than one room with a small bathroom at the back. A man in his late fifties sits behind the counter, his head tilted back in his chair, snoring. There's a small TV on somewhere on the other side of the counter. The place reminds me more of a seedy hotel than an apartment complex.

I rap on the counter a few times, causing the man to choke on his spit as he wakes up. He coughs a few times, then grabs a pair of hornrims from the desk, slipping them on. "Yeah?"

I show him my badge. "We're looking for one of your tenants. Tony Moreno. Seen him in the past few days?"

He shakes his head. "Not for a while. His mail has been piling up," the man says, indicating a stack of letters and bills bound with a rubber band on the shelf behind him. "He better come pick it up soon, renewal's coming up."

"Do you know if he's been in his apartment since Thursday?" I ask.

"Every time I've gone by to try and deliver this, he ain't been there," the man says. "Or if he was, he ain't answerin'."

"We need to get into see his apartment," I say.

He reaches under the desk, pulls out a key and tosses it to me without a word of protest. Normally people start talking about warrants and federal oversight when we try to look at someone's place of residence. Seems like the manager here couldn't care less.

"Just don't steal nothin'," he says. "I got problems enough around here."

I hold up the key and nod. "We'll be right back with this."

It's a short walk over to building one that holds apartment B. "That was easy," Zara says when we reach the door. I place my ear up against the door itself to see if I can hear any sounds of struggle...or anything, really. But it's silent.

I knock on the door and Zara smirks, turning away for a minute. She always gives me crap about how I knock. "Next time you're doing it," I tell her.

"You're the boss," she says, grinning.

There's no answer and no movement as far as I can tell. I make a motion at the door. "Go ahead, let's see how a pro does it," I say. "We'll give him one more chance."

"Fine," she says, and absolutely pounds on the door at least twice as hard as I do. "FBI, open up!"

"What the hell?" I say, "That was so much louder!"

"Oh, you thought I was giving you a hard time because your knocks were loud. No, it's cause they're all wimpy."

"Yeah?" I ask and slam on the door a few times, causing it to rattle in its frame. "How's that?"

"I don't think he's home," she says, ignoring the fact that I just totally out-knocked her.

"Either that or he's standing behind that door with a shotgun." I draw my weapon. "Get ready, we're going in."

She nods, drawing her own weapon. I place the key in the deadbolt and turn, making sure we're both clear of the door before I reach out to open it. I allow it to swing inside and I can already tell all the lights in the apartment are off. "FBI," I call out. "We're coming in." Zara nods and I do a quick check around the frame, seeing only an empty apartment. I move inside quickly, checking all the corners and dark spots as Zara moves in behind me. We turn on lights as we go, until we've checked the entire apartment. It's empty and it doesn't look like anyone has been here for at least a few days. Some of the food in the fridge has already spoiled.

"Well, he's not holding her here," Zara says. "If he's got her at all."

"Doesn't look like he's been back either," I say, closing the refrigerator.

Zara holsters her weapon and I do the same. "So now what?"

"He has to be keeping her somewhere. Did Moreno have any other properties in his name? Places he might have inherited, or other family members that are close?"

She shakes her head. "I'm not sure, I'll have to do some research. Give me a minute, my computer is out in the car." I nod as she heads out. Meanwhile I inspect the apartment a little closer. It looks relatively clean for a bachelor. Moreno has a large TV and surround system set up, along with a lot of gaming consoles. Looks like he passes the time with movies and games, as I don't see much of anything else around. There are a few framed posters of action movies on the walls. The fact that he would even take the time to frame and hang posters says something about this man, that he's not a slob or a burnout or someone without ambition. There's a sizable collection of liquor bottles in one of the kitchen cabinets, and it seems Moreno has a penchant for vodka, as that bottle is the one closest to empty.

I head back into the second bedroom to find it's been converted into a makeshift gym, full of weights and a bench, and a mirror mounted on the wall. He takes care of himself, and he likes to preen. Interesting.

The other bedroom is the primary, and has a king-sized

bed with plush covers. I pull on a pair of gloves and pull the covers back out of curiosity, then replace them back the way they were. Something bright red catches my eye and I bend down, only to pull a pair of women's lace panties out from behind the bed. The closet doors are open, so I make a cursory inspection, only finding men's clothing. Looks like Moreno had a friend over recently, but not someone serious enough to stay very often. Though as I'm turning away, I spot a row of shoes at the bottom. Among them sits a pair of black sneakers, size twelve. I pull out my phone and call Caruthers.

"Hey, it's Slate. Can you send me a picture of that impression you got from behind the house?"

"Sure," Caruthers says. "Do you have something?"

"I might."

"Sending it over now." I pull the phone away from my ear as the notification comes through.

"Hang on," I say. "I want to check this while you're on the phone." I switch over to my pictures and pull up the image from Caruthers. It's a little hard to make out, but I can see a definite pattern in the ground. It's very similar to the pattern on the bottom of the shoes I found. "I think this might be a match," I tell him. "I'm sending you a picture back, let me know what you think?"

"Can't you just bring me the shoe?" Caruthers asks.

"I don't have a warrant here," I tell him. "But if this looks good, I can get one."

"Sure, send it over," he says, though I can hear some disappointment in his voice. I hang up and snap the picture of the bottom of the shoes, then return them to where I found them.

"Hey," Zara says, poking her head in the bedroom. "Here you are. Find something?"

"Might be a match to our shoe print at the scene," I say. "Caruthers is checking."

"Great," she says. "I checked the database for any other

matches on Moreno. He has a sister who lives in Denver, and his parents are deceased. No other properties under his name."

"Damn." I have to consider the possibility Moreno might *not* be our man. There's no sign of Avery, and it isn't like sneakers are rare. It's possible Grant could have the very same pair in his closet. "Maybe you were right, I might have made a bad call here."

She gives my shoulder a reassuring rub. "Don't be so hard on yourself. I just wish I'd made you wager something."

"No," I say. "I'm not betting on anything else with you, somehow I always lose."

"Come *on*," she whines. "One of these days I'm getting you to go rafting. White water all the way, baby."

I shake my head as we leave the apartment, locking it back up. "Don't we have to drive like ten hours to find good rapids?" I ask.

"Yeah, but it's totally worth it. Just think, road trip! And they've got some nice Air BnBs up there too. I've been looking at them online."

I stop short, my mind suddenly firing on all cylinders.

"What?" she asks. "What'd I say?"

Chapter Eighteen

"GOT IT," I SAY, THEN HANG UP, SLIPPING MY PHONE BACK INTO the cup holder in the car. "That was DuBois, they've tracked down Grant, but he's got a rock-solid alibi."

Zara holds up one hand. She's still on the phone with one of the home rental companies. "No, it's Moreno. M-O-R. Like moron." She turns to me, rolling her eyes. As soon as we returned the key to the manager we hopped right back in the car and Zara got on the phone with each of the vacation rental places to see if we can't find out if Moreno has booked himself a getaway to keep Avery. It would make a lot more sense than holding her at his apartment.

I have to admit, it's not a bad plan. He could get a whole house, far away from everyone for a couple of days and all he has to do is make sure he doesn't leave anything suspicious behind. It could look like nothing more than a vacation. But considering he's due to drive for Toscani tomorrow, I suspect the handoff is going to take place today, if it hasn't already.

"Yes, this is official FBI business," she says. "We are pursuing a lead for a missing girl. Are you telling me that I need to talk to your HR department before you give me information that could potentially save her life?"

I'm headed back to headquarters so we can keep doing a deep dive on Moreno. Maybe with more hands on deck we'll be able to find something. What bothers me, though, is I know the assassin is still out there, probably watching all our moves, wondering how far we've gotten. After all, this is technically *her* job. Still, I'm hoping I can find a way to resolve this without getting anyone else killed. We need Liam back, and I don't want the people in this organization to die. They don't deserve it. They deserve to sit in jail cells the rest of their long, useless lives. And if it means I have to work with a killer to find them, then that's what I'll do. But she can only push me so far.

"Really?" Zara says, sitting up straighter in her seat. "Where?" Her laptop is open in her lap, and she types out an address as it's given to her over the phone. "Got it. Yes, thank you for your help. No, this will not be in the papers. I can't— yes, okay, fine. I understand. Thank you."

She hangs up and lets out a frustrated grunt.

"Whatcha got?"

"We might have just hit pay dirt," she says. "They had a Tony Moreno on a reservation made almost a month ago. He's just outside the city in a farmhouse close to the river."

"Got the address?" I ask.

She inputs into my car's GPS, which re-routes us away from FBI Headquarters. "It's only thirty minutes away with traffic."

"Yep," she says, grinning with self-satisfaction. "Let's just hope it's the same Tony Moreno." She dives back into her laptop. "What were you saying about Grant?"

"DuBois said he wasn't even in town when the kidnapping took place. He was up in Pennsylvania with his in-laws for the week, just got back with his wife this afternoon."

"Did he confirm that?" she asks.

"Plane ticket and everything."

"Then I guess Moreno's our man."

I arch an eyebrow. "Like moron?"

She lets out a frustrated breath. "That woman was a moron. She kept trying to tell me she couldn't release that information because of privacy issues. It's a vacation rental, for God's sake, not someone's social security number. Wanted to know if this was going to be on the news tonight, and if so, to mention the vacation rental business."

"Wow. Glad to know she's such a concerned citizen."

"Everyone's out for themselves these days, don't you know?" Zara asks, turning her attention back to the screen. "Best I can tell from satellite photos is this house is pretty isolated. It's set way back from the road, so it's almost on the river, but there aren't any other houses around. Though, looking at the photos online, they've furnished it well. I'd stay here."

"How does that help us?" I ask.

She shakes her head. "I dunno. We'll have to figure out a way to get close to the house without coming screaming down the driveway, because he'll definitely see us if we do."

I check the time: almost five in the afternoon. "We might be too late already," I say, pressing the gas pedal a little harder. "What if he's already made the handoff?"

"But she said—"

"Maybe she's wrong," I suggest. "Or maybe Moreno is in a hurry. He's got that job for Toscani tomorrow. He might want to get this over so he can be back on his normal schedule."

"What do you think she meant when she said they 'prepare' the girls?" Zara asks.

I've been mulling that over as well. I hope it means nothing more than getting them cleaned up and into new clothes. At least I hope there's nothing more to it than that. But there almost always is. We deal with some of the most depraved and disgusting humans alive, who aren't afraid to do the worst things imaginable to other people. I don't know what Moreno's role in all of this is, or how he got involved, but I sincerely hope he doesn't give me a reason to shoot him in the head as soon as we find him; I'm not sure I'd be able to stop myself otherwise.

"Let's just get there," I say. "Call Janice; we're going to need backup."

"But what about—"

"We'll have to get everyone to stay off the main street or the driveway. But if Moreno has Avery in that house, we can't risk it with just the two of us. We need a team, otherwise that little girl's chances get cut in half."

"Right," Zara says, dialing.

I just hope the teams can get there as quickly as we can. Right now, I don't even care about apprehending Moreno, I just want to bring Avery to safety. And where does the assassin fit into all of this? Will she know if we take Moreno into custody before she gets a chance to question him?

Zara puts the phone on speaker as soon as she's dialed. "Simmons," our boss answers.

"We think we've located our guy. Possibly the girl too," I say.

"Good work. What's the situation?" Janice asks. I give her a brief explanation, along with the potential evidence of Moreno's footwear in his apartment.

"I can get forensics over there once you have Avery out of harm's way," she says. "Have you heard from your friend?"

I bristle. "Nothing so far."

"In your opinion, what will apprehending Moreno and saving Avery do to Agent Coll?" she asks.

I have to admit, I don't know how the assassin will react. We were just supposed to find him and then report back to her. But we're right up against the clock, and if we don't get Avery now, before she's handed off, we might never see her again. I can't trust that she'll just be returned one day. Especially not on the word of my husband's killer. "Unknown."

There's a pause on the other end of the line. "And if we do nothing, we're failing in our duty to protect Avery Huxley," she says.

"How should we proceed?" I ask. Zara and I exchange a nervous look.

"Get the girl to safety. We'll deal with the fallout later. But do your best to leave Mr. Moreno alive. We need to bring him in for questioning. Especially if we're going to get to the bottom of this organization."

My heart is in my throat, but I know it's the right call. *I'm sorry, Liam.* "Yes, ma'am. We won't let you down."

"Good luck."

Twenty-five minutes later we're driving along a country road where the speed limit is fifty-five and the houses are far enough apart you don't have to worry about any noise complaints from the neighbors. Most of the houses along this road are either run-down shacks or really nice retreats, like the area can't decide what it wants to be. There don't seem to be any other cars on the road, which I'm taking as a good sign. I'd like to do this quickly and with as little fuss as possible.

"Where's the backup?" I ask.

"Eight minutes behind us. That should give us just enough time to get set up and ready. You got the vests in the back of your car?"

"What do I look like, a rookie?" Since we never know when we'll need to be on a potentially active shooter scene, agents generally keep Kevlar vests in our vehicles in the event something like this comes up. The only times we wouldn't is when our car is part of our cover for an undercover operation, though some enterprising agents find ways to hide them under seats or upholstery.

Zara directs me to an area close to the property, and I pull the car off the road. It's still daylight out there, which won't make this any easier. But at least we'll be able to see our target. We both get out and pull the vests from the trunk, each of us slipping them on. As with most of our other gear, they have giant yellow FBI letters on the back, in case anyone was confused as to who we were.

She pulls her laptop out of the car and puts it on the trunk. On the screen is a satellite view of the area, large enough that I can see the road we just pulled off, along with the house itself, and the river.

"We're going to head along this tree line here," Zara says, "And then cut across here and wait for the other team to arrive. When they get here, they'll come from this side. That way we can have the entire house surrounded and Moreno shouldn't know we're here."

"Works for me," I say, drawing my weapon and checking the chamber as well as my rounds. I slip the weapon back into the holster until I'm ready. "Let's go on ahead and see if we can't get the lay of the land over there before the others arrive. I don't want to run into any surprises."

"What, like booby traps?" Zara asks.

"Like anything."

Taking care not to shut the doors too loud or to make any other noise, Zara and I set off along the tree line, while I send off a series of instructional texts to the other team, letting them know where to pull off. Zara also has a small radio in hand, which we'll use to coordinate when they get closer. The grass is high and if we weren't wearing pants, our legs would probably be covered in bites from all the bugs flying around. But we keep low and fast, sticking to the trees as we trot across the property, parallel to the driveway which sits on the other side of the trees, and which we cannot see yet.

Zara halts us and pulls out her cell phone, checking our latitude and longitude. I wouldn't have thought she'd have a sharp enough signal to get it down to the closest foot, but somehow she has. She knows exactly where we are and where we're supposed to be.

"Here," she whispers, pointing to a small break in the underbrush. "We'll cut through. We should be almost right alongside the house."

I nod, following her lead as we do our best not to make any noise. Thankfully the sounds of the woods cover most of it, including the screams of the cicadas, which are particularly loud out here in the country. I also catch the sound of water, which must mean we're close to the river at this point.

As soon as there is a break in the underbrush, I get a look at the house. It's a modest two-story with a wraparound porch. It looks like an old farmhouse that was fixed up and resold to be a rental property, though it does still contain some of its original charm. A secondary building sits off to the house's left, a garage or barn; I'm not sure which. And parked in front of the barn is a black Camaro Z28.

"Got him," I whisper.

"Looks like it," Zara says.

I pull a pair of mini binoculars from inside my vest and take a look at the house, particularly the windows. Unfortunately, the shades are drawn on every window, which means we'll be going in there blind.

"I can't see a thing. Looks locked up tight."

"Which makes sense if he's got her in there. That house has river views, doesn't it?" I ask.

"It does."

"Then he wouldn't want any nosy people on boats catch a glimpse of Avery in one of the windows. Probably upstairs bedroom."

She turns to me. "Is that where you think she is?"

I scan the house again. No basement, just a crawl space. I hope he hasn't shoved her under there. "If it's his job to get her *ready*, it makes sense he'd do that in the bedrooms. It would be easier to keep her up there too. And hopefully we can go in and catch him off-guard on the ground level. I just hope she's not down there with him. It'll make everything complicated."

Zara checks her watch. "The other team should be here any minute. I'll be able to get them on the radio as soon as they're in position."

Almost as soon as she finishes speaking my phone buzzes. "That's them now," I say, grabbing it and placing it to my ear. "This is Slate, go ahead."

My heart immediately jumps in my throat as soon as I hear the familiar voice.

"Good job, Emily. I knew you could do it."

Chapter Nineteen

I FEEL LIKE I'M FROZEN IN PLACE, UNABLE TO RESPOND. ZARA is looking at me with wide eyes, as if to ask me what's wrong. But I can't speak. How did she know? How did she find us? There's no one around for miles.

"I do hope you're not about to arrest the man who has kidnapped poor Avery," the assassin says. "At least, not until I have a few moments alone with him."

"How did you know?" I ask and somehow, Zara's eyes go even wider. She begins looking all around us, pulling her weapon from its holster.

"I have my ways," the assassin says. "Now. I understand you're about to raid the house where you believe our man is held up with Avery Huxley. I'll need to insist you don't do that, not yet."

"I can't just sit here and—"

"Listen to me very carefully, Emily." I want to put the phone on speaker, but I'm afraid if I do, the sound might carry over to the house. Instead, I lean closer to Zara so we can both hear. "If luck is on your side and that girl hasn't been handed off yet, and you attempt to do anything to interrupt that transference, I can guarantee you that Agent Coll will be dead before you even get your man into handcuffs."

"The deal was we find him; we get Avery and you let Liam go."

"Was that the deal?" she asks, her tone light and airy. "Because I seem to remember telling you to find him and I *don't kill* Liam. That's very different than letting him go. As for little Avery Huxley, her part in this isn't over just yet. I need her for a little while longer."

"To forcibly subject a child to—"

"Trust me, she will be fine," the assassin interrupts. "Anything bad that was going to happen has already happened and won't happen again until she's delivered. And by then I will make sure every single person that is connected to this organization pays. But for right now, I need you to call off your dogs, and keep your distance from Tony Moreno."

I glare at Zara as if to ask how she could possibly know our suspect's name. But then I realize if she's tracking us— tracking me somehow—she may have noticed we went to both Toscani's and Tony's home. It wouldn't be easy but finding out who we've been hunting is within her skillset.

"We can't do that. If we lose Moreno, we lose—"

"You're not going to lose anyone. The transfer will take place there, at your location, if it hasn't already, which I don't suspect it has. They always do these things at night. Moreno won't leave until it's over."

"How can you be so sure?" I ask.

"As I told you, I've seen it before. Now call off your teams or prepare to receive the location where I drop Agent Coll's body."

I grit my teeth and nod at Zara who sends the other team a message. I wish I had time to confer with Janice, but technically I'm the lead agent on this case, so it's my call. "They're pulling back," I say after Zara gets the confirmation.

"Good. Now you two sit tight. I'd hate to ruin the surprise."

I furrow my brow. "What surprise?"

"You'll see. In the meantime, I'd just like to say I knew you could do it. Who else could take an impossible case and turn it around in a day? Maybe it was always meant to be this way. Maybe I should have just abducted you instead and forced you to perform the investigation from the start."

"I don't think that would have worked very well," I say.

"No, I suppose not. Though I can't help but think how much fun it would have been." I can tell she's just toying with me now. She holds all the cards, and she knows it. "Think of it. You, working for me, in the shadows. And what would have happened if you needed access to the FBI database? You couldn't have just walked in, could you?" I can feel my whole body tighten. It's becoming clearer to me now that my first priority needs to be removing this woman from active play. I can't allow her to get away and disappear into the world.

"I have this scene playing in my head," she continues. "Perhaps there's a fancy party in the building next door to your office. We'd have to get you all dressed up—in an actual ballgown—to infiltrate, then we'd get to the roof and rappel over, just like in our own spy movie. We'd use your knowledge to break in and gather whatever we want. It would have been great."

I shake my head. Whatever this woman is smoking, it must be the good stuff. "Let's stick with reality. What happens during the transfer?"

"Moreno will wait for his contact to show up, then hand over the girl for delivery assuming she's been properly prepared for the organization. I want you to follow whoever picks her up all the way back to the organization proper. Like I said, they're decentralized, but she'll be taken to one of them. Then, after that one is done, she will be taken to the next, and so on. I will follow along, at each location, eliminating organization members as we go."

"You said she wouldn't be hurt!" I practically yell and Zara has to shush me to keep Moreno from hearing. I might have already been too loud.

"She won't be, not physically. But the psychological and emotional scars she develops over the next few days will keep her in therapy for life. Who knows, she might even resort to killing as a way of coping. It's not unheard of." For the first time I believe the assassin has revealed something about herself. Whether it was on purpose or not, I don't know. But it helps me understand her a little better. Maybe she sees herself in Avery.

Still, we can't throw her to the wolves. "You know I can't allow that to happen."

"Agent Slate, the only reason you're even in this is because it's what I've deemed necessary. I can take you out as easily as you walk the trash to your dumpster in the evenings. Don't think you're so important that I can't remove you if you become an obstacle."

"I will not let those men use that little girl," I tell her. "I don't care what you have to do, but I'm not living with that over my head for the rest of my life."

She lets out an exasperated sigh. "Ugh. Can you even hear yourself from all the way up there on the moral high ground? You should be thanking me; I'm doing your country a favor by getting rid of these men. Nothing good will come from their continued existence. Even prison is too good for them. All they know is death, so that's all they deserve."

She's determined to see this through, but I can't allow anything else to happen to Avery. If we don't stop this now, we might lose her forever. And I couldn't live with that either.

I shake my head at Zara. She knows it, too.

"You know what?" the assassin says. "I'm not sure I trust you to keep to our arrangement. After all, you are Emily Slate, and your history makes me think you'll put Avery's life over poor Liam's. Perhaps I should just eliminate that obstacle for you now, so you can go ahead and save the girl."

"No!" I say before I can stop myself. "Liam…he doesn't have anything to do with this."

"Now who's living in the fantasy world? Liam is part of this because *you* are a part of this. And because I know you value the life of other people more than your own, it's the only possible way to motivate you into action."

This woman is so maddening I want to tear my hair out. But she's pre-emptively calling my bluff. I can't do anything for Avery without endangering Liam. For the moment, I don't see how I have any other choice, unless Janice is close to finding his location.

"Fine," I say. "We'll sit tight and wait for the transfer."

"Good girl," she says. "I knew I could count on you. Now get comfortable, because it may take a few more hours."

"What do we do once we've tailed the car to its destination?" I ask.

"Don't worry, I'll contact you," she replies. "Enjoy." The phone clicks off before I have the chance to say anything else. I want to slam it on the nearest rock out of frustration, but instead I pocket it.

"Em—" Zara begins.

"I'm not doing it," I say. "As soon as his contact shows up, we arrest them both, and get Avery out of here. Get DuBois back here and his men standing by. We're going in as soon as our other party arrives." I never asked to be this woman's special pet project or whatever obsession she has with me, and I'm not going to let her dictate terms to me.

I have a very bad feeling this decision is going to cost Liam his life. I only hope he knows why and can forgive me. But I can't let this happen. I can't sacrifice that little girl.

I send off a couple of messages to Janice, informing her of the situation while Zara gets back in contact with DuBois.

Thankfully, Janice agrees with my decision, and we get the go-ahead.

Zara and I make ourselves comfortable in the underbrush, while I keep a watch on the house. There's not so much as a flutter at the curtains, which makes me hope Moreno has no idea we're out here. Though I hate the idea that poor Avery is less than two hundred yards from us, and we can't do anything about it. I feel like both Zara and I are spent on words; there's nothing left to say. Instead, we just have to wait and hope that psycho inside isn't doing anything to her.

The more I think about it, the more the whole thing breaks my heart, and I can't believe I've been forced into this position by this *woman*.

"Psst," Zara says, causing me to glance up. Dusk has fallen, shrouding us in complete darkness among the trees. A pair of headlights has appeared at the far end of the driveway, and a vehicle is slowly rumbling down the gravel path. I glance over to the house through my binoculars and see a brief flash of movement at one of the downstairs curtains. Moreno knows his role in this is just about over. But he's not getting away with this. None of them are. I've made up my mind.

"Where's the backup?" I whisper.

"A mile out, standing by."

"Get them to circle in and block the road from out there. We'll box them in so they can't get away in the vehicle." I lean closer to Zara. "As soon as we see Avery, we take both Moreno and his compadre down," I whisper.

"Em, are you sure?" she asks. I know what she's asking me. Making this decision seals Liam's fate.

"I can't let them take her."

Zara shoots me a grin, which is barely visible in the darkness. She pulls her weapon from her holster. "I was hoping you'd say that."

I pull my own weapon and sit in a crouch, waiting for the

car to arrive. But as it draws closer, I realize it's not a car at all, but a pickup truck. Funny, I had imagined the transfer taking place in a Bentley or equally fancy car, at least from the way the assassin spoke about it. These are obviously very wealthy people, strange that they would use a Chevy Tahoe. But then again, I'm not about to question any of this. I just want the takedown.

As the vehicle pulls up to the house, its lights shine on the front porch. The door opens and I see Moreno for the first time. He pokes his head out, his dark hair coming down to his shoulders. As expected, he's a big guy-matching the description Hayden gave us at the hospital. A moment later he emerges with Avery at his side. She's in a frilly dress, like something she would wear to her own birthday party, but I can already see from her face that she's completely crestfallen and broken. Whatever Moreno has done to her since Thursday night has destroyed her spirit, which only enrages me more and tells me we're taking the proper action.

"Get ready," I tell Zara. She whispers into the radio, confirming with DuBois.

The buyer turns off the engine and steps out of the car. It's still dark so I don't get a good look at him as he's turned away from us. But there's something familiar about the way he walks; something a part of me recognizes.

Then it clicks.

"No," I whisper, my weapon dropping by my side.

"What?" Zara asks. "What's wrong?"

As the man walks up to the porch to take custody of Avery, the light beside the front door illuminates his face. And as he turns, I get a perfect view of his profile. One I recognize immediately.

"It's Chris," I say. "It's my brother-in-law."

Chapter Twenty

"WHAT?" ZARA ASKS. "HOW CAN THAT BE?"

To say I'm stunned beyond words would be an understatement. How can Chris be here? Now I realize that's why I recognized his truck; it's the same one I've seen parked at his house every time I was over there dropping Timber off or picking him up.

At first, I can't resolve it in my own head. It's like I'm seeing an elephant flying a jet plane or an upside-down waterfall. It just doesn't make sense. And the more I try to make it fit in my brain, the more it won't go. *Chris* is involved with this? *He's* the one picking Avery up to transport her to God-knows-where?

"Holy shit," Zara says, having taken the binoculars from me. "It *is* him."

At least I know I haven't gone crazy. But at the same time, I don't know how to deal with this information. Does Dani know? Has he been with these people for as long as Matt was? Or was this a recent development? I suppose if Matt was involved with them, it's not a stretch to think that Chris would be too. A family business of sorts.

But then I think back to all those arguments he and I had

—to all those times he accused me of getting his brother killed, of not being there to protect him when he needed it most. He made me feel so guilty for not being there for Matt. And yet, here he is, a member of the same organization that ordered my husband's death. Has he known this entire time?

And yet again I'm faced with having someone in my life who has been able to completely pull the wool over my eyes. It obviously runs in the family. My entire job is supposed to be determining if a person is lying to me or not, and to find out that not only my husband did it successfully for four years, but his brother has now been doing the exact same thing—and so effectively! Every time he'd berated me for what happened to Matt I'd felt terrible, and it turns out that it has all been nothing but a giant *lie*.

I ball my free hand into a fist while the hand with the gun tightens on the grip. "Em, are you okay?" Zara asks.

"Fine," I grumble. Ahead of us, Moreno is ushering Avery toward Chris. This is it. I don't care if he is Matt's brother, I'm not letting him get away with this. None of them are. I'm so mad I can barely think straight. "Give DuBois the go signal. We're taking them down."

"Em—" Zara says, but I'm not paying attention. My eyes are locked on my target and I'm not about to let him get away. This is the last person who is going to pull the wool over my eyes. And if Chris really is connected to this organization, then I can't wait to get him into an interrogation room.

"Get ready," I say. "We go on my mark." Somewhere in my brain I realize Zara hasn't said anything over the radio yet, but that's eclipsed by the fact Chris now has his arm around Avery's shoulder. The girl's eyes are far away; she's somewhere else while Chris and Moreno exchange a few words. I prepare to stand and charge them, only for Zara to grab my arm and yank my attention back to her.

"Em!"

"What?" She points behind me. I turn to see a figure

behind us, clad all in black. I'm startled and think for a second Moreno has made us and sent someone out here to ambush us when I see her face light up when she sucks in on the vape pen, the little electronic device emitting a small blue light that reflects off her.

The assassin.

Her blonde hair is pulled back into a ponytail and she has an assault rifle in one hand, her finger on the trigger, and the weapon is pointed directly at Zara. She places one finger to her lips.

It's as if I've gone numb. None of this is happening. It can't be real, any of it.

"I had a thought you might decide to play the hero," she whispers. "You've taken me as far as you can, Emily. And don't worry, I'll fulfill my end of the bargain. Once the Organization has been destroyed, I'll send you Liam's coordinates so you can swoop in and save him yourself."

I look back at Chris and Avery. He's leading her back to her truck, putting her into the passenger seat while Moreno heads back into the house.

"You knew about Chris, didn't you?" I ask. "*That* was the surprise you wanted me to see."

"I suspected he might be the contact, yes. But the look on your face was worth it, trust me."

I begin to lunge at her, but Zara pulls me back. I notice she's holstered her weapon. The assassin keeps her gun trained on us. "Now, now. We wouldn't want to scare your brother-in-law away. We have to let him think he's made a clean exchange, otherwise he might do something drastic with Avery if he thinks they're in danger."

"You bitch," I say. "I won't let you get away with this."

She just smiles as I hear the truck's engine start. "Don't worry, Emily. Your part in this is done. All you have to do now is go home and put your feet up. I'll take care of everything else."

"You can't possibly think I'm going to let you do this," I say. "We have another team out at the road who will stop them. It's over."

She raises her weapon a little, which trains it right on Zara's face. Kevlar won't do her much good if the assassin shoots her in the head. "I've already managed to incapacitate them. If all goes well, Chris will never even see them." My entire body is shaking with rage and I'm having difficulty thinking straight.

She arches an eyebrow. "I've tried to go easy on you. I've tried to be as fair as I could. But I knew you and I would never see eye to eye. We're just too different." In the distance, Chris is pulling the truck around the driveway and heading off. "That's my cue," she says. She tosses us two pairs of handcuffs. "Lock yourselves to the nearest tree and be quick about it. I need to get back to my car."

I stare at the handcuffs on the ground in front of us and it's as if my vision has gone blurry. I can't focus on anything. But it's not from tears, it's from fury. Everyone and their mother has used me to their advantage, and I'm sick of it. This stops now.

"No," I say.

"Emily, don't test me," the assassin says, glancing out beyond the tree line. Chris's truck is leaving, fast. She's going to miss her window. "If I don't follow him, you lose Avery forever."

"I am sick and tired of being someone's pawn," I grumble, standing all the way up to face her. My handgun still hangs in my left hand. The barrel of her weapon follows me all the way up as she shoots another furtive glance to Chris's truck, which is halfway down the driveway already. "You're not going to follow them. *I* am."

"Don't do this," she says. "I gave you a chance, and now you're going to throw it away? You're supposed to be dead already. I *spared* you."

I take a step forward, and she takes a step back, keeping the same distance between us. It seems she might not be as ready to kill me as she says she is. I make a motion with one hand for Zara to get behind me. She may not be willing to shoot me, but I don't believe she'll have the same level of compassion for her.

For the first time, panic sets into the assassin's eyes. She's about to lose her only lead. I know I don't have long. I'll have to sprint back to the car, which means I only have seconds to apprehend and restrain the assassin. But I promised myself if I was ever face to face with her I would take her down. Now is my chance.

"Lower your weapon and get down on the ground," I say. "You're under arrest."

"Emily," she says, shooting another glance at the end of the driveway. Chris has reached the end, his taillights barely visible.

"Em," Zara says from behind me. "We're out of time!" I realize this might not work out like I'd hoped. I can't apprehend the assassin and track down Chris. Not in time.

"You go," I say. "Stop him, you have his vehicle information, or can get it from the DMV. Pull him over before it's too late. I'll deal with her."

The assassin grimaces and raises the weapon into the air, firing off a series of rounds into the night. The sound is like the crack of a whip in the still of the night. "If I'm not going, neither is she," the woman says, all trace of her former bravado and smugness gone.

In an instant, I decide to rush the woman. It seems to surprise her because her eyes go wide before she can pull the weapon back so its level with my chest. I manage to grab the end of the rifle and yank on it, pulling her toward me. She tightens her grip on it and fires another three-burst round, which strikes the ground to my side. I reach out for a strike with the butt of my gun, but she blocks it with her free hand,

and tries to lock my hand in her elbow. I let go of the rifle and strike her hard in the midsection, causing her to let out a gasp for breath and drop the rifle. I try to train my gun on her, but she lands a hit square across my jaw that I don't see coming, and the ground rushes up to me. There's commotion going on behind me, but I can't tell what it is; I'm just concerned with getting up before she gets her hands on that rifle again.

She scrambles forward, crawling on top of me, muttering something intelligible and I find I can't get her off, no matter how much I squirm. She's like a howler monkey, and she has a death grip in my hair and around my neck. I feel the constriction of air, but I manage to bring up a knee and then my foot, and push with all my force, sending her stumbling back. I jump up, stay low and deliver a surgical strike to her kneecap, which causes her to cry out.

A shot rings out behind me, and I see Zara has positioned herself behind a tree, while Moreno stands less than fifty feet away, a shotgun in his hands. One of the barrels is smoking and he's looking to take a second shot. All the gunfire from the assassin's rifle must have attracted him, which I think was her plan.

But before I can turn my attention back to her, she slams into me from the side, sending both of us sprawling on the ground again. I put my hands up to defend myself as she begins swatting and punching at me with no real strategy. I find an opening and deliver the heel of my palm into her cheek, feeling the crack of a bone. She cries out, falling off just as I hear another blast from the shotgun. Zara cries out and my heart jumps into my throat. I search everywhere for my sidearm, finally finding it laying in the grass. I draw it on Moreno. "Don't move, FBI!"

He's holding a double barrel, which means it can only hold two shells at a time before needing to be reloaded and he's already taken both his shots. "Put down the weapon, right now," I tell him, looking down the barrel of my gun at him. I don't know where the assassin is, but I expect her to strike me over the back of the head at any second. Zara is on the ground, holding herself. I have no idea how bad it is.

Moreno looks like he might not do it, like he wants to take his chances, before he finally tosses the gun to the ground. "Lay down!" I command. "Face down, hands on your head." He does and I turn behind me, only to realize the assassin has used the distraction to make a hasty exit. There's no sign of her anywhere. Instead, I run over to Zara who is still behind the tree. Blood trickles from her pants leg where the buckshot caught her.

"Are you okay?" I ask.

"Just get him in custody," she says, grimacing. I run over to Moreno, keeping my weapon trained on him at all times. When I'm sure he's not about to move, I grab one of his hands and with one of the cuffs the assassin threw at us earlier, I clasp it over his wrist before pulling the other one back and clamping them both together.

"Stay there," I tell him, then rush back over to Zara. She already has pressure on the wounds. "Did he get you anywhere else?" I ask.

She shakes her head. "What about the assassin?"

"Gone," I say, pulling out my phone. I dial emergency services and give them our information. I then call Janice. As I'm speaking with her, I hear people running toward us, and realize it's DuBois and his team, all wearing matching Kevlar jackets. They must have been attracted by the gunshots as well.

"Emily," Janice says after I inform her DuBois is close. "Do you have Huxley?"

"No," I say, deflated. "I failed."

Chapter Twenty-One

I'M SITTING IN THE WAITING ROOM AT GWI WHEN JANICE walks in, followed by DuBois and another agent from his team. I set the cold cup of coffee I've been nursing for the past half hour on the nearest table and stand, smoothing out my wrinkled suit which is half covered in dirt and grime from rolling around the ground with the assassin.

"How is she doing?" Janice asks, indicating the operation ward behind me.

"They said she'll be fine. Nothing more than a few flesh wounds. They're just getting the last of it out now. But she'll be using a cane for a while until she can put all her pressure on it again."

Janice indicates we sit. I take the same seat I've been in ever since I accompanied Zara to the hospital. She insisted I go interrogate Moreno, but I wasn't about to leave her alone in that ambulance. I know how scary that can be. "Tell me what happened. I'm sure I'll read it all in your report later, but I need to know now."

I shake my head. "I don't know quite how to say this, but my brother-in-law showed up," I say. The look on her face says more than words ever could. I've been going over it again and again in my head, trying to figure out what I missed and how I could have been so blind to both Chris and Matt. Who else has been able to fool me? "Apparently, he works for the same people that Matt and his boss did. They're all part of this organization."

"The organization that the assassin is hunting?" she asks.

"So she says. I think she knew we weren't going to let them take Avery, which is why she showed up at the last minute."

"She's still tracking you," Janice says.

"She has to be, she found our location; knew Moreno was our man...she knew everything."

"Give me your phone." Janice holds out her hand and I deposit my phone into it. "We're going to need to issue you a new one. This can't happen again."

"This is my second new one," I tell her. "I think the woman is a witch. We still don't know how she made Matt and Gerald Wright's deaths look like heart attacks with no other lingering evidence."

Janice's hard-lined face stares right back at me. "DuBois informed me the tires of all his team's vehicles were slashed, though they don't know how it happened or when. She got in and out quick. But we'll find her, Slate. No one is perfect all the time. She's going to screw up."

"I let the whole thing fall apart," I say. "All because this woman won't leave me alone. If she hadn't shown up, we could have nabbed Moreno, Chris and gotten Avery to safety."

She leans forward, her forearms on her knees, staring at the ground. "We have Moreno in custody, and there's an APB out on your brother-in-law's car. Though I didn't originally make the connection because of the different last name. We will find him and the Huxley girl."

I shake my head. "Not according to the assassin. She was insistent that once that car was gone, we'd never find it again."

"Have you heard from her since?" she asks. I know she's thinking about Liam. I shake my head again.

"Let's just hope she doesn't do anything drastic."

Now it's my turn to shake my head. "We went hand-to-hand in combat. She could have shot me, but she didn't. But neither of us could follow them because of the other. I think that's what you call mutually assured destruction."

"Slate, you're being too hard on yourself."

I nod. "It doesn't matter anymore. I should have just... the members of this organization, whatever it is, if they really are responsible for my husband's death, as well as Gerald Wright and who knows who else, then they need to be brought out of the shadows and into the light. They don't deserve to die. They deserve to pay for their crimes. And Avery..." I put my head into my hands then turn to Janice. "Apparently that's what they're going to do. They'll pass her around like a party favor, and then when they're done, return her home. Scars and all. She lied when she said Avery wouldn't be hurt."

Janice doesn't say anything, only continues to stare at the floor before checking her watch. "Get back to the office. I want you in there with Moreno. If we were on a clock before, now we're really under the gun. We need to find out how he was hired, who gave him his instructions, and if there's any kind of trail we can follow. He's our only lead to finding that little girl, and hopefully, to saving Agent Coll's life."

"Do you really think the assassin won't kill him after what I did?" I ask.

"I don't know. I just hope our luck turns around soon." I take a look at the doors; I was hoping to see Zara again just so that I knew she was okay. "Go on, Agent DuBois will accompany you back. I don't want you on your own, not with that psycho still out there. I'll let you know if anything develops with Agent Foley."

I take a deep breath and get up. "Thanks." Taking my

cup, I deposit it in the trash can as Agent DuBois and I head out of the operating area.

"And, Slate," Janice says. "Don't hold back."

Chapter Twenty-Two

"HOW LONG HAVE YOU BEEN WITH THE BUREAU?" DuBois asks me as we head in through the underground parking lot.

"A little over four years, why?" I ask, holding the door for him behind me.

"You just seem really young," he replies. He's not a man of many words, these have been his only ones since leaving the hospital.

"I get that a lot." We get into the elevator, which takes us up to the seventh floor. DuBois accompanies me to the interrogation rooms, unnecessarily. I get Janice wanting to be cautious, but I don't need him to babysit me all the way through the building. Regardless, he stays right behind me, silent as ever.

I take a look at the schedule and find Moreno is in room nineteen. Before I head in, I check with the watch commander to see if there's been any update since he was brought in. So far, he's remained silent. I then step into the recording room to get a good look at him for a minute.

Through the one-way window I see a hard man who's had a hard life. He stares at the door, like he's daring someone to come in and challenge him. Moreno sports dark hair down to his shoulders and a goatee to match. A couple of old scars grace one of his cheeks. That could have been from gang-related activity, though his goatee hides part of it. I can also tell he's not a skinny man by any means. When I was pulling the cuffs on him, I was full of adrenaline, but even then I noticed how thick his muscles were under his shirt. While I don't doubt he could have gotten down off that balcony, I expected someone with a little more athleticism. More like a gymnast than a linebacker.

I give the tech a word of thanks before heading back out and preparing myself to speak to him. I do a quick check in the nearby mirror, finding that I have bags under my eyes and my hair is frizzy and untamed. I do my best to pull it back into shape. I'm not exactly at a hundred percent here, but I don't have time to primp and preen. We need answers now.

When I open the door, Moreno barely twitches, he only continues to stare straight ahead. He's cuffed to the table and his feet have been bound around his jeans. "Looks like you're going to miss your driving shift for Toscani tomorrow," I tell him. "I don't think he'll be too happy about that."

"Toscani can eat my ass," Moreno replies. "I just do it for the extra money."

"Good to know," I reply, taking a seat across from him. "You put a federal agent in the hospital. You could have killed her. I'm sure you know how serious this is."

He shrugs. "I was jus' protecting my property. Self-defense. How was I supposed to know you were FBI?"

"From the giant yellow letters on the vests, dumbass," I tell him. "Not to mention when she yelled it at you. No jury is going to buy that story, and neither will I. Oh, and that wasn't your property. Even if it were, Maryland doesn't have a stand-your-ground law."

He sits back, smirking. "Okay. Then who do I need to flip on?"

"Excuse me?"

"I ain't stupid, I know how this works. If you was gonna book me, you woulda done it already. You need me to flip on somebody. Tell me who and I'll tell you my price."

"How about the person who hired you to kidnap Avery Huxley?" I say.

He doesn't even flinch. "Who's that?"

"I thought you said you were smart, Mr. Moreno," I say. "I'll admit, it was a clean grab. But you left one little footprint in the backyard, one that forensics is testing to the sneaker in your closet right now."

He purses his lips, attempting to lean back further, but the chair is bolted to the ground. He isn't going anywhere. "Coulda been anyone's shoeprint."

"We'll see what they say when the dirt samples come back," I say, knowing full well we don't have any dirt samples. How fastidious is Moreno? Is he sure he got all of his clothes clean after that night? "Tell me about Huxley. And I'll see if I can't make this easier for you."

"Even with the shooting?"

"No, that's a separate charge. You don't discharge a firearm at an FBI agent and walk away. It just doesn't work like that."

"Then no deal," he says.

"Look," I say, leaning forward. "I'm offering you the difference between spending seven years in a penitentiary and twenty. You don't want to get out when you're almost fifty, do you?"

He works his jaw a minute. "What do you want to know?"

"Who hired you for the job?"

"I don't know his name. We never exchanged business cards."

"Was it the same man who picked up Avery this evening?"

He shakes his head. "Nah, I'd never seen that guy before. This was somebody else. Real uptight kind of guy. Like a banker."

"A banker?" I ask, pulling out my phone to make notes.

"Yeah, you know the type. Suit, tie, briefcase. Glasses and a sour look on his face like someone had just screwed his wife." He tries to cross his legs, but the chains prevent it, and he's forced to keep them both down. "Real freak of a dude, looked like walking death."

"How many times did you meet with this man?" I ask.

"Two. Once when he approached me for the job, a second time when he paid me."

I look up. "He paid you *before* the job? And you still went through with it?"

Moreno grins. It's an expression I want to smack off that smug face of his. "Yeah. I got the impression if I didn't follow through, I wouldn't be waking up no more."

"So, he threatened you," I say.

"Not in so many words, but yeah. Gave me this list of instructions. Told me when and how to do it, along with the codes to get in the house."

"Wait," I say. "He *gave* you the codes? Didn't Mansfield already have them?"

He shakes his head. "Nah, just the ones for the front gate and the perimeter. Security personnel weren't allowed in the house. In fact, this guy helped me get set up with them for a job," he says. "All I had to do was spend a few weeks getting familiar with the people enough so they could trust me. No one was supposed to know it was me."

"How did he get the codes?" I ask.

He shrugs. "Hell if I know. All that mattered was they worked. Woulda made a clean getaway too, if Hayden hadn't been off his route. He was late on his patrol for whatever reason. Had to take care of 'em."

"It's a wonder you didn't kill him," I say. "The bullet lodged just past his heart. Another centimeter and he would have been dead."

"Lucky him," Moreno says.

"Lucky you. Otherwise, you'd be facing a homicide charge as well," I tell him.

Moreno leans forward. "At this point, Agent, does it really matter? I clearly ain't goin' anywhere anytime soon."

I go back through my notes. "Let's go back. This man approached you. When?"

He cocks his head, thinking back. "I guess about the beginning of the summer. Around Father's Day, I think."

"And what, he just sits down beside you one day and tells you he wants you to kidnap the daughter of a US House Representative?"

Moreno laughs. "Nah, nah, it ain't like that. See what they do is they approach you real sneaky like at first, ask you if you want to be part of some exciting opportunity. Then they show you the cash. Once that's done, they got you hooked in; all they gotta do is reel."

"Why you?" I ask.

He shrugs. "I guess I stand out. People appreciate my skills. I've got a rep out there for some clean work."

"How much did they pay you?"

"Three hundred large," he says. "Plus, I got to keep all the money from Mansfield, *and* I got that vacation home. And all I had to do was take that little twerp and get her dressed up for the ball."

I do my best to hide my discomfort. Instead, I keep my eyes on my notes. "All his instructions to you were verbal? Nothing written down?" He shakes his head. "Where did you first meet?"

"He found me in this bar, Deadly Jack's over off Connecticut. Guy clearly didn't belong in there. But he zeroed in on me. Walked in and sat himself down, started askin' me questions, payin' for my drinks. What was I gonna do, say no?"

"Do you remember what day that was? Exactly?"

He shakes his head. Damn. That's going to make things harder.

"What about the second time?"

"I'd just finished a route for Toscani, and he showed up at my apartment," Moreno says. "At first I thought he was some kind of stalker. But he brought the cash with him. Said he had a job for me if I was interested. Gave me all the details."

"And when was this?" I need to establish a timeline if I'm going to find this banker. I can only imagine he's part of this organization.

"A few days later," Moreno says. "I don't really remember."

I square my shoulders and stare at him. "What were his instructions exactly?"

Moreno lets out a long breath. "He said that I was to get a job with Mansfield, he'd already cleared it so all I had to do was apply. Then I was to keep a low profile, get cozy with the other guys. He'd make sure I had the right assignment. Then, on the night of the thirteenth, I was to use the codes he gave me to get into the Huxley house and take the daughter as cleanly and quietly as possible. He said to use some of the money to rent a place to keep her for a few days, wanted her nice and docile for when she'd be picked up."

"Stop," I say, feeling somewhat sick to my stomach. "Explain that part. What did he mean by docile?"

"Agent, you're not a stupid person. You can guess what that means." He smiles at me with a row of very straight teeth, though one of them has a gold cap.

"Lay it out for me."

He huffs. "The girl was…wild. She needed to be broken. But he was clear that she was not to have a mark on her. I told him that was something I could do."

"Tell me, Moreno. How did you temper a twelve-year-old girl?" I'm glaring at him with the heat of a thousand suns.

He swallows, as if he's nervous for the first time. "Listen, it wasn't nothin' like that," he says. "I just kept her locked down and in the dark for the first day or so. You know, usin' rewards

and stuff like food when she behaved. By Saturday she was...
well, she wasn't fightin' me no more."

"Did you sexually assault her?"

He shakes his head. "Nah. That isn't my thing. I know a
few guys though. Maybe the banker knew that. He wanted to
make sure she was untouched. But he said she was to be pret-
tied up. Told me to pick her up a dress and have her ready by
Sunday. I had to go shoppin' at one of those places in the
mall, pretended like it was for my daughter." He looks
mortified.

"Don't expect me to feel sorry for you," I say, leaning
back. "You abducted a little girl, subjected her to psychological torture, starved her. I should have you castrated."

"You said you was gonna help me out!" he yells.

"I lied," I reply. "I'm going to make sure you get the
maximum punishment possible. You're never seeing the
outside again, Moreno."

He tries to jump up from the table, his large hands out
stretched like he wants to strangle me, but the chains keep him
in place. They don't stop him from jerking back and forth as
he tries to break free of them. "*Bitch!* I know people, I'll get
Toscani on your ass. You think you can keep me in here? I'll
be out and you'll be six feet under."

"I can handle Toscani," I say, standing. "I just wonder if
you can handle a lifetime inside a cell. At least you'll have
plenty of time to think about what you could have done with
all that money. Which we're seizing, by the way."

He lets out a guttural growl and tries even harder to get at
me, but it's no use. I leave the room, not even bothering to
look over my shoulder. He hasn't given me much, but it's a
starting point.

But first, I have a phone call to make.

Chapter Twenty-Three

"HELLO?" THE VOICE OF MY SISTER-IN-LAW HAS ALWAYS BEEN somewhat sultry, but this evening it sounds even deeper, like she's had a cold and is just coming out of it.

"Dani, it's Emily," I say.

"Emily, this is unexpected," she replies. "Are you calling to check on Timber? I'm happy to report he's still in great spirits. He and the other boys spent most of the day outside sunning."

I swallow a lump in my throat. Here I was thinking I had removed my dog from danger by letting him stay with my in-laws, when in fact I'd done the opposite. Just knowing that he'd been less than inches away from Chris these past few weeks makes my heart drop. I have to get him out of there and back into my apartment where I know he'll be safe. But first I need to know if my sister-in-law knows anything about what Chris is doing. It's possible she's involved, but then again, Matt never told me anything. Maybe Chris has been the same way with her. Maybe there's something about being in this organization that says not to involve spouses.

It would sure make me feel better if someone else was in this position too.

"That's great," I say. "Thanks for letting me know. I wanted to check in, how are you guys doing over there?"

"Us? Oh, we're fine." There's nothing in her voice that indicates she's trying to deceive me.

"Enjoying a nice bottle of wine on your deck? The weather is finally starting to cool down." I'm doing everything I can to keep from straight up asking if she knows where her husband is right now.

"No, unfortunately Chris had to go out of town for business this afternoon. I don't expect him back until tomorrow so I'm just taking in a good book, though you're right about the wine." I bite my lower lip and look up at Janice who has an entire team sitting on the other end of the call with me. She motions for me to keep going, to keep her talking.

"Sounds like a relaxing night." I can just imagine her, sitting in that large house with all three dogs piled on the carpets around the couch while she sips from a glass reading. It sounds idyllic, almost too much.

"Would you like to come over? I can't drink all of this by myself, and I know Timber would be excited. He hasn't seen you since you got back from Delaware."

I nod, feeling some of that guilt come back up. But had I not been held up by a master assassin the minute I stepped through my door, I would have stopped by first thing. "I know. Work has been crazy ever since I got back, and I just haven't been able to get away." I shoot a look at Janice who is bearing down on me with her gaze. "While that sounds really relaxing, I can't make it tonight. But could we meet up again for lunch later this week? I'll have some free time then."

"Sure," she says. "How about Thursday? Want to do the same place as last time?" The last time we met up was only two weeks ago, though it feels like a lot longer. It was supposed to be something of an olive branch, after I thought I'd finally started to warm to my in-laws again. The walls between us had all begun to come down, enough that I even got into a drinking contest with Chris. I shudder. I'd ended up spending the night in their guest room that night. To know now that he was involved with the people who killed Matt—he could have very well killed me that night.

But I have to keep my head. I can't what-if myself to death. "The same place sounds great; I'll meet you at eleven-thirty."

"See you then," she says, hanging up.

I let out a breath as the team ends the recording. Janice turns to one of the techs. "Well?"

"GPS zeroed in on the signal, it's coming from her own house," he says.

"Then she wasn't lying about where she was," I say. "Maybe she really doesn't know anything about Chris."

"Still, we need to proceed with caution," Janice says, checking her watch. "I want you to head down to Deadly Jack's. Pull the footage and see if you can't find anything on this *banker* Moreno mentioned."

"It's almost nine-thirty," I say. "On a Sunday night."

"They'll be open," she replies. "In the meantime we're going to keep working on finding your brother-in-law's car. I've got teams searching every traffic camera in the city. He'll pop up somewhere."

"Are you sure I shouldn't—"

Janice shakes her head. "No. And when we find him, I don't want you there. You're too close to this."

"What about the assassin?" I ask.

She shoots a glance at the rest of the team, most who avert their gaze when she does. She slips off the edge of the desk where she'd been sitting and pulls her arm around me, leading me away from the rest of them. "I can't say this out there, but I'm afraid Agent Coll is a lost cause. We have no way of finding him and no evidence to follow up on. We don't even know this woman's real name."

"We can't just leave him to die," I say, doing my best to keep my cool.

"No, we can't. But unless you can figure out a way to reel this assassin in, then I don't see a way to track him down. And don't forget, we still have a little girl out there who is in very deep trouble. I don't know how long we have until she's subjected to these horrors, if she hasn't been already."

I rub my temples, trying to keep a headache at bay. There has to be some way to save them both; I just can't see it. The assassin won't kill me; she needs me. Or she *needed* me. "What if we set a trap for her? A better one this time," I say.

"How does that help us find Avery Huxley?" Janice asks.

"If I can track down this banker, she won't need Chris or Avery," I say. "He'll be enough to give her what she wants: a way into this organization. He'll at least be able to tell her where to start. If we could tempt her with that, maybe we could find a way to uncover Liam's location. That way, when we do find Avery, we don't have to worry about her screwing everything up."

Janice shakes her head. "We've already tried to fool her once; I don't think I have to remind you how badly that went. We're lucky we got you back at all."

"But now she's desperate," I say. "She's not in control like she normally is. Losing track of Chris means she can't do anything about this bounty on her head. She'll take any opportunity she can get to get back on track." If there's one thing I've learned about the assassin, it's that she must be in control. It's how she maintains her power. I saw that façade slip when we were out in the woods. I saw just how important this was to her and that she'd be willing to do anything to get it back. No doubt she's out there right now, trying to track down Chris as much as we are.

"That still doesn't help us find Avery," Janice says. "And right now, I'm afraid that has to be our priority. Agent Coll knew the risks of this job when he signed up. Avery is just an innocent kid."

"I understand," I say, and Janice turns, heading back to her office. "There's something else." She motions for me to follow and I catch up with her. "Moreno told me the banker gave him the codes to disarm the security system in the house; that it wasn't something Mansfield had access to."

"And?"

"He had to get those codes from somewhere or someone in the house," I say. "If Mansfield doesn't have access to them, then they would only be known to the residents of the home."

She turns. "I know what you're thinking and you're not doing it. He's a House Representative for God's sake!"

"I'm not saying Representative Huxley did anything; I'm just saying it narrows down the number of people who could have provided the banker with that code."

"How do we know the housekeeper or caretaker didn't tell one of their friends in passing?" Janice asks.

"We don't. Which is why I'd like the opportunity to question every person in the home, including Avery's parents. It's not much of a lead, but it's something."

Janice checks her watch again. With every passing second, Avery is in more and more danger. But I'm at a loss. Unless he shows up on traffic cameras, we don't have a way to track Chris. His phone is off and can't be pinged. I don't see another way unless we find this banker.

Janice lets out a frustrated breath. "All right. This is your show. But take caution. The last thing I need is someone calling from Internal Affairs saying we've been harassing a sitting Representative of the United States. Trust me, that's heat none of us want."

"I'll be discreet," I tell her.

"But first, find this banker. Then focus on the rest."

"I need my phone. So she can keep tracking me."

Janice retreats into her office and retrieves my phone, slapping it down in my hand. "I hope you know what you're doing."

"Me too," I say, clicking it back on. It shows I've missed two calls and one text. Janice turns and heads back into her office, closing the door.

One of the messages is from the pharmacy about picking up a prescription for Timber. The other is from an unknown number and is just a hang up without a message. But I already know who it's from. The text is from the same unknown number contact. And it's just one short phrase: *we're not done.* While that doesn't exactly make me feel better, at least I know she hasn't given up yet, not that I expected her to. I also have to recognize that maybe the invisible shield that kept her from killing me has now dropped away. I might be going out there fully exposed for the first time.

Damn, I wish Liam or Zara were here.

I begin to make my way for the door when I feel a presence come up beside me. I look over and see Agent DuBois walking in stride with me. "Want some company?" he asks.

"Not really," I tell him, pushing through the doors headed for the elevator.

"I am a great conversationalist," he says. That much I doubt.

I look back over my shoulder. "Did she put you up to this?"

He returns my stare with a sheepish look. "She doesn't want you out there alone."

"How many times do I have to tell people, if this woman wanted me dead, I would be already." Despite what I suspect, there's no reason to panic anyone else.

He stiffens. "I think she's more worried about all the other enemies you're making along the way."

I don't have time for this. I'm sure Agent DuBois means well, but his time could be better spent here, going over the traffic cameras. "Just stay here and hang out in the bathroom or something, as long as you're out of sight. I'll tell her you came alone."

A sad little smile appears on his lips. "I wish I could do that, but I have my orders."

"Fine," I say. I don't have time to argue. We need to get over to Deadly Jack's before they close. As the elevator bell dings, indicating the carriage is there, the doors open to reveal Zara on two crutches. One of her legs is wrapped up good, and she's got on the same sweats I had when they took all my clothing for examination. Her hair is tussled, and she's got bags under her eyes too, but she's alert. She lights up when she sees me and I pull her into a hug right across the threshold, taking care not to hold her too hard.

"Em, I'm okay," she says.

"You might not have been," I reply. "That was too close. I should have been watching your back more carefully."

"You did," she replies. "You got him to put that cannon down. Plus, you were entangled with our surprise guest. Any word on her?"

I shake my head. "What are you doing here? You should be home, resting."

We step aside as she hobbles out into the lobby. "Not until this is over. I assume you spoke to your sister-in-law?"

"I can't tell if she knows anything or not. We have lunch set up for later in the week. Janice can give you a full rundown."

She nods. "You look like you need to go somewhere. Don't let me hold you up." DuBois and I step into the carriage.

"Promise me you'll take it easy," I say as DuBois hits the parking level one option.

She throws me a wink as the doors close.

"You know me."

Chapter Twenty-Four

BY THE TIME WE ARRIVE AT DEADLY JACK'S IT'S NEARLY TEN. The parking lot is a ghost town, with only two cars in attendance, one of which probably belongs to the owner. I haven't received any more calls or texts, but it's only a matter of time. I also can't help but look over my shoulder when we get out of the car and head into the bar. Now that I have my phone back, she's probably out there watching, waiting. I shudder to think what's going through her head at the moment.

Having never been inside before, Deadly Jack's reminds me of the kind of bars I'm used to seeing in old TV shows from the seventies and eighties. The stools and what few booths are present are all in the same old wood, with yellow vinyl cushions. The whole place is lit with string lights hung from the ceiling, which itself looks like a relic from another era, what with all the ornate designs on painted tin tiles. I'd say about a third are missing, exposing metal pipes and the ductwork for the a/c. The bar is long, running about half the space, with a variety of drinks on shelves behind, all backed by a mirror. What look like old, plastic leis surround the mirrors and the frames of any pictures on the wall. It's like the owner couldn't decide which direction they wanted to go with the place and decided to try all directions at once.

A man lies on the bar, snoring, while still holding a half-consumed beer inches from his face. Other than him, the place is empty.

I shoot DuBois a look then approach the bar, glancing back up at the ceiling. Cameras are mounted in every corner, along with one in the center behind the bar. Assuming they work, we should have a good look at our man.

A door to the back kitchen swings open to reveal a woman with a KISS t-shirt that's faded over time. She also wears a trucker's hat which proclaims something about pound town, but I don't give it much attention.

"Sorry, we're closing up for the evening. About to send Earl home." She pounds on the bar and the man on the stool shoots up with a grunt. He looks around, then places his head back on the bar again, never taking his drink from his hand. "Unbelievable."

I show my badge. "I'm Agent Slate, this is Agent DuBois. Tell me those work." I point to the camera above the bar itself.

"They have to. Do you know how much I was losing in stolen liquor before I got them installed?" She points to a series of polaroid photographs on the left side of the bar. There are about fifteen of them, all showing different, surprised faces. "Thieves, all of 'em. Aren't allowed back in here."

I make a cursory inspection of the group, but don't see Moreno or our banker among them. "I'm looking for a patron, someone who may have only been in here once, but it would have been around Father's Day. Late evening."

"Lady," the woman says, leaning forward. "Do you have any idea of how many people come in here each night? *Around* Father's Day? That could have been any number of nights. Like I said, I'm closing up. I don't have time to go through a week's worth of footage for you."

"This is an urgent matter," I say.

"Isn't it always?" She bangs on the bar again. "Earl! Get your ass up and outta my bar before I beat it out!"

He looks up again, then notices his drink. "But I'm not done yet."

She yanks the beer from him then throws it in his face, drenching him. He cries out. "What'dya do that for?"

"I swear to God, Earl, if I have to stay here one minute longer because of your lazy ass—"

"Okay, okay, I'm goin'!" He stumbles up off the stool as she throws him a hand towel, which he uses to wipe his face down. "Just put it on my tab."

"That tab's longer than the Mississippi by now," the bartender says as Earl makes his way to the door.

"Is he okay to drive?" I ask.

She shakes her head. "Earl's fine. He only lives about a block away. Makes it home each night and somehow manages to show up again here every day."

The little bell over the door rings as Earl makes his exit. "As I was saying—"

"That's it," she says. "Bar's closed. Sorry, but you'll have to come back tomorrow. We open at noon. I might have some time then to go over the records."

"Mrs.—"

"Just call me Dickie, everyone else does," she says, holding out a hand, which both DuBois and I shake quickly. "I'd like to help you out, but I gotta get some sleep. I've been on my feet for fourteen hours and they're already complaining."

"Dickie, I completely understand. But we are trying to find a little girl who has been kidnapped. She's only twelve-years-old. Now we think that the man who was hired to kidnap her made contact with his handler in this bar. If we could just take a few minutes to look."

"Ah, shit," she says. "What'd you have to go and say that

for?" She lets out a deep sigh, leaning on the bar for a minute. "C'mon, then."

We follow her through the swinging door which leads to a small galley kitchen. At one end is another door which she unlocks with a key from her belt. Inside is a modest office with a desk, a couple of filing cabinets, and a computer.

Dickie sits down at the computer with a thump and clicks a few things. "Where should I start looking?"

I pull out my phone, consulting my own calendar. "Father's day was on the 21st, which was a Sunday. Let's start on Saturday."

"That'll be a cluster," Dickie says. "Saturday is our busiest night. You really think you're gonna spot him?"

"He won't fit in," I say. "He'll be wearing a suit, carrying a briefcase. Glasses, bald. Looks like a banker. He's been described to us as somewhat gaunt."

"Wait a second," Dickie says. "I think I remember that guy. Gave me the creeps."

"Do you work every night?" DuBois asks.

"I'm the only one to work. We're not exactly Applebees around here. It's pretty much me and the kitchen staff. I'm lucky if I have a busboy most evenings."

"Do you remember anything about him?" I ask, feeling a ray of hope for the first time. It's not much, but it's something.

"Just that he seemed very strange. Never drank a thing, but kept ordering for his friend." She pulls up some footage on her computer. I remember exactly where they were too, at this back booth, being all secret-like." She points to a booth that's currently empty on the screen. A second later she's fast-forwarding through the times until she reaches closing. "Nothing there, let me try the next night."

She ends up going through Sunday and Monday relatively quick, now that she knows what she's looking for. It isn't until she gets to Tuesday does she slow it down enough. "Here he is. Comes in around eight-thirty."

I squint at the screen, seeing a lanky man in a full business suit come in and sit down in the booth. Across from him sits Moreno, nursing a drink.

"Do you have a closer image of him?" I ask.

"I can fast forward to the time he leaves," she says. "The camera above the door should have grabbed him." She switches the angle and fast forwards a good three hours before slowing it down again. Moreno wasn't kidding when he said the guy just kept buying him rounds. As it gets close to eleven-thirty, the banker finally gets up, suitcase in hand, and heads out. On the way the camera above the entrance gets a perfect image of his face, almost dead on, though he's looking slightly down as he's walking under it. His skin seems to hang off his bones and his cheeks are nearly hollow. Moreno wasn't kidding when he said the guy looked like Death.

"Pause it right there," I say and hold up my camera phone, copying the picture. "I don't guess you remember if he paid with cash or credit, do you?"

She shakes her head. "Pretty sure it was cash cause I remember counting a bunch more twenties than normal that night."

I shouldn't be surprised. Someone like that isn't going to risk leaving a paper trail for us to follow. But at least we have a picture; that's better than nothing. "I can't tell you how much we appreciate your help."

Dickie shuts down the computer and stands. "Yeah, well I guess I can spare thirty minutes if it helps you find a missing girl."

"And you haven't seen him in here again since that night, right?"

She shakes her head. "Nope. Not unless he was in disguise. Even then, I think I would've recognized him. Scary SOB. Reminded me of a skeleton."

I take a look back at the picture on my phone and realize she's not wrong. But he doesn't seem that old. Perhaps he's sick, and has been for a while. Details which might help us locate him even faster. "We'll see ourselves out," I say. "Thanks again."

"Good luck," she calls after us.

We head back out into the night air and I immediately begin typing out a text to Zara.

"Are you sending that image in?" DuBois asks.

"I want to see if Zara can pull this guy from the database somewhere. It's a long shot, but you never know. He doesn't exactly fit in with everyone else." We round the building, heading back to the lot in the back where we parked.

"You know, I used to work this area a lot when I came out of Quantico," DuBois says. "Let me take a closer look. She was so quick on that computer I missed it."

"Sure," I say. "Let me just finish this text real quick. I want Zara working on this right away." I begin walking back to the car, typing as fast as I can. She can't use the system we used to track down the assassin since the FBI deemed it a crime to use and destroyed the program, but she can use our new facial recognition software. It's not as good as the program we had before, but at least it wasn't designed and implemented by a serial kidnapper.

As I'm finishing up the text, I sense DuBois walk up closer behind me.

And that's when I feel the steel of a muzzle against the back of my neck.

Chapter Twenty-Five

"DuBois, what are you doing?" I say as calmly as I can. I'm frozen, standing in the middle of Deadly Jack's parking lot, with a gun to my back. And the person holding that gun is supposed to be a fellow FBI agent.

"I'm sorry, Slate, I can't let you send that text."

"What the hell are you talking about?"

"Hand me the phone, right now, or I punch a hole through your throat. Do *not* press any more keys and do not try anything funny. I'm not kidding about this." DuBois has never been a man of a lot of words, but I can tell from the timbre of his voice he's serious.

I swallow and look down at the mostly complete text I have made out to Zara. All I'd need to do is press send for it to go through, unfinished as it is. And yet, I believe DuBois when he says he'll shoot me if I send it.

Still, part of me thinks I should and take the chance. He's obviously a traitor; no wonder he was so quiet in there. I figured he just didn't know what to say. Turns out he's been plotting against me all along. "You work for them, don't you? You're part of whatever this is. How long?"

"The phone, Slate. Now." I turn slowly and hold out the

phone to him. He takes it gingerly as not to accidentally send the message and steps back about two feet from me. He then flicks his eyes down at the screen and taps it a few times. I make a move to grab it from him, but he looks back up immediately, the weapon tightening in his hand.

"How could you do this? You took an *oath*," I say.

"You don't know anything about me," he replies. "In fact, you've barely ever noticed me, unless I was assigned to one of your cases or put on special assignment to track down the killer hunting you. *Saint Emily*, that's what some of us in the office call you, you know. Because you can't seem to do anything wrong. And even when you do, it works out for you."

"It's jealousy then," I spit, disgusted. We've had a traitor in our midst this entire time. What other damage has he caused? I think back to all those times he was assigned to watch my apartment or to work the case trying to find the assassin. Was he sabotaging us all along? Or has he been working his own agenda in the background, waiting for his opportunity to strike?

"No, this is necessity," he says and finishes with my phone before slipping it into his pocket. "Now, let's go. We need to move somewhere quieter."

"If you think I'm going anywhere, you're dumber than you look," I growl.

"Don't think I won't shoot you right here if I have to," he says.

"And how exactly are you going to explain that when you have to turn in your weapon to IA after firing it? How's it going to look when your own fingerprints are on the trigger used to kill me? No one would ever believe I turned on you and it was self-defense."

He laughs. "Oh, you think I'm going back to the FBI. No, all that's done now. You've forced our hand. This has been coming for some time, you just never knew it. The people I work for don't make mistakes. Except maybe letting you live too long. But then again, you were supposed to be eliminated weeks ago and would have been, if not for some unreliable individuals."

He means the assassin, obviously. So that part was true, at least. A lot of good it does me right now.

"You sabotaged your own team, didn't you? You knew about the pickup from Moreno."

He shakes his head. "There was no need. She's good. Had us taken care of and we never even saw her. Otherwise, yes, I would have had to find a way to stop you from interfering. Thankfully, my cover remained intact. Otherwise I never would have been able to keep any eye on you here."

My mind is firing on all cylinders, trying to think of a way out of this, or at least a way to stall DuBois long enough that I can get away. I still have my own sidearm strapped under my blazer, but I can't get to it fast enough to get the draw on him. He's got me dead to rights.

I motion to my phone in his pocket. "Who is that man? You know, don't you?"

"Rossovich," he replies. "He's a low-level recruiter. I really wish you hadn't been this enterprising, otherwise I could have let you stumble along for a while longer. But you're too much of a liability. What are the odds the bar only has one bartender, and she remembers the one person you're looking for?"

"It's like she said. He doesn't exactly blend in." DuBois grimaces, and he motions for me to move to a darker part of the parking lot. "Where's Avery?"

"I don't know. But she's in good hands," he says. "And that's not your concern anymore. All you need to worry about is walking over in that direction. I'd rather not make a mess out here and I want this done before *Dickie* comes to get her car. It's best if they don't know you're missing for a couple hours."

"Why, so you can get away?"

"So things can proceed unheeded," he says. "Now, move."

I can't help but feel a certain level of panic set in. Not only is he cold and emotionless, he's showing no signs of stress. This is just a normal event for him, and he'll have no trouble pulling that trigger. He's too far for me to reasonably rush him and not get shot. But surely someone will hear it. Though, it will probably be too late by then. "You know they won't stop. Zara, Janice. The rest of the FBI. You go through with this, and they'll figure it out. Isn't your organization all about people not knowing who you are?"

"Stop stalling," he says. "You've got five seconds to move."

I scan the area around me. There's nothing. No other weapons, nothing to hide behind. It's just me and him, and he's going to kill me right here. I only hope Zara finds a way not to blame herself once all this is over. I take a deep breath, planting my feet. If he's going to shoot me, I'm not about to make it easy for him.

"Stubborn to the end," he says, raising the weapon. A shot rings out and the smile on DuBois' face fades until he looks down and sees a bloom of red on his white dress shirt. He tries to say something, only for a trickle of blood to come out of his mouth as his eyes roll up in the back of his head. He collapses on the pavement with a dull thud, his fingers still wrapped around the gun.

For a moment I'm stunned, then I realize that someone else is here and I draw my weapon, running to the nearest barrier, which just happens to be a vehicle in the lot. I keep an eye on DuBois, but he's not moving, not breathing. There's no doubt in my mind that was a kill shot.

"What the hell was that?"

I look over the roof of the car to see Dickie come running around the building, her eyes wide. "Get down!" I yell. "This is an active shooter situation!"

She spots DuBois on the pavement and goes white. For a second, I think she's going to faint, leaving her completely open to the shooter. But she holds it together, scrambling back around the corner of the building. I scan the area once more, looking for anyone or anything that might be out there. The shot was loud and sounded like it came from a large caliber weapon. But there are no other sounds out here, not even of cars driving by.

"Give me your phone," I tell her and she automatically produces it from her pocket, no questions. I dial dispatch. "This is Agent Slate at 7600 Irving Street. I have an active shooter situation, Agent down on the scene." As soon as the dispatch relays the information to emergency services I hang back up and return Dickie's phone to her, knowing it won't be long before backup arrives. My shirt is stuck to my back and I'm doing my best to keep my breathing under control, but I can't keep from looking around the car at DuBois. Someone took him out, and they could be anywhere.

But as I sit there, waiting for another shot to come, I realize I can hear something. A soft buzzing, and it's coming *from* DuBois.

Staying in a crouch, I make my way over to the body, keeping my weapon up and steady, looking for anyone high up, which is where I suspect the shot came from. That wasn't a random bullet, and it wasn't a lucky hit. That was a calculated kill, right to the heart.

The tops of the buildings all around are dark, and because this is a commercial area, no one is still around to come out and investigate, which is fortunate. I don't need any more civilians sticking their noses in this. The problem is, I don't even know where the shot came from. It had to have been from either directly behind DuBois, or off to my right or left, considering the shooter would have needed to shoot straight through me to hit him dead center. Maybe that was the plan, two for one. I imagine an organization like this doesn't allow loose ends, and perhaps DuBois was talking too much. But really I have no idea. A thousand things are going through my head at the moment and my main concern is not being the recipient of a second bullet.

When I reach DuBois, I realize the sound is coming from a phone. I reach into DuBois' pocket, retrieving my phone which is vibrating with an unknown number. I glance around again, then pull back into cover by an empty doorway at the back of the building. "Hello?"

"Don't say I never did anything for you." Her words are like ice through my veins.

"This was *you*? You just killed an FBI agent."

"I killed a traitor and the man who had your life in his hands," the assassin says. "Try to be a little more grateful. Now, you have a family member to find. Clock's ticking." The call ends and I look at my phone again. I try dialing the number back, but an automated voice tells me it's been disconnected.

"Dammit," I say, and shove my weapon back into my holster.

"Is it safe?" Dickie calls from around the corner.

I look up at the surrounding rooftops but of course I don't see her. She must have followed us here. I know I should be grateful she just saved my life, but really, I'm more annoyed than anything. How is she always there? How does she always know where I am? "Yeah," I say, reasonably sure she's not going to kill Dickie out of spite. She's done what she's needed to. "It's safe. Come on out." I look down at DuBois, his face frozen in confusion as the tables turned on him at the very last second. I wonder if he knew what had just happened to him.

Dickie comes around the corner and stares at him, splayed out on the ground. "Oh my God. I'm so sorry. Were you two close?"

I stare at the red bloom on his chest. "Not at all."

Chapter Twenty-Six

"I think I'm going to be sick," Dickie says, looking down at DuBois's body.

"You don't need to see this," I say. "Just head back inside and get yourself a glass of water or a stiff drink. I've got backup on the way; they'll be here in a few minutes."

She keeps staring at DuBois and I have to clap my hands to snap her out of it. "Right, yeah. I'll be right inside if you need me."

I give her a reassuring nod as she heads back around the corner and out of sight. I find myself captivated by the sight of DuBois as well. Not because it's a dead body—I've had plenty of experiences with those—but because of what this will mean for my department. A mole working directly in the violent crimes division means a full investigation from Internal Affairs. Which more than likely means every person in our division will be put on leave, or at least temporarily held until it can be determined there are no other moles in the operation. It also means Janice will be under heavy scrutiny, as this happened on her watch.

All in all it comes down to delays, delays, and more delays. And that's time that neither Avery nor Liam have. I can't be

sure of it, but the assassin's actions have led me to believe that
he might not be dead yet. She could still kill me at any point;
that much is obvious. And yet she hasn't. Her tone over the
phone makes me think that she hasn't done anything to Liam
either. Otherwise, what could she still hold over me? Other
than the fact she knows I won't let Avery suffer.

I check my phone. It's a little after ten-thirty. Which means
Chris has a four-hour head start on me. I need to track him
down, find out where he's taken her as I'm sure he's dropped
her off by now. But when I spoke to Dani, she seemed to think
he would be out of town for a while, and didn't expect him
back. That makes me believe that he's either built in extra
time to take care of any problems with Avery, or he's not done
with her yet.

The assassin said that the members of the organization
would pass Avery around, like they have with other children.
What if Chris is the person who takes the victim from place to
place? It would make sense to have one point of contact for
the job, as terrible as that sounds. Part of me can't believe he'd
do something so heinous, but then again, maybe in a way it's
like out of sight out of mind. If he doesn't have to witness it,
he can pretend like it doesn't really happen.

Stop it, I tell myself. I'm making excuses for him because
some part of me doesn't want to believe that someone in my
own family could do this. Because if he could do it, then what
did Matt do? Was he part of this circle of people preying on
children? I shake my head. No, there's no way. I may not have
seen that he was lying to me about this, but there's no way he
was that kind of person. I know that in my core. It doesn't
matter how many lies he told; that's not something he could
have covered up, I'm sure of it.

But still, Chris is obviously involved in this horror show
and needs to be stopped. I doubt Dani has a way of
contacting him immediately; she can probably leave a message
somewhere and he'd call her back. Not that I could convince

her to call him now without alerting her that something is wrong. You don't ask someone to call their significant other at eleven at night unless there's an emergency.

But maybe there's another way.

I retrieve a pair of gloves from my pocket and begin rooting around DuBois' person. I find his phone in his left pocket and pull it out. When I try to open it, it's locked by facial recognition.

"Ugh," I say, and turn the phone to DuBois' face, his eyes still wide open. A second later the phone opens, giving me full access. I start with the text messages. Almost all are to numbers without names attached to them. That makes sense, based on what I know about this organization. The last set of texts he sent was to a number with a Rhode Island area code:

> She's too close. I'm taking care of it tonight.

> Confirmation when finished.

"Shit." I assume this means me. Was he texting with this organization while we were in there with Dickie? How did I not notice that? Oh, right, because I was so focused on trying to get the image of the man Moreno met with. I pull my own phone back out and see the text to Zara has been deleted, but he didn't delete the picture yet. He was probably saving that for later. Good, at least it's a starting point.

I wonder if there's a way I can work this to my advantage.

I turn back to DuBois' phone, typing out a message to the same number.

> It's done. I need a pickup.

I wait a moment, praying that whoever he was talking to, they're not the kind of person to turn in with unfinished business still waiting. A moment later I see the three little dots and my heart jumps.

Why?

Think quick, Emily.

Cover blown, it got messy. Need an extraction.

The three dots appear again.

Corner of Kansas and Powell. Light a match when you've arrived.

I take a photo of the conversation, along with the number it's attached to, then I quickly look through some of the other conversations. Most are just as cryptic. In the distance I hear sirens. I don't have long.

I turn off DuBois' phone and slip it back into his pocket where I found it. I then run back around to the front of Deadly Jack's. Dickie sits inside, nursing what looks like a double whiskey.

"Do you have any matches?" I ask.

She looks up, in something of a daze. "Yeah, um, there's a bunch on the bar."

I head over and grab a pack that says "Come get your BJs at DJs!" on the back. I hold the packet up to her as I'm passing. "BJs?"

"It's a drink specialty. My ex came up with that. I'm too cheap to get them reprinted."

I nod. "Thanks. The cavalry will be here in a few minutes. They'll take care of everything." I say, then head out into the night. The corner of Kansas and Powell is more than two miles from here which means I'll need to take my car, even though that's riskier. I'll have to turn off my phone too, as I'm sure Janice will get on my ass as soon as she realizes I've left the crime scene. But it can't be helped. I'm not leaving Avery to those monsters, and an IA investigation will take too long. They can slap me on the hand when I get back.

I run back to where I parked when DuBois and I arrived and start the engine, pulling out, being careful not to hit the body as I pull away from the scene. I have to run a red light, because I can already see the flashing red and blue's all the way down the avenue. As I'm driving, I power my phone down and I stay off the main roads, just in case I accidentally run into backup coming from the other direction.

I know I'm going off-grid here, but we don't have a choice. If I do everything by the book, it could mean another day or more before I could get back on the case and Avery doesn't have that long. Not to mention we're now dealing with a mole; a murder and we still have a missing agent out there.

I'd really like to talk to Zara about this; but I can't involve her again. She's done more than enough and needs to rest and recover. Not to mention if this ends up going badly, I don't want her or anyone else involved. They all need to have plausible deniability.

As I drive, I try to formulate a plan in my head. I'll need to scope out the scene more before I can make an accurate call; but there's a chance this could work. My thought is if DuBois was speaking with this person regularly, and it seems he was, then I shouldn't have anything to worry about. I just need to trust my own tracking skills.

A couple of blocks away from Kansas and Powell I pull off the side of the road and onto a side street. I cut the engine and leave the car there, then cut across a few lawns and yards to get back out to the main road. Kansas and Powell intersects at the corner of a 24 hour drug store, where someone lighting a match wouldn't look out of place. They'll obviously be looking for DuBois, and the match is the signal, but I only brought them in case of an emergency. If my plan doesn't work. I have no desire to reveal myself to whoever comes to pick him up.

Instead, I crouch down as I come into view of the intersection, staying low behind a row of hedge bushes and benches that line this side of the street. It's a Y-intersection, which helps limit where the pickup car can come from. And while there are some streetlights and some light streaming through the high windows of the drug store, the area is still pretty dark.

I sit, waiting and watching, hoping my luck holds out. After a few minutes I see a black SUV pull up to the stoplight. When it turns green, the vehicle sits there for a moment longer than necessary and turns, heading down Powell. I only caught part of the license plate. Seven-O-H something. I wait a few more minutes and the same vehicle comes back up Powell. The windows are too dark for me to see the driver or how many people might be inside, but I'm hoping it's less than three. Again, it sits at the intersection for longer than it needs to before turning back down Kansas headed the same way it came.

I think that's my ticket.

I run like a bear on speed back to my car, fling open my door and turn it over, keeping my lights off as I tear through the residential neighborhood back out onto the main road. Thankfully there aren't any other cars out here this late on a Sunday night. And while that's good for traffic, it's terrible for tailing someone.

Ahead of me I see the two red taillights from the SUV, about four blocks ahead. Were it not for Washington's straight and narrow streets, I probably would have lost him already. Still, I stay back, not wanting to attract any attention. When the SUV reaches the beltway, it gets on the empty on-ramp for the outer loop. I speed up and flick my lights on when climbing the ramp, and join what other little traffic is on the beltway. It allows me to get a little closer to him without looking suspicious.

When I'm about three cars back I finally get a solid look at the plate. Seven-O-H-one-nine-D-S-A. The familiar yellow and black tells me they're Maryland plates. I'm also thinking whoever this is can't live very far, given they could come pick up DuBois at the drop of a hat. I'm sure right now they're texting and calling him furiously. I just hope no one on the scene is foolish enough to turn DuBois' phone back on yet.

After a couple of miles, the SUV takes the exit and I'm forced to follow. But when it turns right at the light at the bottom of the ramp, I turn left, hoping I haven't blown my cover. I wait a few seconds, then pull a U-turn, turning off my lights as soon as I'm sure I'm out of their rearview mirror.

Putting on the speed, I manage to catch back up with the car as it heads down Democracy Boulevard before it turns on Seven Locks. My heart skips a beat when I realize they might be heading into a gated neighborhood, which will make this much harder. Thankfully, the SUV turns onto Yellowtree Lane. I pull up to the entrance of the subdivision and park the car. Making sure the safety on my weapon is off, I get out, staying low and to the shadows. The houses in this neighborhood are quite large, and most have outdoor lighting, which makes sneaking around difficult. Up ahead, the SUV pulls into the circular driveway of the fifth house on the right. I thought they might pull into the garage, but it seems luck is on my side. I move a little faster, doing my best to stay silent as I watch the driver get out of the car and slam the door. The blue screen of a phone lights up his face.

It's one I recognize.

I quicken my pace and just as the man climbs the steps to his front double doors, I reach him and drive my gun into his back. He stiffens as I press him up against the door to his home.

"Hello, Mr. Rossovich, nice to meet you. I'm Emily."

Chapter Twenty-Seven

ROSSOVICH DOESN'T STRUGGLE WHEN I TAKE THE PHONE FROM his hand; instead, he seems to go limp. As I suspected from seeing the picture and video from Deadly Jack's, he's a frail man and doesn't strike me as someone who could suddenly turn and overpower me. Still, I'm not taking any chances. I pull out a pair of cuffs and link his hands together behind him while pocketing his phone.

"DuBois is dead, isn't he?" the man asks in a strangely soothing tone.

"I didn't kill him," I say. "But yes." I fish around his pockets and find a set of keys. "Which one?"

"The gold one."

"Do you have a security system?"

"Look where I live, Agent," he says. "Of course I do."

"Tell me the code now," I say. "Before we go in."

"How do you know I won't tell you the robber's code, the one that sounds the silent alarm?"

"What good would that do? I *am* the authorities."

He turns his head to look at me for the first time, catching my eye. "So this is a normal procedure for the FBI, then? Completely sanctioned?"

He's got me there. "You know what, maybe we'll talk out here," I say, pulling him away from the doors and back toward the car.

"Where one of my neighbors might see or hear us?"

This guy. As soon as we're close to his car again, I open the passenger door and push him inside, before climbing into the backseat, keeping my weapon on him. "There. Nice and cozy."

"Congratulations, you've managed to best me," he says. "I supposed you better call the paddy wagon to take me away."

"Very funny," I say. "Tell me where Avery Huxley is."

"How would I know?" he asks.

"Because you're the man who hired Tony Moreno for the job," I say.

"While I applaud your investigative skills, I'll have to refuse," he replies, looking back over the seat at me again. "I'm sorry to inform you that you've made it to the finish line only to trip before crossing the ribbon."

"You know you are looking at multiple charges, right? Conspiracy, kidnapping, child abuse, stalking, second-degree murder—"

"Wait a moment, I haven't murdered anyone."

"I'll take that as an admission to the other charges," I say. "And while you might not have pulled the trigger, I have at least two murders I can trace back to the organization you work for. You help me out, and maybe some of these charges go away."

He chuckles, which turns into a coughing fit, enough to make me worry. "Look at me, Agent," he says once it finally abates. "I won't be around long enough to even see the end of one of those charges. So if you're going to arrest me, do it already so we can get on with this."

I sit back, deflated, though I keep my weapon trained on him. "Why do you do it? Why be part of an organization that hurts children like this? What's the benefit?"

"You must realize that every organization in the world contributes to the degradation of society in some way. Some do it by poisoning water supplies for higher profits, others curtail rights for political power. Some companies use their vast wealth to prop up dictators, while others find ever-increasingly destructive ways to raise the temperature of the planet. Everyone does this, Agent Slate, so why not find the company with the largest profit margins and become a part of it?"

"Really? It's just all about money to you?" I say, disgusted.

"Trust me, it's all about money to *everyone*. People see what's coming out there, and let me clue you in: only those with money will survive. The rest will tear each other to shreds for the scraps while the wealthy sit atop their glass towers and bemoan it all. But unless you have that access, you'll find yourself down at the bottom with the animals. And when the time does come that you're forced to kill another man for nothing but a cup of water, you will have wished you did more to secure a better future for yourself."

"You're talking about the apocalypse." I wouldn't have taken Rossovich for a religious heretic, but they come in all shapes and sizes.

"No, I'm talking about the inevitable conclusion of the human experiment," he says. "We are born to split ourselves into social groups and we will do it until we expire. Rich, poor, young, old, powerful and weak. We cannot escape it; we can only adapt to it. I have decided that obtaining a vast amount of wealth is preferrable to clawing for scraps in the slums, that is all."

"You said yourself you're not long for this world, so what do you care?" I ask.

"Look at that house up there, do you think I live there all alone? I have a family to care for, to provide a future for. My family will have the advantages of money and power, and will rise to the top when everything falls apart. Can you say the same for yourself and your loved ones?"

"How would your family feel if they knew you were part of a child trafficking operation?" I say, not bothering to tamp down my disgust. People like this enrage me, but I can't lose my cool right now. He's my only link to finding Avery before it's too late. "Maybe I should go in there to tell them."

"You won't do that," he says, more confident than I would like.

"And why not? Don't tell me they're in the family business."

"It is our policy not to involve our families in what we do," he says. "But the minute you tell them, I will not only deny it, but I will also sue the FBI for harassment. You have no evidence of wrongdoing, and I will never be convicted in a court of law. Not only that, but you will never get another word out of me." In the rearview mirror I catch the self-satisfied smug look on his face. He believes he's holding all the cards, and that I'm just here for his amusement. But it's not going to work that way.

"You know, it's funny," I say. "Every single person who's ever told me that has always ended up giving me exactly what I needed. I have to assume your buddies in this organization are some well-connected individuals, am I right?" He doesn't reply, only gives me a curious look in the rearview mirror. "How loyal do they think you are?"

"It has never been questioned," he says.

"Okay. But if we were to keep you, detained, without a trial, do you think they would continue to count on that loyalty?"

"Nice try, Agent. But I'm not a terrorist. You owe me due process."

I shrug. "I dunno. You just told me about how you are preparing for the end times. About how only the strong will survive and those with the most resources will rise to the top.

Do you know who else talks like that? People who wish to topple the government. People who are looking to implement a New World Order."

"Wait just a moment," he says. "I did not say we're actively attempting to destroy the governmental structure in place, just that we're taking advantage of it while it still exists to enrich ourselves."

"You know, the definitions aren't really very specific on what constitutes domestic terrorism. Usually all I'd need to do was prove you were a threat to the United States Government, in any capacity. Then we can hold you indefinitely. You'd die awaiting your day in court. Trust me, I know a lot of people too."

"I must say, I wasn't expecting this level of ruthlessness from you. They told me you were one of the incorruptible ones. Another reason why you had to go; you were never going to bend to a bribe or coercion."

Damn this man and his organization. I can't help but think about how many lives he's ruined, including my own. He may not have been able to get me, but that doesn't mean he didn't go after someone close to me. "Is that what happened to my husband? Is that how you got your claws in him because he wouldn't take your money?"

He laughs aloud. "Certainly not. Your husband never had a choice."

"Tell me what that means," I demand, my concern for Avery temporarily slipping from the primary spot in my mind.

"Only if you guarantee that I'll be given fair treatment under the law."

"You want fair treatment, so you can use your unfair advantages to beat the system?" I ask, incredulous. "Not happening."

"Then I'm afraid it's something you'll never know."

"Fine," I say, pulling out my phone. "Then it's mutually assured destruction. I lose any chance of finding out what

happened to my husband, you die in prison. Sound good?" I
power the device back on.

"Wait," he says. "New offer. I give you the location of
Avery Huxley, and you release me, and forget all about this
little mix-up."

"You know I can't do that," I say. "You're a primary
suspect in a kidnapping case."

"Of course you can," he says, his eyes squinting almost
like they're the eye slits of a snake. "You already have the real
kidnapper in custody and with the information I give you, you
will be able to retrieve young Avery and arrest anyone else you
find at the scene. It's quite the opportunity."

"So much for loyalty," I say. "Do your other partners know
you're willing to stab them in the back to save yourself?"

He tries to turn in his seat, as if telling me this next part is
of the utmost importance. "It's part of our creed: that we shall
endeavor to protect ourselves at all costs before others. This
business with the child…it's nothing more than a distraction
for some of our more…eccentric members. Honestly, I would
not mind if they were…removed from the playing field, as it
were."

"Who the hell are you people?" I ask.

"Some call us concerned citizens. Others…well, others
tend to think of us as the hand of fate." I don't like anything
about this. I also don't like how he's dangling Avery out on a
line for me, just waiting for me to bite. What if it's nothing
more than a trap? I'm on my own, and I doubt I'd be able to
call for backup given the situation with DuBois. My entire
department will be bogged down in paperwork and internal
interviews for at least forty-eight hours. It's times like this
when I need a couple of friends outside the Bureau; people
who can operate beyond the confines of the law.

"*If* I agree to this, what assurances do I have from you?"

"None," he replies. "This is an exercise of faith. I want to
prove to the others that you're not as incorruptible as you

seem. Believe it or not, that's a good thing. It means we may not have to kill you after all."

I'm trying to think but it feels like my mind is in a vice grip. I can't abandon my principles, can I? If I let Rossovich go, I'll be showing them I can be bought for a price. But at the same time, I might be able to save Avery. Isn't that worth the cost? Or will these people commit even worse atrocities because I allowed this man to go free? Isn't there some way to stop them *and* save Avery too?

"You better think quick, Agent Slate. My wife expects me back from my errand. If she happens to look outside and sees my car but not me, she may become concerned."

I have so many unanswered questions, but none of those matter right now. All that really matters is, am I willing to compromise my principles to save a little girl from a lifetime of atrocities?

I don't see that I have any choice.

Chapter Twenty-Eight

STUPID, STUPID, STUPID.

I can't help the words on constant repeat in my brain as I floor it. I can't believe I let Rossovich get to me. This is all probably nothing but a trap, or a complete waste of time. But what choice did I have? If I'd had more time, I could have gotten him into an interrogation room and eventually pulled the information out of him. But it's closing in on eleven p.m. and Avery is out there, probably already experiencing the worst humanity has to offer. I need to get to her before it's too late. There's no other choice.

I'll be arrested, that much I'm sure about. Probably charged with failing to uphold my duty. Maybe even sentenced. I won't even contest it. If it helps save this kid, then it will have been worth it. And honestly, maybe behind bars is where I belong.

The streets are still empty and I'm blowing through red lights in an attempt to get to my destination faster. Every second counts. I just pray Rossovich was good on his word. The thing that finally clenched it for me was the disgust I heard in his voice regarding the other members of this little club of his. He wants them gone. And that means there's at least a fifty-fifty chance he was telling the truth.

On the other hand, it gives him time to flee.

My phone trills in my pocket, causing me to swerve and almost sending me off the road. I'd forgotten I'd turned it back on. I look at the screen and groan. Gritting my teeth, I press the accept button.

"Slate! Where the hell are you?" This sounds like the Janice I'm used to.

"Tracking down a lead," I reply.

"A lead about what? You were almost shot this evening. You need to get your ass back to headquarters for your debrief and statement. Then you have about a dozen meetings with Internal Affairs tomorrow. And don't tell me you can't make it. All casework is temporarily suspended until we get this mess worked out."

"Sorry, boss, but I can't make it," I say.

"Agent Slate, I swear if you are—"

"I think I know where Avery Huxley is," I say. "I'm on the way to get her right now."

"No, you're not," she replies. "You're going to turn around and come straight back. Do you understand me? That is an order, Agent Slate."

"I can't do it, I'm sorry," I say. "I'm willing to accept the consequences of my actions, but I'm not letting them do anything else to that little girl."

"What's your source?"

I grimace. Part of my deal with Rossovich was I wouldn't reveal his location. He must know that won't hold forever, but I'm also very much aware that if he sees flashing lights in his driveway he could call these people up and warn them that I'm coming, giving them time to take Avery and disappear. I need to make sure she's safe before revealing him. "I'll be able to tell you when I've secured her safety," I say.

"Dammit, Emily," Janice says. "This is not a game!"

"No, ma'am," I reply. "But I didn't make the rules. I'm just following them. If we want her, this is the only way I can get to her. I'm not even sure…" I trail off.

"What?" she asks, her tone softening just a bit.

"Nothing," I say. "Do whatever you have to do. I know you're tracking my phone. I'll probably need backup." *If Rossovich wasn't lying through his teeth to me, that is.*

"You're putting me in a very precarious position here, Agent Slate," Janice says. "I'm already under fire for DuBois. This isn't helping things any."

"I'm sorry, Janice, I really am. But this girl needs us— needs me. No one else is coming for her. And I owe it to Agent Coll, whether he's dead or alive. It's the right thing to do." I press even harder on the accelerator, pushing the car past eighty on roads with a posted speed limit of forty-five. "I'm almost there. The address is 506 Hidden Fields Lane. It's out in the middle of nowhere, so it'll take you a bit to get here. I hope to have the situation under control by then."

"You are digging a very deep hole for yourself, Agent," Janice says.

"I know. But it's not about me," I say. "I'll see you when you get here." I hang up and power the phone back off. I don't need any more sudden surprises.

Following the car's GPS, I turn down another deserted road and find myself crossing over into Rockville. A few miles beyond the border is the road I'm looking for. I slow and turn onto Hidden Fields, which is little more than a gravel road that disappears into a thicket of woods.

As I drive down the dark road, keeping my speed as fast as I dare go over gravel, I notice the GPS on my car begin to freeze up. It no longer is updating as I'm driving, which means it's lost the signal. I'm not sure if it's the thick overgrowth of trees or what, but it doesn't make me feel very good about getting a cell signal out here either.

Suddenly, though, the trees part and the sky opens up to

reveal a series of rolling fields on both sides of the gravel road. According to where the GPS *was* sending me, I should be right on top of it, but there are no house numbers anywhere. However I catch sight of a faint glow coming from just over one of the hills, which just happens to have a dirt path that splits off from the gravel road. I turn down the path, switching off my headlights, and proceed slowly. When I crest the hill, I'm greeted by the sight of a decaying farmhouse which looks about ready to collapse, along with a large barn and silo nearby. Close to the barn are two vehicles and I can see light through the slats of the wood while the house itself is empty. I kill the engine and get out, leaving my car right on the edge of the ridge, where hopefully Janice and the others will see it when they arrive.

Thankfully, though, the barn is a good hundred yards or more away, so I don't think anyone knows I'm here. But there's absolutely no cover out here. I'm in the middle of a field with low grass and it's a clear night, the moon shining bright in the sky. Out here in the country it's acting like a spotlight, and I know if anyone happens to look, they'll see me coming. It's as quiet as the grave, the only sounds are the crickets and other night creatures singing their rituals. Which means I can't make any noise if I hope to reach the barn without being detected.

I don't have a choice. I pull my gun from its holster and stay as low as I can while moving closer to the barn and house. My footfalls are silent in the grass, but more disturbingly, I don't hear anything coming from the barn. When I'm only about fifty yards away I stop short. One of the vehicles is Chris's Tahoe. The other I don't recognize; it's a dark blue sedan. At least I know I'm in the right place. My approach brings me up to the fronts of the vehicles, which are both pointed away from the barn itself. The other car has government plates, which doesn't make me feel any better, but I snap a quick picture of the license plate for later. On instinct I look behind me and I think I see something moving across the ridge, but I can't be sure. It could be a deer or other wild animal.

Whatever it was, it's gone a moment later. My heart is pounding in my chest, but I can't afford to wait any longer. There's no telling what awaits me in that barn, but I'm sure Avery is in there, being subjected to something terrible. I close my eyes and take a deep breath. Once I'm ready I swing around Chris's truck to head for the barn's entrance.

Stars explode across my face, and I hit the ground, hard. There's someone else here, someone standing over me, and I try to scramble back, even though my head feels like someone cracked it open with a hammer and all my brains are spilling out onto the grass.

I've lost my gun; it went flying from my hand when I was blindsided, which makes my primary concern getting away and regrouping. I can barely even feel my cheek, but then the white spots begin to subside, and I can see in front of me again. As I'm attempting to pull myself away from my attacker, his blurry form finally comes into view.

"Chris," I say.

"Goddammit, Emily," he says, holding a long rifle with the butt of it out. That must be what he cold-cocked me with. "Why can't you just leave something alone?" He rotates the gun, so the butt is up against his shoulder and the barrel is pointed directly at me. I dive to the right, scrambling as fast as I can as he squeezes off a shot, which kicks up dirt beside me. Scrambling, I make it back to the cars just as another bullet clips the front headlight of his vehicle, shattering it. I get back behind his car, using it as a barrier between the two of us. Shaking my head, I try to regain my bearings.

He knows I'm somewhere behind the car, but not exactly where, and I'm not about to help him out by shouting at him. I can hear his boots on the packed dirt leading up to the barn, though, and he comes around the right side of his car as I

crouch and move around to the other side of the other vehicle. "This isn't personal, not entirely," he says. "You should
have just let it be." As he's talking I keep a full vehicle between
us, circling to remain opposite him without him seeing me. "It
was supposed to look like he died naturally, and it was my job
to keep an eye on you, to make sure you didn't suspect
anything." Chris laughs, something I haven't heard in a long
time. "But it turns out you're just as good of a liar as I am.
You knew all the way back in March, didn't you? When you
came back from that little town in Virginia. I could tell something was different about you, even then."

To think it has all come down to this. Back before Matt
died, Chris and I were close. Really close. Considering all the
time we spent with him and Dani, the four of us were just
about inseparable. After I got married they were like my new
family, my only family. And this is how it ends for us. I have a
million things I want to say, I want to *shout*, but I'm not that
stupid.

He moves around the left side of the other vehicle on the
property, but I've already circled back to his car, but this won't
hold forever. Eventually, he'll catch up to me. So instead I
wiggle underneath his truck, watching his feet move slowly
around the other vehicle.

"We really tried to let you live, Emily. I know Matt
wouldn't have wanted you dead. But at the same time, you
were too much of a liability. Had you continued to believe the
lie, I think things might have been different. We could have
gotten back to that place where we used to be, out on the deck
drinking margaritas and enjoying each other's company. Dani
and I even would have supported you remarrying.

"You realize all of that was for your benefit, right? We
could have killed him any way we wanted. We could have
shredded his body into a thousand pieces where no one would
have ever found him. But I knew. I knew you'd never stop
looking. So we had to make it look like he died of natural

causes. That was the only way to keep you out of it. And believe me, it wasn't easy or cheap. And yet, somehow, you still managed to find out."

He's approaching around this side of his car again. I can practically smell his aftershave as his boots clomp closer. I'm doing everything I can not to think about what he's saying, and instead trying to focus on what I need to do in order to survive this. As he passes again I slip out from under the truck as fast as I can, except I must hit the underside or something because he spins, his eyes wide, but calculating. I'm close enough that I tackle him, and the rifle is too long for him to get off a shot at me in time. We both hit the ground and I feel the sharp pain of being hit over and over again, all while I'm trying to get the weapon out of his hand and find a way to restrain him. But he's too strong and his hits are quickly draining what energy I have. Finally, I get a hefty punch to his kidneys, which causes him to stop for just a split second, long enough for me to knock the rifle out of his hand. But that opens me up to a headbutt that sends me onto my back. I know if I don't do something quick, he'll recover that gun and I'm dead. I roll to the side and kick at the rifle, sending it back up under his truck. Again, it opens me up to another blow, this one from his boot as it connects with my face.

I roll onto my stomach, feeling like a rag doll that's being batted around, but adrenaline is surging in my veins and I'm not about to let this asshole best me. I manage to get on all fours and turn to see Chris grabbing for the gun under the truck. I grab one of his ankles with both hands and twist it as hard as I can, hearing the snap and he cries out in pain, all thoughts of the gun forgotten. His eyes are full of rage as he turns back to me and tries to kick again with his good leg, but this time, I'm ready and I dodge. Instead I grab the leg and shove it up and out of the way as I deliver the *hardest punch I can* right to his nuts.

It's as if the entire world goes silent for a moment and

then he screams like a banshee, high and wild. He curls into a fetal position, both his hands on his damaged privates, which gives me enough time to pull out a pair of cuffs and crawl back over to him. I grab one of his arms and wrench it behind his back as he howls in pain, before rolling him over and taking the other arm, and cuffing them together. Strangely, these are the same cuffs Rossovich was wearing not more than half an hour ago.

Chris is on his stomach, writhing in pain, rocking back and forth. I'm sure I caused some permanent damage, but as far as I'm concerned, it was deserved. I stand up, all the energy draining from my body and retrieve the rifle from under the truck. I then find my revolver over in the dirt a few feet away from the other vehicle. As much as I would like to believe the hard part of this is over, I know it's just begun. Avery is still in that barn, and I'm not about to let her stay there.

I take a deep breath, and I head for the cutout door in the large rolling door, resolved to end this, one way or another.

Chapter Twenty-Nine

THE INSIDE OF THE BARN IS LIT WITH MODERN LIGHTING, which is surprising. I'm not sure why I expected it to be all oil lamps and torches, but I guess the state of the accompanying house made me think no one had been in here in years. But that's not right at all. This barn is more modern. A large aisle runs down the middle, while two rows of eight stalls line each side of the barn. The floor is solid concrete, and all the stalls look to be made of recent pinewood. And while it looks like it's a two-story barn from the outside, the whole space is open at the top.

The stalls themselves seem to be completely enclosed, which I've never seen in a barn before. There are doors, but the windows at the tops of the doors where a horse would normally stick their head out has been covered with what looks to be thick glass. I walk over to one of the stalls and look inside, but it's dark and I can't see anything. I still don't hear anything in here, which makes me wonder if I'm in the wrong place; or maybe they've already left. I open the door to the closest stall, only to be greeted with the sweet smell of perfume. When I flip on the light, my stomach bottoms out.

The room is decorated like one would be for a child, the

walls covered in colors and designs that make it look like a forest. There are also a bunch of animals painted on the walls, each with bright, smiling faces. A couple of pieces of furniture occupy the room, including a dresser with a lamp, a couple of shelves full of stuffed animals and a bed. But what's more disturbing is the bed isn't child-sized, it's a king-sized bed, taking up most of the room. I walk in and open the top drawer of the dresser, only to find it filled with a variety of sex toys.

"Oh, my God," I say as a chill runs through me.

I bolt out of the room and run down the stalls until I find one with a light on. But the window is covered from the inside, and I can't see what's going on in there. The door has been bolted shut at the top and I unlock the latch, swinging the door open.

This room is decorated completely differently than the other one. If I had to name it, this one would be a princess theme, complete with a four-poster bed. In the center of the bed sits Avery Huxley, shaking and crying. She's still wearing the dress she had on at Moreno's place.

"What the hell is going on? I told you not to disturb—" The other occupant of the room, a heavyset man who is mostly naked, save for a pair of boxers, stands at the side of the bed, his clothes on the floor. He stops cold when he sees me, his face going sheet white. "Who—"

"Shut up, Mr. Chairman," I say, recognizing him immediately. Jack Hirst, Representative Huxley's boss and the House Committee Chair, it turns out, is a pedophile and a deviant. I stow my handgun and pull out a second pair of cuffs. "You're under arrest for soliciting a minor for sex and child endangerment."

"Now wait a minute, you can't do that," he says. "I'm protected—"

"By your position? No, you're not. And if you think your buddies will come get you out of this, I'm afraid to tell you but they're the ones who ratted you out." His face blanches again as I place the rifle up against the doorframe. I grab one of his meaty arms and pull it behind his back before grabbing the other one. He smells of sweat and barbeque, which turns my stomach. Once I have him restrained, I push him to the ground where he lands, then sort of rolls to his side.

I rush over to Avery who pulls away from me. "Avery? Are you all right?" I ask. Even though I'm usually terrible with kids, I can't let that get in the way of this right now. She needs me to be strong.

She shakes her head back and forth, tears streaming down her face. "Did he do something to you? Did he touch you?" She's holding herself tight but shakes her head again. "Are you sure? It's okay to tell me if he did. You're not in any trouble. I'm here to take you back home, okay?"

"Okay," she squeaks out.

"Who the hell do you think you are?" Hirst says, managing to sit back up.

"I'm Agent Emily Slate, FBI," I tell him. "And you're about to enjoy prison for the rest of your life." I don't want to wait for backup to arrive, but I'm facing a conundrum here. I want to get Avery out of here as quickly as possible, but I don't want to leave Hirst alone for even a second. And I still have Chris out there to deal with, though I doubt he's going anywhere anytime soon. As much as I don't want to, I think it's best if I leave Avery for just a minute to get Hirst in the back of his own car, where I know he'll be secure.

I lean down to look at Avery again. "I'm going to take him out of here and you never have to see him again, okay?" She nods. "Then I'll come back and get you and take you back home. Can you stay here for just a minute for me?" Her eyes flit to Hirst, then back to mine and she nods again. "Good girl."

I walk over and grab Hirst by the wrists, forcing him to get up or break his arms. He manages to get to his feet with some effort and I lead him out of the room, grabbing the rifle as we pass by. "I'll be right back, sweetheart, okay?" Avery gives me another nod and I escort Hirst back to the aisle that divides the stalls. "You better hope I don't find out you did anything to that little girl, otherwise this only gets worse for you."

"Fuck you, Slate," he spits. "You have no idea how many connections I have."

"And I don't care," I reply. "I will make it my life's mission to take you down for this if I have to. You and this little organization you belong to."

"How about this," he says as we pass the animal room. "You tell me who gave me up, and I offer you a lifetime of protection against any enemy. I know the organization has been gunning for you for a while, but I can protect you from all of that. You'll never have to look over your shoulder again."

"And what, I'm just supposed to forget this?"

"There's a cost to everything in life," he says.

"That's too high a price," I reply, forcing him out the door and into the night. Chris remains on the ground where I left him, groaning in pain. I try the door to Hirst's car, but it's locked. Internally, I groan. The keys must be in his pants inside. Looking at him, Hirst isn't the kind of man who looks like he can run very far or fast, especially with his arms strained behind his back. I'm hesitant to take him back inside just because I don't want Avery seeing him again, but I don't want to leave him out here unattended either. I pull out my phone, checking the time. Janice is still probably a good ten minutes away, but at least Avery is out of danger now.

"C'mon, we're going back inside to get your keys."

"Agent Slate, you are making a fatal mistake," he says. But as we turn to head back to the barn, I stop, dead in place as I see Avery standing there, with the barrel of a gun pointed at her head. It takes me a second longer than it should to realize the person holding the gun is none other than my sister-in-law, though she doesn't look much like herself. She's clad all in black, with her hair pulled back out of the way. I've never seen her like this before, but the stern look on her face tells me that she's not messing around.

"Emily, let him go," she says.

"No," I say, more stunned than anything. I had thought Chris hadn't involved Dani in this mess, though it seems the "no family" rule didn't apply to them. More than that, it looks to me like Dani is comfortable holding a Glock to the head of a twelve-year-old, like pulling the trigger wouldn't bother her in the slightest.

She pushes the gun harder into Avery's skull and the girl cries out. "You won't get another warning."

I wince, knowing she's got me. I let go of Hirst and he stumbles back over to her. "About time you showed up," he growls. "Where the hell were you?"

"Inspecting a disturbance," she says. She nods to me. "Lose the guns, both of them." I toss the rifle at her feet and pull my service weapon out, adding it to the pile. I can't have come this far just to have her kill Avery in front of me. "I found your car." She must have been the shape I saw as I was approaching the barn.

"Let her go," I say. "She's got nothing more to do with this."

"And how will that go, Emily?" she asks, mocking me. "You two just leave together? Go off into the sunset? I don't think so." Chris groans from the other side of his car. "Plus, I have to make you pay for what you did to my husband."

"I should have done it to *him*," I say, indicating Hirst. "Just to make sure he couldn't ever hurt anyone else."

"You think you're so clever," Dani says, her face twisting into a snarl. "I can't believe I actually thought we could still be friends. After what Matt did—"

"I don't think we need to go into detail," Hirst says. "Just take care of this quickly so we can get back to business. I have a vote in the morning and I want to be well-rested before I need to be back."

"Does Huxley know? Is he part of this *organization*?" I demand.

Hirst laughs. "Of course not. He has no idea. The fact that he's a prick makes little difference. His daughter just happened to be the right age."

"Right age for what?" I ask.

"Kill her already," he says. "And get me out of these things." He turns around for Dani to remove the cuffs. I grimace as for the second time tonight I'm looking down the barrel of a gun. I wish—

A gunshot cuts me off and Hirst spins a little before falling face-first into the dirt. Avery screams and Dani turns to him, momentarily distracted. I see my chance and begin to charge her, only for her to reassert herself and put the gun back to Avery's head. "What was that?" she demands. "What happened?" Avery is still screaming. "Shut up!"

"It's okay, Avery," I say with both of my hands up. "It's okay, I promise."

"Emily, you better tell me what you did before—"

"I can't feel my legs!" Hirst cries out. I notice blood begin to seep from the hole now visible in his back. The bullet must have impacted his spine.

"It wasn't her," the assassin says, emerging from the darkness.

"Camille," Dani says, surprise in her tone. "What—"

The assassin—or Camille—stands over Hirst and points her high caliber assault rifle at the back of his head and pulls the trigger, cratering the Speaker's skull and killing him instantly.

Avery begins hyperventilating.

"What the hell do you think you're doing?" Dani yells.

"Don't pretend like you don't know," Camille spits, her blonde hair swishing as she speaks. "I've been on the kill list for a good week now. A kill list that you people authorized. Now you're going to tell me the names of the other members of this organization, otherwise I will finish what Emily started with your husband."

Dani looks to me and back again. "You two are in this *together?*"

"Not exactly," Camille says.

"Where did you even come from?" she asks.

Camille nods in my direction. "You had me track her, so that's what I've been doing. And she led me right here."

"How?" I ask. "My phone has been off most of the time."

Camille sends me a glance that is full of pity. "My dear sweet child, did you think I would use something so crude? No, I embedded trackers in all of your shoes the day I set up all those surveillance cameras. It's low-tech, but it works. And surprisingly, you wear the same pair almost every day."

"Enough of this," Dani says, still holding onto Avery. But she seems more inconvenienced than upset about Hirst. "Camille, you've put me in a difficult position. And if you're here, then I'm sure she's got the rest of the FBI on the way, which means time is short."

"Yes, it is," Camille says.

"Then I'll offer you a new proposal. How about a fresh start? One where all is forgiven?"

Camille arches her eyebrow. "In exchange for what?"

"A simple task. Kill Slate."

Chapter Thirty

"You people," I say. "You're all about making deals, aren't you? First Rossovich, then Hirst, and now you."

Dani turns to me. "Then Rossovich is the one who informed you about this place."

I shake my head. "Does it matter? You're clearly all willing to stab each other in the back at the slightest provocation. It's good to know this organization doesn't operate on any kind of real trust."

Dani sneers, turning back to Camille. "I know you're upset, but we can still salvage this. We can proceed on schedule as we've only lost a little time here. Kill Emily, and your record will be wiped clean. You'll be able to go anywhere, do anything without fear of retribution from us."

Camille looks over at me and it seems like she's really considering it. I can't condone her actions, but I'm glad Hirst is dead. It means he can't wiggle his way out of a trial, though it also means there will probably be a coverup. "A clean slate?" she asks. "Pun intended."

Dani smiles. "Of course. It's better this way. It was only because you refused to kill her that you were targeted anyway. It's like you'll be repaying your debt to us."

"You can't trust her," I say. "She pretended to be my friend, my family. She watched my dog and always lent a sympathetic ear whenever her husband came down hard on me. She played the role perfectly, and I never saw it. If there's one thing I've learned, it's that these people are masters of deception. She'll just kill you whenever it's no longer convenient to keep you alive." I truly believe in my heart of hearts that Dani will do and say anything to get Camille to her side, which means I have to as well. Or at least stall long enough for Janice and the others to arrive.

"Like you'll never stop hunting me," Camille says derisively. "I'm the person who killed your husband. Do you really expect me to believe you'll let me go on my merry way, with no more pursuit by the FBI or any governmental agency?"

"We can offer protection from that," Dani says. "We have people in some very powerful positions. They can make sure you're always safe."

Camille looks down at what remains of Hirst, then at Avery, and then at me. I can't tell what's going on in her head; I just know that if she decides Dani is right, I'm dead and Avery is as good as. I have to do something.

"Why didn't you kill me?" I ask.

This seems to snap Camille out of something. "What?"

"Why didn't you kill me when you had the chance? You could have done it at any time; you had plenty of opportunities. Why let me live?"

"Does it matter?" she asks.

Dani looks from me back to Camille. It's like all three of us are in a Mexican standoff, except I'm the only one without a weapon.

"I just figured you could be more useful alive than dead." She turns to Dani. "I suspected you might turn on me one day. Figured I needed some insurance."

Dani cocks her head. "*Really*. Insurance. Let's not forget what you've done for us, Camille. You've killed a lot of people,

including her husband and Gerald Wright. You've assisted in
these matters before"—she gives Avery a shake and the girl
only lets out a whimper in response—"and yet you've never
had trouble completing an assignment before. Did you know
the partners were planning on inducting you, once you killed
her? That was your final job, and you would have been set for
life."

"What?" Camille says, raising her eyebrows.

Dani shakes her head. "No, I didn't think you knew. We
don't tell you that sort of thing beforehand because we want
to make sure you are committed. Some of the other members
said it was too easy a test. You managed to kill Matthew, why
not his wife as well? Of course, that's off the table now. All I
can offer you is a clean record and protection from the US
Government, should you need it." Camille furrows her brow.
"Think of it, I know you have bank accounts everywhere. You
could leave this life behind, retire on a beach somewhere, and
never have to worry about looking over your shoulder again."

I don't like how this is going. It's too tempting for a trained
killer. Who wouldn't want that opportunity?

"Conversely, if you side with Emily here and decide to kill
me, you will be hunted for the rest of your days," she says.
"Even if you let us both live, the organization will never stop
pursuing you. And if you think the FBI can protect you?" She
laughs aloud. It's a sultry, seductive sound. "Let's just say they
can barely keep their own people safe when we're *not* targeting
them."

"So I've noticed," Camille says, and my mind immediately
goes to Liam.

C'mon, Janice, c'mon. I hold out my hands. "She's right. We
can't offer you protection. In fact, the FBI will want to arrest
you. Perhaps in exchange for vital information we could put
you in witness protection, but realistically I think that's
unlikely."

Dani narrows her gaze at me.

"The FBI will charge you for the murder of two people, in addition to any other charges they can bring against you. Even if you help me here today, it won't be enough to wipe out everything else you've done."

"What are you doing?" Dani asks.

"Agreeing with you," I say. "Her best option is to keep working for you, to get the money, retire, and know that she made the smart choice by sticking with the people that stabbed her in the back. It's a risk, but it's the smart risk."

"Nice try," Dani says. "But once you're dead, we'll have no more reason to pursue her. It'll be a non-issue."

"Okay then," I say. "But what about her?" I look at poor Avery, who has closed her eyes, having almost gone limp against Dani's grip.

"What about her?" Dani spits. "She'll be returned to her family…in time."

I turn to Camille. "I'm sure she will. And I'm sure there will be no lingering scars from this experience. I'm sure she'll have a completely normal rest of her childhood, one full of fun, friends and new experiences. And when she goes to bed at night, she won't be visited by the nightmares of the horrors about to be inflicted upon her. Even decades later, when she hasn't thought about it for years, a certain smell or sight won't be enough to send her into a full-blown panic. I'm sure she'll be absolutely fine."

Dani grimaces, holding on tighter to Avery. For a second, I'm sure she's going to shoot her right there, but she still needs her. There are more members of this organization out there, waiting for their turn. Were I not about to die, I think I'd have a hard time keeping my lunch down.

But when I look at the assassin, I see her face twisted in pain. I may have just used the only piece of leverage I have. Finally, something resolves itself in Camille and she raises her weapon to Dani's chest. "Let her go."

"You idiot," Dani sneers and I'm suddenly aware of

someone coming up behind me. I turn to see Chris, his arms still clamped behind him, charging Camille.

"Look out!" I yell and Camille turns at the last second, firing three short bursts right into Chris's chest.

The world slows down as everything seems to happen at once.

Chris begins falling backward, the bullets having penetrated right through where his heart and lungs are. I'm sure he's dead before he even hits the ground. Dani screams something unintelligible, releasing Avery so she can steady her gun, as it's pointed at Camille. As soon as I see Dani let Avery go, I rush over, grabbing the little girl just as Dani squeezes off two shots at Camille.

Camille doesn't have time to turn and reset, and one of the slugs slams into her shoulder, while a second goes right into her kidney. But she doesn't even seem to notice. As I'm pulling Avery away, trying to get behind Chris's truck, I hear Camille squeeze off a couple more rounds, but they hit the wood of the old barn as Dani ducks behind it.

Avery is crying and whimpering, and I can only hope that she'll block all of this out and completely forget the past few days. I poke my head up above the bed of the truck as things speed back up. There's no sign of Dani, but Camille is standing there, still holding the rifle. She looks over at me, then drops the rifle before collapsing on the ground. It's then that I look up and see the familiar blue and red lights of the cavalry, cresting the hill where I parked my car. They come tearing down the hill.

I want to go to Camille, but I don't dare leave Avery, not after all of this. I reach down and pick her up, carrying her in my arms to the other side of the car, keeping my back to the vehicle as the police cars come down the hill, followed by an ambulance and four unmarked vehicles.

The first car that arrives is Rockville Police and I already have my badge out as they get out of the cruiser, weapons drawn. As soon as they see my badge, they rush over and take Avery from my arms as one of the unmarked cars comes skidding to a stop and Janice gets out.

"We have an armed hostile loose on the property!" I yell. "Danielle Hunter, five foot nine Caucasian, dark brown hair in a ponytail, dark clothes!"

"Where?" Janice asks and I point to the barn. She rounds up the cavalry as I watch the officers take Avery to the ambulance. Now that I know she's in good hands, I run over to Camille, who is still lying on the ground, the rifle beside her. Even though I know she's not going to use it, I kick it away anyway as she looks up at me. Her blonde hair is caked with dirt and I try to find the wound in her side, putting pressure on it.

"I need a med team over here, now!" I yell, putting pressure on the wound. She winces and blinks a few times.

"Just let me go," she says. "It's only fair after what I did to you."

I shake my head. "I can't do that, and you know it."

She seems to have trouble getting her breath. That bullet might have punctured a lung, in which case she doesn't have long. I see a team from the ambulance rushing over as more officers fan out around the barn, looking for Dani.

"It was because I saw myself in you," she says. "That's why I couldn't kill you. You were like me, alone against the world, no family, no connections, out there on your own. I know...how hard that is. I respected you for it. You didn't deserve what I did to you."

"Camille," I say. "Where's Liam? Is he still alive?" I have to know before she goes into shock and can't tell me.

She rattles off an address, then smiles. "He's fine. Maybe hungry. I just needed to motivate you." She grabs hold of my collar. "Find them. You have to find them and kill them. They can't be allowed to continue..."

I take her hand just as the medics reach us. "Save your

strength, the medics are here. They're going to take care of you."

"Emily," she says with a weak breath and I can tell she's fading. I don't have a lot of confidence she'll make it. She reaches for my head and pulls me down so she can whisper in my ear.

"Excuse us, ma'am, we need to get to her," one of the medics says.

I lean back, somewhat stunned, allowing them to get to work. There's a lot of blood and Camille has closed her eyes.

"She's going into cardiac arrest!" one of the medics calls out. Another comes rushing over from the ambulance and I step back, allowing them to work.

"Slate!" Janice calls and it takes me a moment to bring myself back to the situation at hand. I glance back over at the ambulance as a second arrives. Avery is sitting in the back with a blanket around her shoulders as one of the medics inside leans down, talking to her. Janice isn't far away, motioning for me to come join her in the field.

I take one last look at Camille—the woman who destroyed my life, then saved it, and join my boss.

"Who is that?" she asks.

"That's her," I say. "The assassin."

"Did she give you the location of Agent Coll?"

I nod and repeat the address to her.

"We'll get a unit out there right away," she says, then continues after a pause. "Doesn't look like she's going to make it." I shake my head; she's probably right. "I guess you're pretty glad about that."

I watch as the medics' movements become faster and more urgent, before they realize there's only so much they can do. One of them looks at his watch; they're calling the time on her.

"I'm not sure," I finally say. "Not anymore."

Chapter Thirty-One

FOR THE FIRST TIME IN MY LIFE, I'M THE ONE SITTING ON THE other side of the interrogation table. After the events at the barn, I was relieved of my weapon and driven back to headquarters in the back of one of the unmarked vehicles. Since I don't wear a watch and there's no clock in here, I can't say for sure how long I've been here, but it feels like a couple of hours at least. Janice didn't say much else, except to confirm there was no sign of Dani, but they weren't going to give up looking.

I let out a long breath and stare up at the ceiling. Interrogating Moreno in a room identical to this one feels like a lifetime ago. So much has happened in the past few hours, it's hard to wrap my mind around it. But at least Avery is safe; I know that much. I just hope Camille was telling the truth about Liam.

Thinking about her brings mixed feelings. It's strange to finally have a name to go along with her now. One of her aliases was a woman named Kamilé Michael. It's possible *Camille* was just another alias, or it could have been her real name and Kamilé was just an offshoot of that. Regardless, I don't have her real last name, so I'm not sure we'll ever find out who she really was, unless the team that finds Liam manages to uncover something.

I lean back down, looking at the table. I can't believe things went down like that. Chris is dead. Dani is on the run, and both of them worked for the same people Matt did. They knew this entire time what really happened to him. I was the only one out of the loop.

Not only that, apparently the House Committee Chair was a member of this organization, whatever it is. And now he's dead too. How all of this doesn't turn into a massive scandal is beyond me.

The door to the room finally opens to reveal Janice. She gives me a stern look before turning and closing the door again. In her hand she holds a file folder, but it's too small to be my personnel file.

I sit up, adrenaline surging through my veins once again. "I need someone to go over to Chris and Dani's house," I say. "My dog is there, along with their dogs. They need to be taken care of."

She nods, holding up a hand. "A team is already on their way over there, despite the fact it's—" she checks her watch "four in the morning."

I was wrong, I've been in here longer than I thought. I wonder if I blacked out there for a little while.

Janice pulls out the chair opposite me and takes a seat.

"Did you find Liam? Please tell me she gave us the correct address."

She nods. "He's already headed back home to get some rest. They found him in a shipping container on the property —though there was a bed and a bucket in there as well. Thankfully he was only in there less than a day. He's a little dehydrated, but no worse for wear."

"Thank God," I say, laying my head down on the table. "And Avery is okay?"

"She's undergoing evaluation at GWU before going back home with her parents," Janice says.

While I don't revel in knowing she's back in her *father's* loving arms, at least she'll be headed back home where she knows she's safe—or at least feels a little better. Still, that kid is going to need a lot of therapy to help her understand and cope with what's happened over the past few days. Moreno swears he never touched her, other than giving her clothing. And from everything I could tell I got to her before Hirst had a chance to put his hands on her. But more may come out in the near future; it isn't like she was going to trust another stranger in that situation. I just have to be content knowing I did the best I could to save her. And now I have to face the consequences.

Janice clears her throat and looks down at the file folder in front of her. I have a bad feeling it contains a letter terminating my position with the FBI. "You disobeyed a direct order from me and put yourself in harm's way after almost being shot by a fellow officer," she finally says.

"All of that is true," I reply.

"How did you know where to find her?"

I take a deep breath and explain how I went through DeBois' phone to lure Rossovich out, then tailed him back to his place before making the deal with him. And while it led to the result I wanted; it doesn't sound very good coming out of my mouth.

"So you entered into an agreement with a criminal. Someone who instigated the kidnapping of the very person you were trying to save."

I nod. "I did. I don't believe it was the wrong call."

"Until he goes out and abducts the next child. And another and another."

I sit up, nodding. She's absolutely right. But in the moment I felt like I didn't have a choice. "I'm sure he's in the wind by now. But I know this much, he's sick and he has a family. Which means he's vulnerable."

"And dangerous," she replies. "I know I've given you broad latitude these past few months after your stellar performance on some very tough cases. But you should have run this by me."

"There wasn't time," I say.

"So it had nothing to do with the fact that I'd already ordered you to stop engaging in any further activities as a federal officer and return for a debrief?" I don't reply. We both already know the answer to that question, and I don't want it on the record.

"We don't have much on DuBois yet," she replies. "Who shot him? The caliber didn't match your service weapon, it came from a much larger gun."

"Camille," I say. Then: "The assassin. She was watching from a rooftop, I assume. When he pulled the gun on me, she took him out."

"Your very own guardian angel."

"I don't know if I'd go that far." The woman has been the source of all my stress ever since I first passed her in the elevator back in Virginia. That was almost six months ago. It's strange to think now that she's gone. That I'll no longer have her hanging over my head, threatening everything I do.

I reach down, pulling my shoes off. "That reminds me. Get these to tech services. Apparently it's how she was tracking me. She put devices in all of my shoes. It was never my phone."

"Clever," Janice says, taking the shoes and setting them beside her chair. She nods to the plate glass window for someone to come get them. A moment later an agent walks in wearing gloves and retrieves them. I wait until he's left before speaking again.

"Am I being fired?" I ask.

"That's not up to me," she says, looking at me over the

rims of her glasses. "That will be Cochran's call. But he's not due to be in for a few more hours. I'm sure they'll pull me in front of the review board regarding DuBois, but his record has been spotless. There were never any signs."

"I know the feeling," I say.

Janice leans forward again, folding her hands together on the table. "Emily, I'm not going to sugarcoat this. You have seriously jeopardized your position here. Had you not uncovered that mess back at the barn, I have no doubt you'd have already been fired and probably arrested. As it is, things are still…messy."

"You mean Hirst," I say.

She shakes her head. "Jesus…Hirst. Who would have thought it?"

"Had you ever met the man?" I ask. "He was vile. It didn't take a genius to see there was something off about that guy."

"We had to bring in reinforcements, especially since our department is under review now," she says. "I don't even want to think about what's going to come out in the next few days regarding who and what has been in that barn."

"I got the distinct impression it has been used more than a few times by a few different people," I say. "It's not going to be easy to nail them."

"Fortunately, that's not our concern at the moment. As much as I'd like to let you go back home, you're to stay here to give formal statements regarding the events of the evening, as well as undergo a psych evaluation to determine your mental state."

"You mean to determine if I'm still loyal and not a traitor like DuBois," I say.

"We all have to do it, me included. IA is going to be all over this place for the next few days. Then I would expect a call from Cochran's office. He said he'll be handling your case personally. Whether that's a good or a bad thing, I don't know." She looks at the door behind her. "There's going to be a lot of fallout from this."

"Can I at least get a shower and a couple hours sleep?" I ask.

She nods, motioning to the plate window to cut the recording. She takes the folder and stands, returning to the door and I follow. "It's going to be a hard few days, Slate. I hope you're up for it."

"As much as anyone who has been accused of treason can be," I say as the same agent as before opens the door for us from the other side.

"You haven't been accused of treason. Just disobeying orders and endangering your personal safety. There's a big difference. But if Cochran determines you're too much of a risk, that you can't follow orders in a crisis, I don't see how you could expect to remain here. The one good thing you have going for you is he's career motivated. And this is a big deal, what with Hirst and everything. It could go either way."

"I understand," I say, following her out into the hall.

She places a reassuring hand on my shoulder. "I know why you did it. And maybe I would have made the same call in your position. But the ends don't justify the means, not in this job." I nod. "Give your statements, get clearance from IA, then go home. At least now you know you're not under surveillance anymore."

"What a relief," I say as if I have nothing else to worry about.

She gives me a sad smile. "Good luck. You're going to need it."

Chapter Thirty-Two

I TEST THE WATER, IT'S RIGHT BELOW SCALDING, WHICH IS exactly the way I like it. Not enough to burn me, but enough to work out all the knots covering my body. After the past twenty-four hours, I feel like I could sleep for a month. But first, I need to feel clean. I remove my dirty clothes and slip into the tub, the heat absorbing me like a sponge. I don't even notice the heat, I'm just happy to get into something warm and comforting for a while. After the physical ordeal of fighting Chris and the mental ordeal of dealing with Dani and Camille, I need this more than I think I realize.

It takes me only a moment to get settled, right to where my nose is barely above the heated water and the humidity envelops the small room. Looking across the still surface of the tub, steam rises up and disappears and I feel like I'm in my own personal Emily soup.

Just as I close my eyes and begin to relax, the knots in my neck and back beginning to work themselves out, the doorbell rings.

My eyes snap open and I glare at the bathroom door, as if I can make whoever it is go away by sheer will alone. When it rings again, I grumble and pull the plug to the bath. "Can't even get five freaking minutes."

I barely have my robe on before it rings a third time. "Hang on!" I call out. My hair is soaked and I'm still half wet, but if it's someone from the Bureau—either IA or the review board—it's better if I get it over with now. Though I don't know what IA would want, I already spent the better part of nine hours with them earlier today, going over every interaction I ever had with DuBois.

I pull my hair up in a towel and exit the bathroom, grabbing my revolver from my bedroom side table out of habit. Timber is already in the living room, looking at the door, wagging his tail. When I went in to take a bath he'd been asleep on the bed. He doesn't know what's happened, but he can feel my stress. It's been a lot for him too. I'm just glad he's home for good.

I reach the front door I check the peephole and freeze, wishing now I'd just stayed in the bath. "Shit," I say reflexively.

"Emily?" comes his voice from the other side of the door.

I grimace, then put my revolver on the kitchen counter before returning to the door and throwing the deadbolt. When I open the door, Liam stands in front of me. He's got some deep bags under his eyes and his eyes are bloodshot, but other than that he looks okay. "Hey," I say. Timber walks up to him, wagging his tail as he sniffs Liam.

"I'm sorry," he says, patting Timber's head. "I didn't realize you'd—I mean, I didn't want to interrupt your shower."

Right. I forgot I'm in nothing but a robe and a towel. I give him a smile. "It's fine, I just got back a while ago. I've been rolling in the dirt all night it seems like." I feel that same surge of adrenaline I felt when I was being interrogated by Janice. Except this is different.

His face is tight with worry. "I should have just called. I'll come back later."

I shake my head. "No, come on in."

"But you're—"

I step over the threshold and wrap him in a hug, holding him tight. I'm not sure what compelled me to do it; maybe I just didn't realize how much I was worried about him. A second later I feel his strong arms wrap around me. "I'm so sorry," I whisper.

"It's not your fault," he says. "I'm fine."

"But you might not have been." I pull back from him. "There was a point in the investigation where I had to make a decision. And I knew if I made the call I needed to, it would put you in danger. Very possibly get you killed. And I made the call anyway." I blink as my eyes begin to well up with tears.

"Emily, it's okay," he says. "I understand. This is part of the job. You couldn't control what happened any more than I could."

I shake my head. "But I could. I could have just given her what she wanted."

He holds me at arm's length by both shoulders. I'm so tired I just want to let him hold me up. "And allow Avery to be put in further danger? I've spoken to both Janice and Zara. They told me everything."

I avert my eyes. It might have been the right call, but it's hard to look someone in the eye when you know you're the reason they almost died.

"Emily," he says. "Listen to me. It's not your fault that woman did what she did. I never should have let her get the drop on me, but she got me when my guard was down. She's the one who put you in that situation; it isn't like you chose to be there."

"No, I guess not," I say. "Would you like some...I have coffee or tea."

"Let me fix it," he says. "You've been through enough."

I can't argue with that. I step back and his arms fall away from me. Timber continues to wag his tail as Liam comes in and follows him into the kitchen. I retrieve my revolver and put it in a drawer in the living room.

"Expecting trouble?" he asks as he gets out the tea kettle.

"When you never know if you're going to wake up with a gun to your head you tend to start carrying one through the house."

He nods. "I guess that's a good point. What does it feel like knowing that you don't have that hanging over your head any longer?"

I take a seat on the couch, pulling my legs under me. I feel a little odd wearing a towel while he's here, but also comfortable enough that I'm not embarrassed. But really, my thoughts are on what Camille whispered to me right before the medics made me back away. Even now, goosebumps form on my arms as her words repeat in my head. I haven't been able to stop thinking about it. I want to tell him, but some part of me feels like it's better to keep this close to the chest. Maybe it's better if no one finds out.

"Em?" Liam asks again as he's filling the kettle with water. Timber trots around him, looking for a treat.

"Timmy," I say, and he comes back over, laying on his bed beside the couch while I try to refocus on his question. "I haven't had time to get used to it yet. The past few months have been...stressful. Knowing that she's not out there anymore doesn't feel right."

He comes around the island and perches on one of the stools while the water boils. "Do you feel like you've gotten justice for your husband at least?"

That's something I've been pondering ever since I learned there was more to this than just one random person's actions. "There's an entire organization behind his death. I'm not sure I'll feel anything until they've all been brought to justice."

He gives me a solemn nod then tends to the kettle again, pouring two cups of tea. "Bags?"

"Upper right cabinet," I say. He retrieves a few and steeps them, bringing both cups over to the couch. I take one and hold it in my hands. It's no bath, but it's better than nothing. I realize all our discussion has been about me, when he was the one who was kidnapped and detained for almost twenty-four hours. "What about you? How are you feeling?"

He shrugs, sipping at the tea. "A little sore. Nothing I can't handle. After all this stuff with IA is over I'm going to take a few days off. Maybe drive out to the coast. I was wondering… if you'd like to join me."

I stop short of sipping my own tea. "You mean, like a vacation?"

"Nothing so formal. Just two friends out of town for a few days. When was the last time you went away that wasn't on business?"

Thinking back, I'm not really sure. My job has taken so much of my life over the past few years. And after Matt died, I literally threw myself back into my work, as much as they would let me. Zara and I went down south, but that was only to find Camille's trail, which ended up failing. Everything else has been on the job, nothing else. "I don't know."

"You don't know when you took a vacation, or you don't know if you want to go?" he asks.

"Either. I mean, getting out of town for a few days sounds great, but Cochran is going to put me through the wringer this week, regardless of what IA finds. I disobeyed an order from a superior, and potentially jeopardized a case by making a deal with Rossovich. I don't think it's a good idea to leave town until after."

He takes another sip. "But you'd like to go?" he asks, hope in his voice.

"Liam," I say, not sure how to begin.

His face falls, but he recovers quickly. "That's okay. I

understand. I'm pushing too hard."

"No, it's not that," I say. "What happened when we were in Delaware—that was really special to me. I thought I could just brush it off, pretend like it was nothing more than a one-night stand, but then when you were taken and there was nothing I could do…" I trail off, then manage to reset myself, placing my tea on the coffee table. "I realized my feelings for you run deeper than I was willing to admit."

"Oh," he says, and puts his cup on the table as well. "So what does that mean?"

I take a deep breath. "It means I would very much like to take a trip with you. Once all of this is over. As it is, this organization is still operating without any kind of oversight or knowledge, Dani is still at-large, and I don't know if I'm even going to have a job by the end of the week. From what Camille told me, I wouldn't expect this organization not to retaliate just because I'm not in the FBI any longer."

"C'mon," he says. "You're not going to lose your job."

"I don't know," I say. "This will be strike two for me. After what happened back in January after Matt died, I swore I'd never screw up like that again. I'm not sure I'd blame Cochran if he decided to terminate my employment."

He places his hand on my shoulder gingerly. "Listen. You made a judgment call. You're not perfect, and you saved a little girl from something that would have scarred her for life. Give yourself a break. If they decide to call in character witnesses, you know I'll be first in line."

I smile, feeling the warmth of his hand through the fabric of my robe. Suddenly I feel my cheeks flush. "I appreciate that."

He seems to realize he's still touching my arm and pulls away, clearing his throat. "Well, I should go. Let you get back to relaxing. You deserve some time to yourself before we have to be back in the office." He stands, and Timber reflexively gets up as well.

A strong part of me wants to grab him by the lapels and pull him into the bedroom, but I manage to restrain myself. My emotions are running high right now, and I haven't slept in over twenty hours. Now is not the time to be brash. "Thank you for the tea," I say.

Liam heads for the door, chuckling. "I should be thanking you, it's your tea. I just wanted to make sure you were okay after…everything."

"You're sweet," I say, accompanying him to the door.

"Bye buddy," Liam says, leaning down and petting Timber on the head. He wags his butt in response. Just as he's standing back up something compels me to grab that collar of his anyway and a half second later our lips are locked. His breath is hot and I can taste remnants of the herbal tea on his lips. Pulling away is like wrenching two magnets apart, but somehow I manage. He stands there, stunned and I can't help but grin.

"Thanks again for coming by," I say. "I'm glad you're okay."

He blinks a few times, clearly dazed. I have to admit, I'm a little lightheaded myself. "Sure," he says. "See you tomorrow?"

I smile. "Tomorrow."

A grin appears on his lips, and he leaves, trotting down the stairs in front of my place with what looks to be an extra pep in his step. I close the door behind him, locking it and exhale, leaning against the doorframe.

Timber stands at my side, panting and looking up at me with a big grin on his face. I rub his head. "I know bud, I like him too." Despite everything weighing down on me, I feel lighter. I feel like I can breathe again. It's going to be a tough week ahead, but instead of dreading it, I'm looking forward to the challenge.

Because no matter what happens, I know things will be okay.

Epilogue

DANI RACED DOWN THE ROAD, CURSING WITH EVERY BREATH AS she pushed the speedometer past ninety. She was aware everyone from the State Police to the FBI was looking for her, but she just needed to get to the safe house to regroup. She'd managed to evade them for thirty-six hours so far, but she was tired and dirty, and she was running out of resources. She only had so much cash left, and she couldn't risk being picked up by security cameras at a grocery store or convenience mart.

That was fine, the safe house would have supplies. She could regroup there and figure out her next steps.

She never should have let Camille make the choice; she should have just shot her there and been done with it. Then Chris would still be alive, Emily would be taken care of, and no one would be the wiser. Chris had already blown his cover, obviously, but hers had still been intact.

Now all that was over. She needed to check in, then make her report before being shuffled into the system so she could leave the country. The life she'd made for herself here was over anyway, what with Chris gone. She'd loved him, sure, but losing him hadn't been the worst thing in the world. It gave her a chance to start over. Anyway, it was his own fault. He never should have been so sloppy as to let Emily track him down.

Dani worried about Rossovich, though. He'd given them up, and for what? To save his own hide? She wondered what the rest of the group would say about that when they heard. Would they take the same action they took against Gerald Wright when he threatened to talk? Rossovich hadn't outed the organization, just one small piece of it. But it had ended up getting Hirst killed, which now left a vacancy. Dani wasn't presumptuous enough to think she could fill that vacancy, but she would at least alert them to Rossovich's betrayal. He might not be a full member; neither of them were, but they still worked for the organization. There were consequences.

Finally, Dani got off the interstate and back on the surface roads of downtown Baltimore. It was late, past two a.m. and most of the streets were deserted. She didn't need to look for directions; she already had this place memorized. Though she lamented never being able to go back to her house in Washington again. She'd miss that life, the slow mornings filled with nothing but sex and coffee, the days sitting out on the deck with the dogs, or the afternoons when she could sit down with a good book. It was the perfect assignment, and it had fit Dani well. She still did her work, obviously, but that took very little of her focus, considering she'd been trained for something much more strenuous.

When Chris had first told her about the organization, before they'd been married, she thought he'd been joking. And when he swore her to an oath that she would die if she ever told anyone, she still hadn't been sure it wasn't all part of some larger practical joke. But when she'd been in the presence of them, she truly understood that she'd stepped into something far larger than she'd anticipated. She'd been trained as a watch operative, her duty to keep an eye on certain people and intervene if necessary. Chris had been doing it all his life, as had Matt, and Dani was just getting started when Matt began dating Emily. She thought that Matt would bring Emily into the company just like Chris did, but every time she brought it up with him, he vehemently refused and ordered her never to speak about it in front of Emily. She'd kept that promise, even after he'd died.

Maybe Matt had known that Emily never would have gone for it. She was too rigid regarding the law. Something to do with her mother's death. But it put the three of them at odds with each other, and Dani watched as Chris and Matt grew apart.

But what really clenched it was when Matt confided with her that he was going to leave the organization. That he was going to reveal the truth to Emily and expose the entire thing. He'd told Dani in hopes to give her time to cut ties and move on before he brought the whole thing down.

But she couldn't do that. She'd seen what those people could do, and she knew the price of turning against them. Matt should have too, considering his family had been members for years. He'd miscalculated.

Dani finally pulled into the back alley, parking her stolen vehicle underneath an overhang to shield it from above. She got out and trotted over to the only door on this side of the building, a metal security door with a small keypad beside it. She punched in the code and the door clicked, allowing her entrance.

Inside she was greeted by a studio-sized room, complete with bed, desk, and computer. There was a small kitchen in the back and an en-suite bathroom, which had the necessities. No frills.

She pulled off her jacket and went over to the computer, logging in. She'd left everything behind, her wallet, keys, phone, all of it. Anything that could be used to trace her. All she had was the couple of remaining bills from her wallet.

After logging on, the computer clicked to life, the screen split into nine equal parts. Her face was at the center, and in the square below hers was the face of Rossovich, already online. His skeletal face smiled when he saw her.

"Hello, Danielle. The others will be just a moment."

"You bastard," she says. "You ratted me out."

"Please wait for everyone before you begin," he replied. One by one, the other squares filled with the faces of the Organization's head members. All except for the lower left-hand square. That had belonged to Hirst. Now all it showed was a blank screen.

"This is Hunter, coding in," Danielle said, using her last name.

The man in the upper right-hand corner glared at her, his eyes stern. "Report."

"Boyle is dead. So is my husband. Slate exposed the barn; all the cops know about it now. Huxley is out of play. For good. I've been compromised."

"No shit," another man said. "Your face has been all over the news."

"I need extraction. And to issue a formal request to kill Rossovich. He exposed my operation; he's the reason it all went to hell."

"Seems to me like the reason it all went to hell is because your husband was stupid enough to get himself found out," the man directly left said. "Slate found him before Rossovich was even involved. By the time she got to Rossovich, it was too late."

"And who do you think helped her?" Dani, said, trying to keep her anger at bay. "Obviously Camille knew about Rossovich, enough to out him."

"No," Rossovich said. "She never had that information."

"Then what? Emily found him on her own?"

"She used DuBois as cover," Rossovich said. "Lured me into the open. I had no other choice. It was either give her what she wanted, or risk everything. If she had stepped into my house before I had a chance to clean it out, it would have meant the end of this entire organization."

"It is our view that Rossovich did the only thing he could to salvage the situation," the man in the upper right said. "None of which would have been necessary had your husband not been so sloppy. His death saves us a bullet."

"You've got to be kidding me," Dani said, slamming her fist on the desk. "He was loyal to you for his entire life! As I've been! You owe me an extraction."

"We owe you nothing," the man directly above her said. "You failed in your mission. You compromised the Organization; you got one of our primary members killed."

"That wasn't my fault!" Dani protested. "Camille—"

"—would have been dead if you'd done your duty," the man directly to her left said. "Yet she was left alive to wreak havoc."

"That was because I couldn't find her." Dani was beginning to panic. She didn't like where this was going. "Chris and I searched for weeks, neither of us could ever pinpoint her. She was like a ghost!"

"Then you weren't up for the task," the man in the upper right square said.

Dani heard a noise behind her and turned to see a man in a dark trench coat standing at the door to the studio. She turned back to the computer, tears already streaming down her face. "Please! I've been loyal! I've done everything you've asked of me!"

"Not everything," Rossovich said. "Once this business is done, I would like to nominate myself to primary member status. I believe my contributions to the Organization outweigh those of any other competing members."

"That will need to be tabled," the man in the upper center square said. "Due to Mrs. Hunter's incompetence, we must go silent until the heat has died down. All further business is suspended."

Dani gritted her teeth. They'd already made their decision; there was nothing she could do. She remained glued to the chair as the man in the trench coat approached. She watched as he retrieved a Ruger Mark IV with a suppressor attached from inside his coat. His face was blank as he raised it, so the barrel was level with her temple. It was all Dani could do to squeeze her eyes shut.

"Now you have done everything we asked," one of the men said, though she wasn't sure which without looking.

It was the last thing she heard before the pop of the gun.

THE END?

To be continued...

Want to read more about Emily?

It's All Come Down to This...

Following the massive revelations about her family and the Organization that killed her husband, Special Agent Emily Slate had hoped she was finally on the right track to take them all down and finally find the answers she needed.

But due to the fallout from her actions regarding the same Organization, Emily has been relegated back to desk duty, and is given a new ultimatum: she's being transferred to a new office in a different part of the country.

Fortunately, before her transfer goes through, a new case comes in, one that's suited to her particular talents. A teenage boy has been brutally murdered, mutilated and staged, and Emily's new boss wants her to take a look before she's sent off somewhere else.

Except, when Emily dives into the details of the case, nothing seems to make sense. The evidence isn't lining up, and she can't make heads nor tails of who could have done this. All she knows is, if she doesn't do everything she can to solve this case, she'll be forced to move and leave everything and everyone she loves behind.

It's only when she makes a startling revelation that Emily realizes the true motives behind this heinous crime. And they will wreck her to her core. She will find herself alone with the greatest threat she's ever faced.

And there's no guarantee she'll make it out alive.

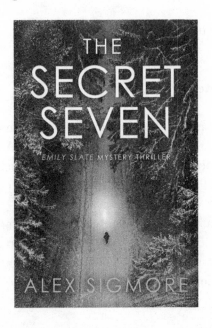

To get your copy of THE SECRET SEVEN, CLICK HERE
or scan the code below!

FREE book offer!
Where did it all go wrong for Emily?

I hope you enjoyed *The Lost Daughter*. If you'd like to learn more about Emily's backstory and what happened in the days following her husband's unfortunate death, including what almost got her kicked out of the FBI, then you're in luck! *Her Last Shot* introduces Emily and tells the story of the case that almost ended her career. Interested? CLICK HERE to get your free copy now!

Not Available Anywhere Else!

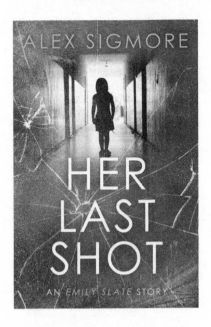

You'll also be the first to know when each book in the Emily Slate series is available!

Download for FREE HERE or scan the code below!

The Emily Slate FBI Mystery Series

Free Prequel - Her Last Shot (Emily Slate Bonus Story)

His Perfect Crime - (Emily Slate Series Book One)

The Collection Girls - (Emily Slate Series Book Two)

Smoke and Ashes - (Emily Slate Series Book Three)

Her Final Words - (Emily Slate Series Book Four)

Can't Miss Her - (Emily Slate Series Book Five)

The Lost Daughter - (Emily Slate Series Book Six)

The Secret Seven - (Emily Slate Series Book Seven)

A Liar's Grave - (Emily Slate Series Book Eight)

The Girl in the Wall - (Emily Slate Series Book Nine)

His Final Act - (Emily Slate Series Book Ten)

The Vanishing Eyes - (Emily Slate Series Book Eleven)

Coming Soon!

Edge of the Woods - (Emily Slate Series Book Twelve)

The Missing Bones - (Emily Slate Series Book Thirteen)

A Note from Alex

I hope you enjoyed *The Lost Daughter*, book six in the new Emily Slate FBI Mystery Series. Talk about some serious revelations! My wish is to give you an immersive story that is also satisfying when you reach the end.

But being a new writer in this business can be hard. Your support makes all the difference. After all, you are the reason I write!

Because I don't have a large budget or a huge following, I ask that you please take the time to leave a review or recommend it to fellow book lover. This will ensure I'll be able to write many more books in the *Emily Slate Series* in the future.

Thank you for being a loyal reader,

Alex

Made in the USA
Las Vegas, NV
13 November 2023

80778976R00152